This is for Goines, Goodis, and Thompson, fine gentlemen who practiced their trade only too well.

SWITCHBLADE

switch·blade (swĭch´blād´) n.
a different slice of hardboiled fiction where the dreamers and the schemers, the dispossessed and the damned, and the hobos and the rebels tango at the edge of society.

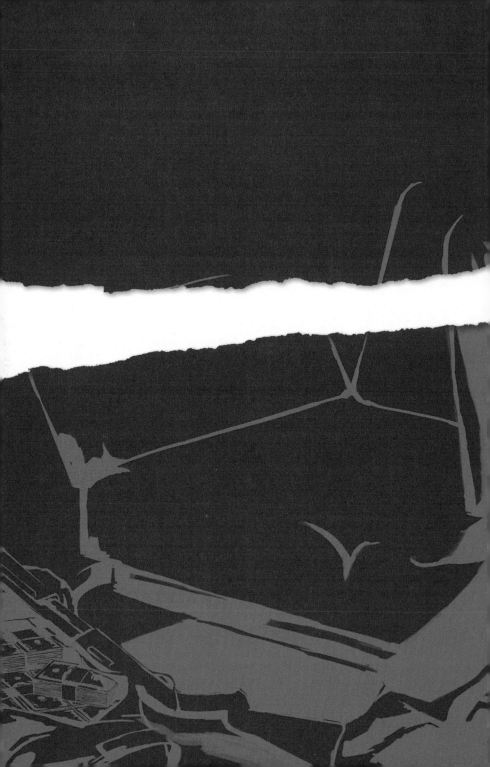

THE JOOK

GARY PHILLIPS

PM PRESS

THE JOOK
By Gary Phillips

Copyright © 2009 Gary Phillips
This edition copyright © 2009 PM Press
All Rights Reserved

Published by:
PM Press
PO Box 23912
Oakland, CA 94623
www.pmpress.org

Cover Illustration by Roderick Constance © 2009 www.shadowshapes.com
Designed by Courtney Utt

ISBN: 978-1-60486-040-5
Library Of Congress Control Number: 2008905962
10 9 8 7 6 5 4 3 2 1

Printed in the USA on recycled paper.

"Every sin is a result of a collaboration."
–Stephen Crane, *The Blue Hotel and Other Stories*

≈

"Just win, baby."
–Al Davis

*i*t was hot as an Alabama outhouse when I got off the plane from Barcelona. LAX was busy like the mug as I stood online for customs. Time was, people would have been sweating me to sign something cute for their granny, or some boob-job chick would have been asking me to write my number on the topside of the tit poking out of her halter. Now all I got was them sideways looks, that frown that said, 'You look like you used to be somebody.'

"What was your business in Barcelona, Mr. Raines?"

The bureaucratic dude gave me the once-over like I was any other square. 'Cept white boys were always a little curious about brothers not in the service who traveled overseas, thinking we were all hooked up with Farrakhan on a trip to pick up the IEDs in Iraq or some shit.

"I was playing ball with the Dragons. You know, NFL Europe League." I said it as if he, or any other of the hundreds of people running around, had actually taken the time to watch one of the games. Hardly.

He looked at my passport again, which he'd placed on top of his computer terminal. "Zelmont Raines." There it was in his watery blues. A few seconds ticked by, then he said, "You used to play for the Falcons."

He didn't finish it. Didn't go on about the Super Bowl where I blew off two defenders and caught the game-winning pass while doing a spin in mid-air. The Atlanta Falcons had only been to the Super Bowl twice since the club was founded. The first time they'd been skinned by Denver. They were on their way to losing a second time against the Jets but for me.

Yet here I was coming back from Spain, after playing six games in a league even the guys at Fox who broadcast us didn't watch. The games had been moved later into the summer to try and catch the excitement that always built up for the NFL pre-season – the real NFL, I mean. But still no one tuned us in.

"Yeah," was all I could give it.

He tapped my passport against his cocked thumb. If it had been a slower time of day, he might have gone on.

Asking me about all them stories of girls in Day-Glo vinyl mini-skirts with no underwear on leaping off my roof into a pool full of whipped cream and cafe au lait. And, if the conversing went on long enough, it always wound around to how I pissed it all away like a sailor on a three-day drunk.

Instead, he just asked his routine questions then said, "Have a good day, Mr. Raines," handing me my passport. I nodded at him as I picked up my equipment bag. The one that was the signature brand I'd endorsed in my last year in the NFL. I went down to baggage claim and waited another hour before I got the rest of my gear.

Time was there'd be a limo waiting for me, Courvoisier on a rack in the back, and maybe some mama with pouty red lips warming up the leather seat. Now, standing outside in the steaming night air, I had my choice of which airport van to catch. I flashed on rolling by the pad of my shortie, Davida Orlean, but nixed it 'cause I was beat and wanted some solitude.

I got in a shuttle driven by some Middle Eastern dude with a dead tooth. First he tooled a fare – two firm sorority babes – to Westchester. I made eye contact with one of 'em, but her friend cock blocked. What you gonna do? Then he took this old girl smelling minty over to the Roosevelt on Hollywood Boulevard. 'Course I had to help her ass out of the ride. Finally, he got me to my crib in the Hollywood Hills.

"That'll be $40, sir." He was gazing at the pad, trying to figure out who I was. "You work in the music business?"

"Head ringer, baby." I was inclined not to tip, but wanted to show I was still the man.

The cat didn't look at the Jacksons and Lincoln for the tip as he hefted my bags out of the back of the van. "I see you in the papers, right?"

"Not so much now, man."

"Oh yes," he said, shaking a finger at me. "You've been in movies too, I know."

"TV. Sports commentary." I was in a few flicks. B efforts where I was fifth billed or more likely a cameo.

Build-up roles, my agent – well, the agent I had then – called 'em. Even shot a show for syndication. Me and this Asian actor were supposed to be troubleshooters. I was the burned-out alcoholic ex-cop and he was the idealistic software designer. The setup was that even though we dislike each other, we naturally have to work together to solve the case. We did three episodes. The CW aired two and canceled us. Didn't even get enough ratings on a network that keeps shows ranking in the 70s.

"Take it slow, champ." I picked up my stuff and made my way up the slope of the walkway past the iron gargoyles planted on either side of the dried lawn. One had a twelve-inch tongue poking out of its evilly smiling snout. The other had claws and wings raised like it was swooping down on a fat, juicy cow. I loved those beasts. Called them Dandy and Candy. Don't know why, just liked the way it sounded.

Inside, the mail had been stacked on the coffee table by Adrianna, the cleaning lady. I used to pay her to come twice a week without thinking about it, but not these days. I was pretty sure there weren't no offers or a letter from the 49ers requesting my services. Later for the pile.

I poured some V.S.O.P. from the bar, punched in 92.3 on the stereo, and laid on the couch. As a Mary J. Blige number bumped from my JVCs, I stared at my row of honor over the fireplace. It was lined with trophies from Pop Warner on through the pros. One of my girlfriends said she thought I was being juvenile. Said I ought to have put them in the study, a back room or something. Shit. Any motherfuckah who comes into my house has gotta go with the flow. I ain't never asked nobody to light candles in front of them statues. But those are things I've earned, makes something solid of what I've done.

Anyway, that chick always acted like she had her nose up. Correcting my use – she'd say improper use – of words in public. Them trophies is still here, and she's long gone.

I shifted and felt a twinge in my fibula. My upper leg had been throbbing something fierce since halfway through the long flight from Barcelona. I'd gotten up to stretch it so many times, people must have thought I had some sorry-ass bladder infection to need to go to the can that often. It was like grinding gears in the upper part of the leg just to slip off my docksiders.

The phone rang and I had a good idea who it was. The machine picked up the call on the third ring. "I know you left Spain on Friday, Zelmont. I bet you layin' up there now with some blonde heifer when you should be sending some money down here for your son. I know you must have been making more than $100,000 for each game you played. You better do right or I might have to mention it to Daddy. Call me." The machine clicked off, then the red light started blinking, taunting me.

I took a long sip. Who'd have figured some big-legged nineteen-year-old high school dropout sports groupie would have a bougie lawyer for a father? Let alone that I would be the pathetic motherfuckah among a platoon of cats who banged her – and I only did her twice – who had the DNA that matched the baby's? It had been four years of steady bullshit from Terri. I felt sorry for the little kid she's supposed to be raising.

A Dragons game was on Fox Sports West, but it wasn't like I had any reason to watch them fools. The brandy and jet lag crept up on me and I dozed off, not dreaming of a goddamn thing.

The next day I was running after Kelrue Cummings on 56th Street, just east of Avalon. I'd been driving around for a while looking for him that morning. I tackled his fat ass and shoved his over-large ears and head into a cyclone fence above one of those little signs wired to the links advertising braiding.

"Fuck, Zee. You ain't got to clown me on my own block."

"Get up, Kelrue." I had my fists balled as I stood over him, up on the pads of my feet. Mad not 'cause he owed me plenty – he was just one of a bunch who were into me for some serious green. I was mad 'cause he assumed his overweight, waddling self could outrun me with my gimpy hip.

He sat against the fence, his flabby chest straining the buttons on his Karl Kani shirt. "I'll get your money." He held up a protesting hand with a gold ring on each fat finger.

"Gimme those for collateral."

"Aw, home, moms gave me these as family keepsakes." He rubbed the rings with his other hand like he was gonna transport somewhere else.

"Look here, Kelrue. I put up 40K for your rap record label thing and ain't had nothing to show for it 'cept reaching a disconnected number when I try callin' you these last few months."

He finally stood up, squawking. "Shit, Zee, used to be you wouldn't blink about no chump change thousand dollars or so."

He was right, which just got me madder. On my last go-round on a crack binge, I'd signed a check to Kelrue while I was more focused on getting my pipe lit. He used to be one of my go-boys – go get this, go get that – and hell, it had seemed like a good plan. Then.

"It's been two years. You played me, man." I backed off some in case the chump tried to book again.

"Aw, brah, you was handin' out cash to them hang-on punks on the gp. Me, I had a for-real business plan for In the Cut Records. We had talent lined up, fine-ass girls for the videos. We even put together a couple of CDs."

Kelrue's features were tiny, swimming in the round baby fat of his overstuffed head. There was something about the way he screwed up his face that always made me want to believe him. "Yeah, I remember going to a release party or some such."

"Yeah," Kelrue shook his big head, doing the sad act. "But you wasn't the only one to put money in, man. Napoleon, Scottie, DeJesus, they all ponied up the ducats. Hell, I put my own bank in too." He tapped his chest over and over like Mighty Joe Young to show me how sincere he was.

"So what, man? I have to hear from the streets you was back in Philly a few months ago." I leaned against the fence, my mad-on cooling down. "You should have told someone."

"What could I do, Zee? Them sharks in the record business butt-fucked me with no Vaseline. Studio costs, engineer costs, processing the videos, plus putting homies on the mic who was one day slangin' and the next thinking jus' 'cause they made one record, they was all that. What did I know about running a business?"

"But the business plan was tight on paper."

"You didn't think I did that, did you?"

"You showed it off like you did." A cop car rolled past, the uniforms mad-doggin' us. They made the corner and went on.

"Man, you know you got to front. Got a cousin in the MBA program at 'SC. She helped me write it up. But I thought I had the contacts to make it happen. Pretty soon, I was in deep. What could I do but keep tryin' to get something out that would bring the rest of the company up?"

"Yeah, keep going forward." I'd actually forgotten for a while about the money I'd loaned Kelrue. I was so doped up, a lot of what happened then is buried in brain fog. Three years ago I'd been bounced from the Falcons for failing my random drug test. The following year, I'd gotten a month-to-month with the Ravens, but then blew out my hip again in a game against Pittsburgh. And I was shoveling out buckets of money to lawyers fighting a charge of statutory sodomy rape. "But now's different, man."

"I thought you was still overseas." He scratched at his head.

"Just got back yesterday." He looked like he was expecting me to go on, but why in hell did I have to explain anything to him?

"Oh, I see," he said, as if he did. "Look here, Zee. I ain't got your funds no more than I can make a toad go meow. Why you think I been layin' low for all these months?"

"The point is I invested in you, Kelrue. You suppose to be responsible."

"Why just me?" he squawked. "Shit, you lent money to Choo Choo, Lemon, Big Pockets…"

"Nigga, I know who the fuck's got my money," I shouted. "Don't you think I'm gonna collect on all them punks? You just been the easiest to find."

"Aw," he did a turn on his heel, grabbing the top of his head. "That motherfuckah Danny finked me out, didn't he? He's still upset 'cause I messed with Tori, that fine Filipina Baronette he's been tryin' to get next to."

Danny Deuce had left a message on my machine. Two weeks ago he'd actually seen the cable broadcast of the game against the Rhine Fire where my hip had been knocked out of place again. Now I knew why he'd dropped a dime.

"Zelmont, I ain't got it. And it don't seem like I'm gonna get it anytime quick. Why the fuck would I be livin' here back in the 'hood if I was still a player? You can see I ain't got shit."

"What about what you owe me? How do I recover?"

"Zee, all I can say is you need to see your partner, Napoleon. He opened a club called the Locker Room downtown near Staples." That was where the Lakers, them sorry-ass Kings, and the pathetic Clippers played. "The place is jumpin', homie," Kelrue went on.

I hadn't seen Napoleon Graham since last year. At the time, he'd been talking about maybe opening a nightspot. "What's that do for me?"

"You and he is boys," Kelrue snapped.

"Gimme two of them rings."

He stamped on the ground. "Damn, Zee."

"Damn nothing. You signed a contract, son. You gonna honor that paper. We gonna work out a payment plan, and this is the first install-ment." I stuck out a hand and gave him my game face.

He was deciding whether to swing and see where it got him. But I knew he wouldn't. Kelrue started to twist off the ring on his little finger.

"Not that gangrene turning bullshit," I said. "Gimme the one with the diamond shaped like a triangle in it and that rope gold, baby."

That fight look came back and I grinned at him to say bring it on. Kelrue grumbled but forked over the two rings.

"Next month, let's have some cash," I said. I put the items in my pocket and started to walk away.

"You used to be the one, Zelmont. You used to have me lookin' up to you," Kelrue whined.

I used to have a $15 million deal and get a signing bonus worth more than my entire Barcelona Dragons salary. I used to not have to settle for $17,000 a game like I did playing for the third-rate Dragons. I used to be a lot of things.

I drove past the rear of the Coliseum on Vermont, the home of the Barons. Last season they were nine and six, and word was they'd take division this season. The retracting dome with the hole in the top they'd put over the joint was sparkling chrome-gray in the daylight. Soon there'd be large crowds in there to see the third season of the expansion football team that had been formed in L.A. A homegrown team more loyal than the Raiders, who, like the scrubs they were, left town. I could almost hear people cheering and high-fivin' as the receiver makes a spectacular catch and cakewalks into the end zone.

There were some black and Latino kids playing touch football on the grass on the Exposition Park side of the stadium. I pulled to the curb and watched them for a while.

Then I went over to the Four Stars pawnshop on Western and got money for the rings.

*d*avida was bent over the chair in the living room, her purple skirt hiked up over her tight brown butt. She had on a pair of those black silky panties that only made me harder, and I was yanking on them as I jugged her coochie from behind. The muscles in her buffed arms stood out all sculpted like as she braced against the top of the chair.

"I missed you, Zelmont," she gushed.

I slapped that ass and she moaned. I slapped that sweet mound several more times, making it jiggle and blush. She moaned some more as I kept doing her from behind. That's my girl. Damn. I felt like a million bucks. "I'm about ready to bust, baby."

She grabbed my johnson and eased me out of her. She turned around and dropped to her knees, taking me in her mouth. Shit. I got all lightheaded as I shot my load while she worked her lips all over my rod.

"Damn, girl. You been watchin' those Penthouse videos or something." I just stood there gasping, my pants down around my ankles. She laughed and sashayed over to the coffee table. I watched her as she bent down and straightened her muscled body up, taking a drink of juice. She made a big thing of running her tongue over her lips, knowing it was driving me wild.

"Now I come over here to say hi, and you go and ravage me." She smiled, moving back toward me. "You know I have an appointment with a producer over at Def Ritmo Records at ten." She started to play with my balls.

I slipped a hand under her skirt, putting my finger between her wet legs. "You show him what you got there, Davida, and he won't know how phat to write your check." We kissed as we stood there, feeling each other up.

She took my hand and sucked on my finger. "There's a party for the NFL owners over at Napoleon's new club on Thursday. Want to go?"

"Stadanko gonna be there?" I was getting hard again. Maybe the hip wasn't the best, but I could still make it rain when it counted.

Davida walked backwards, holding my member. She unzipped her skirt and took it off carefully so it wouldn't get wrinkled, then folded it and placed it on the coffee table.

I pulled off her panties and bit on them between my teeth. She lay on the couch and I got on top of her. "Him and his self-actualization wife." She nibbled on my ear. "Plus some City Council people and the Coliseum commissioners."

"Cool," I grunted between thrusts. "I'll be on the down low, smile and laugh at his weak-ass jokes."

"Get on his good side," she whispered in my ear.

I sat back and put the panties around the back of her neck. I tugged on them, rocking her head as we banged. Slowly, I crossed the panties around her throat. Her eyes got wide as she held onto my rib cage. I pulled tighter.

"Faster," she hollered.

I pulled the panties even tighter, her breath gurgling out from her throat. I got scared and excited and let up. She hit my arm with her fist – her signal for me to continue. I pulled tighter again and her dark eyes got so round they all but swallowed me up. She pulled me close, driving her tongue into my mouth. I still had hold of the panties, my arms pinned against her. Davida could barely breathe, but she grabbed my forearms as I tried to right myself.

She dug her nails into my butt and I bucked like a mule in a stall, letting go of the panties. She held onto me and we crashed onto the floor. We finished there, scooting around in heat.

"Shit," she said, rubbing her butt as she got up. She looked over her shoulder, turning her leg to try and get a look at the red mark on her butt. "You big ol' panther." She gently pushed the point of her shoe underneath my balls.

I laid on the floor, looking up at her and laughing. "Hey, is Weems gonna be there too?"

She gave me a funny look as she marched off to the bathroom. "You must have taken too hard a hit in Germany, Zee. What the hell would that Christian creep be doin' in a den of sin like Napoleon's club?"

"He's the football commissioner." I got up, disoriented. Rough sex did it to me every time. "His holiness might be there to keep everybody in line." Where the hell did my Jockey's go? A quick pain went through my leg, and my knee went out from under me for a second. I sank down, leveraging myself against the coffee table.

"What you doin' in there, son?" Davida called from the bathroom.

"Nothin'," I said, "just looking for my underwear." I massaged my upper thigh.

"Make some coffee, will you, baby?" She got the shower going.

"Okay." I tried to keep the strain out of my voice. I got up and made my way to the kitchen, hoping to work out the kink in my hip. The socket was grinding and I took a punch at the cupboard, frustrated.

"You ain't going nuts out there without me, are you, Zelmont?"

"Yeah, that's it, Davida." I leaned my butt against the drain, working my leg up and down until the hip joint moved back into place.

Later, I left Davida's apartment in Lennox and went over to the NFL offices on Century Park East. I signed some papers for my pension. I had about fifty grand in the bank. That's what I had left after living expenses and fronting the high life in Spain. That might be a lot to some, but I was used to a certain lifestyle, and that wasn't gonna get it.

Plus I knew I couldn't get out of sending at least ten or so to that ballbuster Terri in Savannah. It had been damn near a year since I'd last mailed her a wad of dough. And there was no way a judge, let alone her low-rent Johnnie Cochran of a father, would let me plead poverty. But the mortgage on the pad was kicking my tail, so the half a hundred wasn't gonna last long at the rate I was going.

I spent the next couple of days trying to chase down the other people who owed me money. Most of them were unfindable or just plain gone, no forwarding address. In a pool hall near Lynwood, I ran down Harper "Lemon" Carroll who owed me 20Gs.

"Eight in this pocket." He tapped the hole with his cue, glancing past me. Like I was some bitch he never intended to call again.

He stroked the white ball and it angled against the eight, sending the ball against the cushion. The black ball banked and sunk just where he'd predicted. The guy he was playing, an older gent in a brown leather jacket, handed over two Jacksons.

"You got nothing to say, man?"

"What?" he barked. "I'm supposed to be lighting up firecrackers 'cause you strolled in?" He held the cue in both hands like he was gonna do a Jackie Chan on me.

"Where's the money you owe me?" People were watching. Brown jacket moved back. I moved in on Carroll.

"You gettin' all in my business like I'm some mark."

"I want my money."

"Shit, Raines, everybody knows you ain't nothing but yesterday's news." He looked around, grinning and seeing if he got a reaction from the others.

"The twenty grand that belongs to me is fresh in my mind." I didn't wait for a reply or for him to swing the cue. I straight hit him in the jaw, knocking him back against a table. I jumped forward, but Carroll tripped me with the cue. Off balance, I fell against a stool, crashing to the floor.

"Who the fuck you think you is?" Carroll screamed, pulling out a gun from underneath his loose-knit shirt. He had it pointed at my head, sideways like he saw gangstas do it on the *Shield*.

There was no way I was gonna do the backdown in front of a crowd. "You better get that thing out of my face, fool." I got off the floor.

"The only thing I'm gonna do is bust some caps in your ego, you arrogant motherfuckah. Like I'm supposed to be all intimidated 'cause you think your reputation is gonna scare me." He shoved the Glock alongside my cheek. "Now what you better do, Zelmont, is walk the fuck out of here and see if you can make like Adam Sandler and be the waterboy for the Barons or some shit." That got a laugh from the dudes standing around the joint.

I held up my palms. "Okay, man. You the one with the gun. I guess that makes it your world."

Carroll grinned and I knew he was caught up in feeling superior. I faked with my right, then grabbed his gun hand with my left. Doing what I knew he would, he tried to pull back, freeing his gat. I let his arm go in that direction, bringing my elbow up and into his nose in the same movement.

"Dammit," he hollered.

The whack made him loosen up and I snatched the gun away. I backhanded him with the business end of the thing. There was a line of red where the skin had broken open over his nose. There was respect in his eyes as he looked at me over the hand he held to his wound.

"Look, Zelmont."

"Shut the hell up." I was enjoying this. The tingling I got in my gut was like sex with Davida. "Don't say a goddamn thing unless it's how soon you gonna have my cash."

"What you better do," a voice croaked from behind me, "is take your niggerish behavior out of my establishment."

The man with the frog voice was a round-bellied brother in suspenders and athletic T-shirt. His ugly, greasy face had a Barons cap pulled over his activator-starved tired Jehri curl.

There was a Mossberg pump laying on the counter with a choke on the end of the barrel. He stood behind it, a pudgy hand resting on that bad boy.

"I didn't pull the piece," I said, eyeing Carroll again.

"Say, man, I don't give a fuck who did what. Take your bullshit outside." The Mossberg was in his hands.

"Come on." I motioned to Carroll with the pistol.

He tucked in his lips.

"Don't try to be slick. Do what I tell you."

We marched past the slit eyes of the owner and came out into the sunlight on Atlantic. Several of the dudes from inside also tagged along. I put the gun in my back pocket since it didn't seem too good an idea to broadcast the piece.

"Well, what about it, Harper?"

He looked from side to side as if an answer was floating around in his lopsided head. "I know you heard about my mama."

I put a finger in his face. "Your mama ain't the one that signed a loan agreement. She can't read no way."

"You think I don't know you been ridin' all over town lookin' to collect your debts?" His voice went up higher with fear and anger. "But if I ain't got it, I ain't got it."

He was gonna step to me and see if I was ready to up the play. I cracked him hard on the jaw with a jab. He went down on one knee, sobbing like the princess he was.

"Oh God," one of the men watching said.

"Now what you got to say?" I kicked Carroll in the face.

He dropped over like a kid's doll on the pavement.

"Hey, you gonna kill him if you keep that up," somebody said.

I didn't care. Motherfuckah tried to bitch me up in public. You don't do that to Zelmont Raines. Unlike some wide receivers who were scared to take a hit, I didn't sweat that kind of action. You didn't get your name in the record books 'cause you couldn't perform. Art Monk, Warfield, them dudes didn't hear footsteps. They kept their minds on the ball, getting banged up time and time again as they caught the pass. No matter, they got up and went back to the job.

"'I ain't got it' won't do, Harper." There was a new gash over his left eye and he had a hand over it as he looked up at me. Blood leaked out between his fingers. "I decide who owes me and when they owe me. You get my fuckin' money together."

"Okay, Zelmont, okay."

"That's right, man. You better make it okay."

I walked away with all eyes on me. I felt good. I'd handled my business and I knew this was a sign things were bound to get better. I felt so good, I drove over to the Pico Union district near downtown and copped a dime bag of rock. I wasn't getting back into bad habits. The thing about being in rehab three times was I knew the signs, I knew when I was getting out of control. This little jolt was just to give me an edge, to keep me sharp. After I smoked up at my crib, I changed to my sweats. Then I jogged over to Runyon Canyon Park, not too far away.

I forgot there would be kids around, it being summer. Usually it was only on the weekend where you had to put up with the crumb snatchers and their yacking and goofing while their parents walked or ran with the family dog. But there weren't too many of them, plus I had my buzz on. Naturally there were the forty-something blonde types talking about the latest colonic or how they had to get the dishwasher fixed or some other ordinary bullshit.

There were a few hotties, models and wannabe actresses trying to keep their shit tight. Out and about, too, were a few fags, cruising for a set of hairy, buffed legs to wrap around come nightfall. And, of course, a few Hollywood studs, execs of some sort getting their workout on while trying to figure out how to screw the next shithead on the ladder.

I was going up the path that went around the big mountain. A young Latino in very short blue shorts and a Yale logo sweat top, his black hair colored with streaks of bright red, was walking down with his cocker spaniel and gave me the once-over as I moved past.

"Excuse me, didn't we meet at one of Napoleon Graham's parties?" He had a long earring dangling from one ear. It was shaped like something that fell off a chandelier.

Great, now the bungholers were the only ones who recognized me. "Could be, man. I gotta hit it. Sorry," I mumbled, churning my knees hard. My hip socket began to ache as I rounded the bend. The grinding pain made me want to stop several times, but I kept putting one foot in front of the other. Sweat was making my lips salty, and every time my right leg came up it was like a jab with the point of a knife in my upper thigh.

Come on, Zelmont, it ain't nothing to do but to do it. I huffed, then grunted, clamped my teeth, and kept moving, eyes straight ahead.

I made the bend, where the path leveled off and you could see out onto the city in several directions. I stopped, bending over more from the pulsing in my hip than being out of breath. Straightening up, I wiped my face with my old Falcons top. Not far away to the left I could see my house tucked up on its hill. The thing looked solid and safe, like the day I first spotted it running this mountain. I was up for Rookie of the Year and knew I had to have a pad like that.

People assumed I did it to have the fly chicks and swinging parties. Have me a cool address and be able to look down on the city where I was raised. Well, I guess there was something to that. Hell, my mama never had nothing but the hot cramped apartment me and my two sisters were raised in growing up near the Coliseum.

We didn't skip no meals, but there wasn't too much extra either. I made do with out-of-fashion kicks when all my friends were getting the next new thing. When I made it to the pros, I set my sights on getting used to things I never had as a child. I should have been smarter at holding on to the money. I could have listened to people, including my mother. But there was always the next pass I was gonna catch, the next product I was gonna pimp.

Them days ain't done yet, I promised myself. I took a deep breath and started a slow jog down the other side.

Thursday, me and Davida, in her used Mercedes Kompressor roadster, went over to the NFL owners' set at the Locker Room. Graham's place, on the corner of 11th Street and Georgia, was real classy. Across the way was the Staples set-up with its glass and metal arena, hotel and Nokia auditorium. The arena itself was shaped like a giant 'q' knocked on the side.

There had been a lot of rigmarole in getting the NFL owners to agree to bring a team back to town. They pretty much wanted the City of L.A. to kiss their collective butts and mortgage the public piggy bank to build a new stadium complex, like Cleveland and San Francisco had done. But the crew of local high rollers who'd put the deal together, along with city representatives, played it cool. They knew the NFL needed the number-two media market – their ad revenues had been down for several years. So they held out for a better deal, and got it.

Ellison Stadanko, who'd made his money in solid waste retrieval, was a pal of one of the movers and shakers and got the inside track on being the main backer of the Barons. And the Coliseum, built for the Olympics in '32, fixed up for the traitorous Al Davis in the '80s, got a new life and a dome to go with it. The Sports Arena next door had been hollowed out and turned into a food and bar court that led to a four-story parking structure.

To the south side of the Staples arrangement was the Convention Center. Nobody was at any of those venues that night. And the Joe and Jane six-packs who kept the machinery of pro sports going by buying the tickets and getting a snack at the Denny's or Wolfgang Puck's alongside the complex weren't invited to the Locker Room. This set was reserved for players, coaches, agents, and others in the loop.

The outside of the club was done up in polished steel panels with rivets showing. The roof had goalposts on one end and a gigantic hoop on the other. There was a two-story-high TV monitor on one side of the building. An old Jim Brown, Fred Williamson flick, *Three the Hard Way*, was showing on the giant screen when we walked up from the parking lot.

People were backed up at the entrance. "Zelmont," I heard as a hand the size of the end of a shovel rose from the crowd chatting and standing around.

"Napoleon," I said, making my way over. We hugged. "This ain't making you hard, is it," I only half-joked. His dreads were tied back, the last inch of each dyed bright blond. He was wearing blue-green mascara and his eyebrows were V'd up like Mr. Spock's. Other than that he looked normal in a black double-breasted suit with white pearl buttons, a white no-collar shirt, and a ruby stud at the neck.

"Nigger, please. I may be a switch hitter, but I got good taste."

"That's what I mean."

Napoleon pretended to ignore me and kissed Davida on the lips. "You lookin' good, girl."

"Always a pleasure when I'm in your company, Nap." She touched his buffed chest, scoping the scene as we entered.

Chicks in short, tight black skirts and black and white striped halter-tops passed out drinks on trays to the crowd.

"Sorry about Barcelona," Napoleon said.

"Hey, you know how it gets. But I'm on a program, getting stronger every day. I've got a couple of years left yet."

"Right on."

I wanted to get off the discussion about my hip. Napoleon was a nut for those goddamn "reaching-your-full-potential" courses. He even was a speaker at some of the conferences. I remember after he'd been busted with his boyfriend, this Hollywood director of big shoot-'em-ups. They had been tossing their salads at a resort in Palm Springs, and the tabloid fucks had been stalking him, trying to prove the rumors about my boy. But rather than hide and deny, Napoleon went on Tyra Banks' show preaching the virtues of bisexuality. Jesus.

Me, I don't give a shit who's doin' who. It's about can you trust a mufu or not, and I could trust Nap.

"I best mingle."

"Cool. I want to talk to you about something later." Some dude in loafers and a Prada suit came up to Napoleon. He was talking in some foreign language on a cell phone, and at the same time shaking the former All-Pro tackle's hand. Davida had drifted away and I did the same.

"Mr. Raines, hope you enjoy your evening." The waitress' healthy chest strained the material of her top. I barely noticed the martinis on her tray.

"I will now that you've said hello." I took a glass and toasted her. There was a R&B band playing on a raised stage supported by clear cylinders off to one side. The backdrop was glowing footballs that swirled around and around in a black sky. A spread was laid out on several tables, with an ice sculpture of downtown L.A. surrounded by some huge shrimp as the centerpiece. Monitor banks on one wall of the place played NFL and NBA game films.

Mama said never turn down free food, so I headed for the grub.

"Yo, Zelmont, how'd it crack in England?"

"Spain, Danny, it's a whole other country." Danny Deuce was standing with a couple of his boys, chilling along one of the walls.

"Spain, Mexico, it ain't the real pros, is it?" he cackled. One of his homies put his hand in front of his mouth, giggling. The other dude was too busy zeroing in on the honeys.

"Catch you, man." I walked off, knowing he was watching me as I did.

I got some food and spotted Davida talking with a roly-poly short guy in a turtleneck and silk sport coat. He was glancing everywhere but her direction. His face had that uncomfortable look I'd seen on owners' faces during contract negotiations. She circled around him, gesturing with her arms. I went back for more shrimp. I loves me some shrimp.

I reached across a cute Korean chick in a slit dress and bumped shoulders with somebody else grabbing for a prawn.

"Raines," Julian Weems said. His pinched looks were as sour as ever.

"Commissioner." I rubbed my tongue over a side tooth. "Surprised to see you here."

"What have you been doing these days?" He turned his head, concentrating on fetching his chow.

He knew I'd gone to play in Spain – sumabitch had to sign the league transfers. "Not much. But I've been working out, staying healthy."

"Oh, why?" Weems gave me his Moses-on-the-mountain glare behind those Ben Franklin glasses of his. He chewed on a piece of broccoli.

"I'm going to get back into football."

"Have you been offered an assistant coaching job?"

I should have pimp-slapped him. But it was his tune to call and I had to shuffle to it for now. "I aim to play for the Barons. I grew up here, this is where I went to the pros from Long Beach State, and this is where I'd like to finish out."

A fade-cut white boy in a three-piece pinstripe with planed-off shoulders slipped beside Weems. The guy walked like he'd just taken three Ex-Lax and was holding it back. He passed his blues over me, daring me to breathe. There was a small flaming cross tattooed on the left side of his cheek. His jaw muscle bunched and unbunched.

Weems gazed at this corn-fed husky like he was his favorite pet. "I didn't realize how droll your humor could be, Mr. Raines. You are a known child molester, sir. Our league is in the process of rebuilding its stature as America's sport after men like you worked overtime to tear it down. Dope parties, fornication, beer bashes on team flights, trashing hotel rooms, bar fights." He chomped on a shrimp. "Even if by some cruel test of the Lord you were healthy, and I read the account from Barcelona, do you think I'd allow you back in?"

I shoved a finger at him. "That girl in the wheelchair said she was twenty. And if you recall, commissioner, I wasn't convicted of that statutory rape charge. Although I know you was prayin' real hard that I would be." I leaned into him, his dog flexing. "I'm gonna be a player again."

"Sure you will."

The two of them walked off.

Davida came up. "I can't believe this shit."

All I got was a couple of blowjobs for all the goddamn trouble that handicapped chick caused me. She was waiting in the cold drizzle outside my pad one night. Said she was left by her friends, that they'd been teasing her for having a crush on me. Damn, she initiated the sex. She'd wheeled over and grabbed my crotch while I was dialing her a cab. I lost my endorsement contracts with the auto parts chain and the video game. Plus I spent a fuckin' armored car full of money on lawyers keeping my black ass out of jail.

"Zelmont, are you listening to me?" Davida was digging her nails into my arm.

"Yes," I said, pulling back.

"What'd I say, then?" Her top lip curled over her capped teeth.

"You was going on about how that producer in the turtleneck over there was supposed to get your CD together for the fall, put money into promotion, downloads and so forth. But now he's givin' you static that some of the cuts ain't slammin.'" The ability to have my mind in two places at once came from years of hearing everything the QB was saying in the huddle and still making eye contact with a babe on the 30-yard line.

"You don't have to be so fuckin' smug."

"Sweetmeat," I said, "I'm in your corner, you know that." A long tall sally walked up behind Davida. She was fine as bone china.

Davida ran a hand through her black hair and shifted in her high heels. "You take me for a plaything, don't you?"

"No more than you do me." She looked at me like she was trying to penetrate my mind. I kissed her, running a hand over her firm backside.

"Excuse me," said the good-looking sister. She'd been standing there listening to us and now had come around front toward the ice sculpture and shrimp. She wore a blue shimmering number with specks of dark orange spattered all over the material. The hem was a few tasteful inches above her knees. Her hair was frizzed out around a high-cheek-boned face, silver teardrop earrings hanging from her chocolate-colored ears.

"Mind if I get to the shrimp?"

"Knock yourself out," said Davida, pulling on my sleeve to let her pass.

I was careful to not take my eyes off Davida. "Did you see that big clown standing next to Weems?"

"Yeah, he's one of his Internal Truth Squad bruisers," she said. "Napoleon told me that Weems had recruited these guys from groups like the Promise Keepers about a month ago."

"To do what?" The woman in blue got her shrimp and walked across the dance floor to a table where Stadanko sat with some others.

"Keep things kosher," Davida answered. "Keep bad boys like you from messing up the program."

"Some kind of spies?"

"I guess," she said, irritated. "What am I going to do, Zelmont?"

"It's going to work out, Davida. You got other contacts besides this dude, right?"

"Yeah, but Jansen can make things happen without a whole lot of bullshit." She began gesturing again. "The songs are almost mixed. This album can put me over. This is my career we're talking about, Zelmont. It's very important to me. I ain't going back to what I used to do, you understand."

I looked around, hoping to change the subject. This broad was wearing me out with her going on all the time about the work she was putting in to get her singing career going. Three years ago, she was the choreographer for the Laker Girls. And like all them other air-headed babes from Youngstown and wherever, she thought just because she could shake her tail feather and had a halfway okay voice, she was going to be the next Janet Jackson.

"Zelmont," Napoleon yelled from a balcony with a gold rail. He signaled for me to join him.

"I'll be right back, baby. Fact, I'll ask Napoleon if he's got some ideas for record people."

"Whatever," she said, throwing me a glare.

I copped another drink on the way up to the big fella. There was a white dude in a Zegna suit talking all excitedly to Napoleon. He stopped when he saw me. Then he walked away, smoking a thin cigar as he went past. "This set's live, home," I said to Napoleon, who leaned on the rail, swirling the ice in his drink.

"The honest always pay up." He straightened to his impressive full height and took a large swallow.

"Huh?"

Napoleon smiled and held the drink out. The waitress who'd talked to me when I'd come in was there in a flash. "Another, Nappy?" The way she said it made me think of jam on a hot biscuit.

"Not now, thanks, Dora."

"Okay, Mr. Graham." She smiled real nice at him and threaded her way back into the pack.

"You hittin' that, Napoleon?"

He put his hands on his hips. "It's men this month."

"Wonderful." I sipped and watched the woman in the blue and orange speckled gown down below throwing her head back and laughing at something Stadanko said. Ysanya, Stadanko's missus, was rubbing one of her goddamn crystals, looking here and there like Timothy Leary's ghost was gonna show.

"Who's the hammer at Stadanko's table?" I asked.

"If you think she's gonna give you some trim, you might do better in a dyke bar twirling your dick."

"Huh?"

"That's Wilma Wells, lead attorney for the Barons. She's the one that put together the package the City and the team owners went for. She knows her stuff."

Smart women and me went together about as good as Clarence Thomas and Al Sharpton on a double date. Plus she must have been a couple of years older than me. "What it be then, brah?"

"You need work?"

"That obvious?"

"I been there, remember?"

I nodded and drank. A dark guy in a dark suit with black slicked-back hair eased behind Stadanko's old lady. He put a hand on her shoulder, and she put one of hers on his. Damn, Stadanko into some kinda threesome? Then I noticed the thing dangling from his ear. It was the gay boy I'd run into on the mountain who said he knew Nap.

"That a friend of yours?" I pointed my drink at the dude. He was bending low, whispering something to the space lady.

Napoleon rubbed a finger across his upper lip. "Pablo is a corrective ch'i color consultant."

"The fuck is that?" I said, chuckling.

"About a thousand pretty little green ones a week from Ysanya."

Pablo was looking around and spotted my broad-shouldered buddy. The fidgety fellow blew Nap a kiss.

"How about you become the Locker Room's utility man?" Napoleon said, making a gesture like a duke or something to his boy down below. Pablo got all squirmy, and Ysanya's lids got real tight.

"You wouldn't mean I got to be one of them bathroom towel-holdin' motherfuckahs in a bow tie, would you?"

"Negro," he whined.

"I ain't so hard up I want to be a greeter like how Joe Louis finished his days. Or how Tyson went out." A bad feeling exploded in my stomach even as I said the words. I hoped I wasn't predicting anything.

"No, I have something more, ah, appropriate for you, Zelmont."

I leaned my backside against the railing. "What in the hell are you talking about, Nap?"

His mouth closed as fast as he'd started to speak. I could sense the man coming up beside us.

"Good party, Napoleon," the dude with the accent and Zegna suit said. "You are making a good go of things. A good go." He squeezed one of Nap's broad shoulders like they was tight. "This another of your football friends?" He gleamed his teeth at me.

"Zelmont Raines, All-Pro and Super Bowl winner," Nap said. His body was rigid.

"Pleasure, Mr. Raines." The man lifted his eyebrows at Nap and trotted off after a redhead.

"Who's that?" I asked.

Nap bit the inside of his mouth. "Rudy Chekka."

"So who is he?"

"Stadanko's cousin," he answered but didn't go on in his explaining. "Look, Zee, I'll call you tomorrow. We'll talk then." He clapped me on the arm and hauled his large self down the stairs.

What was up with that, I wondered. I put my empty glass on a table and started back down to the main floor too. Wouldn't you know it but Stadanko and that stacked Wilma Wells were at the foot of the stairs, talking.

"Mr. Stadanko." I stopped on the second step from the floor.

"What are you doing these days, Zelmont?" Stadanko was a bear-sized man. He was almost my height, with a wide middle and a flat face that wasn't improved much by his bushy mustache. Stadanko was wearing a gun-gray drape coat, black slacks, and some old school black and tan Nunn Bush like my Uncle Gene used to have.

"Not through with playing some ball yet."

"I heard you fired your last agent."

"The Barons have a walk-on period in the next few weeks," I tossed out.

He grunted and looked at the Wells woman. "That's cause our counselor, who is conscious about the team's public image, finagled that with the Coliseum Commission to get them to give us the new sky boxes. Encourage local talent and all that. Personally, I've never seen a good prospect come along that way."

He glanced hard at me. I knew he wasn't waiting for me to flinch.

"Anyway, I have to go schmooze our favorite politician," he said to Wells, his personality picking up when he talked to her. He waved to Councilman Waters and pretended like I wasn't there as he went off to do his thing. Stadanko put his arm around Waters, whose district included the Coliseum and who was head of the Coliseum Commission.

"Having a good time?" That was lame when I was in junior high. But them brainy chicks always threw me off. Never knew what to say, or how to say it.

"Business," she said softly. "I'd rather be home reading a book or listening to Etta James and sipping a glass of Merlot."

Fuck. Last book I read was the thing that explained my NFL pension and benefits. "I know what you mean." I was dying. But she hadn't moved off.

"I saw an interview you did while you were on the Dragons for the British Channel 4."

"You doing better than me," I said, impressed. "How'd you stumble on that?"

"Interesting people always interest me."

"Uh, thanks." Damn, could I have been any geekier?

The muscle boy who'd been shadowing Weems all of a sudden decided to make himself handy.

"This man crowding you, Ms. Wells?"

"You better get back to the kennel, fang."

He got in my face, huffing and puffing. "You are a nuisance." He put a hand on me and I slapped it away.

"It's okay, Trace, Mr. Raines and I were simply conversing." She smiled at me.

"Yeah, you know what conversing means, don't you?" I said, taunting the chump. Let him go off. I'd wind up with a couple of million in my pocket from the league if he did.

The muscle beneath his flaming cross throbbed, and we did the stare-down for a few seconds. "As you say, Ms. Wells." Fang stomped off.

"I wish you luck with the Barons, Mr. Raines. You should know that Jon Grainger and Tommy Earl are also doing a walk-on for the wide receiver slots."

"I appreciate the tip." I wanted to ask her why she was giving me the heads up, but nixed it.

"I better work the crowd myself," she said.

"Hope we have a chance to converse again."

"Surely."

I watched those hips moving underneath the clingy dress and forgot all about my problems, at least for a few minutes.

hat I need is some real support from you, Zelmont." Davida kicked at one of her throw pillows. "You say you're down for my career, but you don't act like it."

"I'm sorry, was I supposed to have your picture tattooed on both my arms instead of one?" A big jet zoomed overhead.

"Asshole." She threw a magazine at me.

"Be cool," I warned, wondering how the hell she put up with living near the airport.

She threw another magazine at me, a thick one – must have been a *Cosmo*.

"What I tell you?" I shoved her down on the couch.

"Oh, the big bad wide receiver likes to beat up on the poor Chicana from Boyle Heights?"

I made like I was playing a violin. "Yeah, the one who used to catch three buses to dance class and then go to work to help her mother and chucklehead brothers?" I folded my arms. "That how you gonna sell it to the tabloid shows?"

"Maybe. Could be the jumpstart I need for my singing career."

I laughed without thinking.

She sat up in a hurry. "What the fuck's that mean?"

"Come on, let's go get some breakfast."

"No, pendejo, what did you mean?" She was right under my nose, shaking a red nail at it.

"Davida, ain't neither one of us exactly at the top of our game."

"Yeah," she said real quiet, waiting to spring.

"Look," I moved around her living room, "you yourself have said you knew you didn't have the strongest voice in the world. Damn, all kinda singers use, what do they call it, recording over their own voice a couple of times to beef the singing up." Come on, Zelmont, talk your way through this. Don't blow this thing where you can jug this fine mama any which way but loose anytime you want.

"My voice is refined, Zelmont, like a precious vase. It isn't brassy like Tina Turner's or Christina Aguilera's." She was following me around.

"If they's harsh, maybe you ought to get your nana to light one of her prayer candles so you can run up on some of that." I knew I shouldn't have said it, but she got me mad, talking down to me and all.

She popped me in the chest and was about to go for two when I caught her wrist. I bent it hard.

"Shit. Bully."

"You like it."

She kicked at me but I scooted back. "That's old, and you're slow."

"Let go, motherfucker."

"No." I forced her back and bent to kiss her. She slapped me, stinging. I got a look from her 'cause I could feel my mouth twist on one side. "You don't want that."

A shade of fear flashed in those black eyes of hers.

"Zelmont, let go."

"Hmmm." I was going to back off, but then she gave me a certain smile. Like she was playing me. Outside she was scared, which I liked. I wanted respect. But inside she was marking me for a chump.

I put my hand on her face, my triceps tightening. I blitzed her head toward the wall, letting go right before she made contact.

"Puta," she screamed.

I watched her, chewing on my bottom lip.

"Get the fuck out of my apartment, bitch," she yelled.

I felt like doing something else to her. I got a warm rush in my gut, like the time I beat Henderson's coverage on me for the Bears in 20 degree weather. I cakewalked into the end zone, having outrun a dude who the sportswriters said was gonna make me eat muddy ice. I was getting hard, like I did back then too.

"Leave." The worry was in her voice.

I came closer. "Why, late for your singing lessons?" I put a hand on her chest, rubbing those puppies.

She stared at me, not blinking.

I brought up the same hand like I was going to strike, getting a gasp from her. "See you, Davida."

I was hungry, but too worked up to eat. I started driving over to Napoleon's club for our appointment, knowing I'd be early. It was one of those gray, funky days that hit L.A. sometimes. I got off the Harbor at 9th, going around the one-way block. I went down Flower to 11th, then cut back west. I parked next to Nap's Lincoln and knocked on the metal door. Also on the lot was a silver Prowler with shiny black rims and one of those limited edition Nissans done up like a '34 Ford Coupe hot rod. Both had yellow running lights.

"Nap," I said, knocking again. I didn't get an answer, so I tried the latch. The door was unlocked and I went inside. A bottle of something exploded upside the door, spraying glass inches from my head. I leaped over a low rail, slamming a foot into a dude in a long leather coat. He fell back, knocking over a cocktail table.

He said something that wasn't English or Spanish, but I wasn't taking a language lesson. As he tried to get up, I brought one of Nap's thick ashtrays down on his skull and heard a satisfying crack. He wilted to the ground as I went forward.

Two others had ganged up on Nap. A third one was draped against the bar, his belly pointing to the ceiling. One of the two spun my way, bringing up an arm like a ref making a call.

His gun clacked, but I was already diving behind a fat pillar.

I hunched there, heard a grunt, and came around the pillar.

The gunman and Nap were mixing it up, Nap ramming one of his molded forearms under the dude's throat. The other one had been swatted against a potted plant. He now had a blade out and I lifted one of the small round tables.

"Yo, man." I threw it and tagged his ass in the sternum. I rushed over and stomped him twice in the face before he could spit.

"This is not good relations, Napoleon." The dude with the gun was holding one side of his head in pain. The gun was at his feet.

"Zelmont," Nap said, throwing the cat off his bar. He groaned as he hit the floor. "Help them find the exit." Nap picked up the gun and pointed it at the guy on the floor.

I made the suffering one and the one I'd hit with the ashtray carry the one I'd stepped on outside. Nap bum rushed the fourth one, the gunman, outside.

"You must learn to relax," the guy said. "Discuss these matters in a rational manner."

Nap tossed the gun back to the cat, and I about peed on myself.

"Nigga, is you crazy?" I screamed, not knowing what to do.

Nap walked back inside. I hurried after him, shutting the door and locking it. "What in the fuck was that all about?" I was happy to hear their rides fire up.

He walked to the bar, and for a second it looked like he was gonna actually pour himself a real drink. But he was true to his tofu-loving ways and got one of those liter bottles of Ginger Ale from underneath.

"If you want something with more kick, help yourself, brah." One of his knuckles was bleeding. He closed his fist on some ice and tossed the cubes in a thick glass.

"Naw, I'm cool." I copped a seat on a stool at the bar and watched him.

Nap tipped his glass and poured his soda carefully, like a scientist mixing a secret formula. He held it up to the electric lights and swished the ice around. Nap's gift as a tackle was his calm.

His life off the field was as wild as a sixteen-year-old nympho on meth pulling a train in the back of a 6-4 Impala. But in the game, Napoleon Graham was famous for not blowing his top. Offensive linemen from various teams compared notes in the off-season on how to get underneath my man's exterior. When he was contained like that – that's when the brain power was churning, his mind snapping shit into place.

"Little Hand," he said, taking a gulp from his glass.

"Your new nickname?"

Nap smiled, leaning on the bar next to me. He scratched the side of his face with a long turquoise nail. "I'm into them for some large bills, Zelmont."

"Your partners in this?" I waved a hand around.

"Yeah." He tipped his glass, looking at the bottom.

"Say, Nap. You was the one always advisin' me to get off the pipe and blow and save my scratch. You was the one who made all the good investments."

He straightened up, his biceps flexing and loosening as he placed his hands flat on the bar. "And I did too. But don't forget I've got two ex-wives and had my share of palimony suits, women and men." He showed his horse teeth. "I know you understand how it's tough keeping your dick out of trouble when junior gets an itch."

"That guy on the cell phone the other night, the one with the accent," I said.

"Chekka. He's the local don, or whatever the hell the Serbs in Little Hand call the leader."

"And they came to you? Black folks, even brothers like you, don't run in that crowd, do they?"

"They do if, like me, they've put some money into a certain commercial waste hauling business headquartered in San Pedro."

He poured more Ginger Ale, letting it sit in the glass. He picked up a swizzle stick whose head was shaped in the Heisman Trophy pose, then started tapping it on the bar.

I always had a problem learning my playbook. My degree in communications from Long Beach State said more about my worth to the athletic program than it did about my focus on schooling. But once I got my mind around the information, I was on it, baby.

"You mean Stadanko's in on this too?" The solid waste retrieval business he owned was called Shindar. Hell, 'cause of Napoleon I used to have some stock in the company myself.

Nap stopped tapping the swizzle stink. "I'm not sure to what extent Stadanko is involved on the criminal end. His cuz Rudy seems to be the one true gangster in the family. Near as I can tell, Chekka launders cash through Shindar and other legit enterprises."

"Then Standanko is his front man," I said. "But he must know what Rudy does and gets his cut off of the strong-arm stuff."

"Yeah," Napoleon agreed, shaking his head, "there has to be

something to that. It appears that on a day-to-day basis, Standanko runs the franchise and Rudy runs the solid waste business as a way to control his other businesses. I checked, and on paper, Stadanko is supposed to have sold his shares to Rudy."

"That would make sense," I said. "Stadanko can't be linked to any thug shit, what with Weems on the warpath."

"True," the big man added, "gives him plausible deniability."

I wasn't sure what that meant but I went on. "And he's got the city officials watching his every move too. But why'd you have us invest in his trash business in the first place?"

Nap made a sound with his tongue. "What better way to get in tight with the dude? Remember, back when I said it was a good idea to invest with Shindar, he was only one among several who might get the nod to be the majority owner of the Barons."

"Always keeping that back door option open, huh?" I cracked.

He gave off with a big ol' grin. "Why not? When I got out of football I had enough to live all right on."

"But you wanted to stay in the zone, still be an operator," I finished.

Nap hunched his tackle's shoulders. "You know what I'm talking about, Zelmont. Doing that play-by-play thing on ESPN wasn't gonna get it."

"And an upscale club kept you high steppin'. But you could have gotten a regular loan, couldn't you?"

He finally drank some more. "That means straightening out some credit them ex-hos of mine fucked up. That means collateral and a business plan. That means time to line that shit up, get through the bank committee, and so forth.

Meanwhile you had some other ballplayers backed by new money kids in Newport Beach salivating to get this land 'cause it's right by the new sports complex."

I adjusted my butt on the stool. "So you had to move quick. Now what?"

Nap looked at me dead on. "I need you and Danny to watch my back."

I laughed. "Why don't you get your brother and his Victoria Avenue poot butts to roll up on this Little Hand?"

"Come on, Zelmont," he said, annoyed. "Those gents ain't got enough discipline to walk in a straight line if there was free Olde English at the other end. But I got to put Danny in on this, otherwise he'd get insulted."

"We wouldn't want that."

"But you got the savvy to keep him in line. And we can put him and his boys in motion when it's needed."

"You sounding like that's a for sure thing."

"I expect to get out of this box I'm in. Come on."

We went into his office. The room was done up in dark woods, and there were different kinds of African carvings, gargoyles and demon statues all over. On top of a tall bookcase was a row of Nap's trophies. Of course there was a frou-frou touch, with a pink and blue toilet set on a marble slab, an umbrella over it. Modern goddamn art. Through a large arched window I could see the Staples Center.

He walked over to a large squat stone head sitting on a thick wood shelf. It had those ancient Mexican features with black blood in its face. He stuck his index finger in each eye, then touched the nose followed by the left ear.

I heard a panel slide open somewhere in the room. Nap crossed to a curtain pulled back from the arched window. He reached behind and, like Blackstone the Magician who my mom took to see me once, produced the rabbit that made me smile. He laid two thousand in cash on me.

"Every week I can pay you the same. No reporting, no trace. And if things go right, there'll be a bigger payoff."

"Like how?"

"Be in the moment, my brother. All will be revealed."

It got on my nerves when he spouted that Phil Jackson Zen shit. But the two grand was looking good about then, so what could I say? "Now you know I gotta be workin' out, Nap."

He banged his swizzle stick against his bottom lip.

He seemed to be considering something else, but said, "That can be handled. You seen Burroughs since you been back?"

Burroughs was a doc a lot of the guys went to for help in establishing a rehab program. Especially if you needed to be clean in a hurry. He was also useful in several other ways too.

But I didn't want to get into why I hadn't. "I ain't gonna be standin' in the entrance in a top hat and one of them long coats like some doorman?"

"You're repeating yourself, son. And don't change the fuckin' subject."

"It must be your feminine side which sets you to worrying so much. I'll take care of my hip."

Nap pushed his hands up like a homie pulled over by the Highway Patrol on the Harbor Freeway at 3 a.m. "Be here tomorrow 'round six. Me, you and Danny need to go over a few things. I have some photos of the Little Hand slobs I want y'all to become familiar with like your old lady's snatch."

"I'm in as long as I ain't got a contract. But once that happens, I'm outta here faster'n one of Madonna's husbands."

The big fella chewed on the end of the swizzle, breaking it off in his teeth. "That's good, Zelmont," he said, again keeping what he was thinking to himself.

We shook hands and I went back out into the parking lot, careful like. Maybe Chekka's boys were waiting around, figuring to smoke a brother before lunchtime. They weren't and I got in my ride with no particular place to go. I could have gone to find Davida, try and make up. But she'd see through that. She knew me well enough to know I would just be doing it to get a celebration fuck out of her. She could wait.

I had butterflies with razor wings doing loop-the-loops in my stomach. I was psyched up and couldn't quite figure out why.

The danger of them gangsters had me sharp, but that wasn't it.

Motherfuckahs who thought with their guns were cowardly punks anyway. You had to respect a piece, but not the fool packing it. Guns gave 'em a false sense of security. That could be handled.

Maybe somewhere down below the usual bullshit going on in my brain I felt I had turned a corner down a hall and couldn't come back the same way. I knew I had to get to the end, wanted to get there, in fact. It was the doors along that hall I had to be up on. Those doors were going to open any second, and I didn't know what might be spilling out at me.

I could have gone to the Canyon to work out. Or I could have gone over to Gold's Gym in Venice and done some reps, hit the stationary, maybe catch a bouncy little something looking for an afternoon diversion before she got to her acting class. Yeah, I should have done one of those things. Instead I went and found me a slanger on Figueroa and bought two vials of crack. Sumabitch recognized me too. He'd be telling stories to his partners later.

I didn't wait until I got to the crib to light my shit either. I got a room at a hot sheet motel. The chunky Indian chick behind the glass looked at me as if I'd lost my mind. I'd strolled past two hos out at the curb like they were invisible and hauled my big ass into the courtyard. Standing there alone at the counter behind bullet-proof glass, I shoved the forty under the slot, grinning like I was natural-born country.

Inside the room the air wasn't moving. It was like all the quickie stranger sex had been soaked into the cinder block walls and was seeping out a little bit at a time, getting absorbed into the skins of the users, then recycled back into the room.

And the women like the ones prowling outside were living off the energy like it was anti-matter in *Star Trek*.

I clicked on the TV. An adult flick came on.

The stem of the pipe was warm and comforting in my fingers.

Narcotic vapors went up from the bowl, and that smell wasn't new in the room either. I took a pull, then another, then let the shit out. Amateurs will try to take in too much on their first suck like crack was marijuana. But the deal is to take it slow, draw it in like you're baiting a trap. Then I took a third pull and look here, that was the bomb.

The hit had arrived, and I was riding on top of the engine car of the locomotive, the fumes coursing through the corpuscles in my arms, my legs and into my skull. My ears started tingling. The buzz was on. I laid back on the bed, staring at the mirrored panels attached to the ceiling. The moaning of the couple on the screen became the cheers of the crowd. I was running for the goal line in my Barons uniform, my hip rising and falling like a well-oiled piece of machinery down the moist grass of the Coliseum.

Nothing could stop me.

i pretty much sleepwalked through my gig the next few days at the Locker Room. It wasn't like I had to roust the clowns looking to grab some booty on the sly or talking too loud in one of the four bars of the club. Nap had plenty of swelled-up dudes, and a couple of beefed body-building chicks, to take care of that. My thing was to float, do a little backslapping, laugh and nod my head with the out-of-towners, pose for a picture now and then. And keep on point.

On the third night, I peeped a couple of dudes that had to be with the Little Hand. They mumbled in that language of theirs, and like Chekka they wore way too much Hugo Boss cologne. Like they were trying to hide the rotting smell their corrupt asses must naturally give off.

But these two laid in the cut, assessing things for Chekka, I figured. Me and Nap watched them on the monitors he had behind a sliding section of wall fronted by those crazy statues in his office. He had several mini-cameras hidden about the club. Nap was a smart cat, always thinking ahead.

"His name is Ondanian," Nap said, sipping on a glass of fizzy water. He tipped his head at the taller of the two on the monitor screen.

"That don't sound like one of them Russian names like the rest of them." I wanted a hard drink but didn't want Nap to think I was slipping. My tryout was next week anyway.

"He's Armenian," Nap said for my education. Like I knew where Armenia was compared to Bosnia. "I understand he and Chekka may be doing some business together."

"You mean he ain't on homeboy's payroll?"

47

"Freelancer," Nap answered. "Seems he made his money in black market arms dealing to places like North Korea and Iraq."

The two walked off and Nap killed the power to the wall of monitors. "Let's keep a watch on Ondanian, Zee. Could be he'll prove useful as a block on Chekka."

"Cool," was all I could say. To me he was just one more hungry mountain lion circling to try to get his piece of the bull. If I got a contract, I intended to buy in with Nap, and then we could open Locker Rooms in other cities. First, though, I had a few brothers who'd kill their mamas for bus fare I was gonna stick on Chekka, Ondanian, or any other chump with a hard-to-pronounce name who was trying to roughshod my boy. "Davida have any luck on that record thing?" We were walking back to the staircase.

"Man, I ain't talked to that silly ho since we went at it over her so-called singing career the other day." I started down the stairs. At the main entrance, which was done up like a tunnel into a stadium, a man in a hat like Sinatra used to wear on those album covers came in. He flashed something to Rory, the doorman. Me and Nap exchanged a look.

"I'll go see what's up." I was already in motion as I talked. I hit the bottom of the staircase and zigzagged my way through the clubbers to where the cop stood near the stage.

"Can I help you, doc?" He was a little over average height, a Tiger Woods looking stud. Could be he was part Samoan like Dwayne Johnson. His pearl gray suit was crisp but out of fashion by years. Somehow, without him even talking, I knew his threads matched his personality.

"Superstar." He leaned back against the pillar, his coat falling open to show the butt of his piece and the badge he'd clipped back on his belt. A goofy smile pulled his mouth apart to show the gap in his front teeth.

"Well aren't you somethin'," I teased.

"I caught a couple of your European games on Fox."

This chump was starting to get on my nerves, what with his half-finished sentences. "We card 'em if they look under twenty-five." I assumed he was vice the way he was dressed.

"How old was Davida? Oh yeah, twenty-seven."

"You her new squeeze?" I didn't know if I was relaxed or stressed. He played with the top of his hat but didn't take it off.

"You been in trouble before, haven't you, Zelmont?"

I knew that tone meant it was time to lawyer up. "Say what you came here to say, man."

"Fahrar – that's FA-RAR." The cop squared me up. Until then I hadn't noticed, but it seemed like one of his eyes was darker than the other, or maybe it was just the low lighting.

"So you came to sweat me?"

He put a hand on my arm and my first instinct was to pull away. He wasn't applying any pressure, his thumb in the crook of it, his fingers on my elbow. "Davida's dead, Zelmont." He sounded like one of those fake-ass undertakers in an old Western on TNT.

"That girl's healthy as two horses." I knew that for true given the way I'd been ridin' that ass.

Suddenly he pulled himself closer, tugging on my arm. "She was murdered," he whispered into my ear. I could feel his mismatched eyes scanning me, hoping for some sign.

"I didn't do it, man. That's all I got to say, you understand?" Me and him stared at each other for a few ticks, then he leaned back again.

"Her neighbors say you were over there four days ago and they could hear you two going at it."

"Yeah?" Be cool, Zelmont. This is like the time you got busted in that motel in Decatur with the two broads and the coke. Don't say shit.

"You O.J. her, homeboy?" Fahrar fooled with his hat again, his off-colored eye shining at me.

"What's a matter, man?" I said, moving closer to him.

Cops hate it when you invade their space. They call it challenging their authority or some shit. "You ride the pine in high school and can't stand to see a brother who's successful?"

"Was successful," he hurled back at me. "You got someplace you were this morning?"

"You mean after I left your mama's house?" popped into my mind, but unlike that time in Decatur, I didn't say that.

'Course I was high then and almost didn't feel the cop's baton as he'd rammed the butt end into my stomach. "I told you, man, we ain't havin' a chat. Either arrest me or jet."

"You haven't had nothing but experience with the law, ain't that so, Zelmont?"

He was just getting to me now and it's going on ten-thirty in the evening? "Working out in the hills above my pad, man. That's what I been doing a lot of."

"Yeah?"

"Yeah."

"Don't suppose you talked to any honeys or somebody while you were doing your road work?"

"Not particularly, Fahrar. I wasn't there to get my swerve on. I got more important things in mind."

He scratched a nail at the base of his close-cut hair.

"That's weak, brah. You could be like Rumpelstiltskin, here there and everywhere. Can you do better?"

"I ain't got to do better. How'd she die?"

"Strangled with her own panties. Laid out on the hood of her sports car. Body wasn't discovered until late this afternoon."

"And that's all you have to harangue Mr. Raines?"

We both turned to the sound of the voice. It was Wilma Wells, and she was looking fine in a pants suit thing that had off-center gold buttons going up the jacket to wide lapels. She strolled over and smelled good doing it.

"Ma'am." Fahrar finally took his hat off and kinda waved it at her. "This is police business."

"I'm a lawyer, officer, my name is Wilma Wells." She handed him a card from the authentic Louis V clutch bag she carried.

The cop worked hard not to show any change. 'Cept I knew inside he was weighing his options like a second-year man during contract negotiations. "Yeah, and?"

"And what was the approximate time of her death?"

He didn't want to say but he knew he was boxed in. "M.E. guesstimates around eleven or noon yesterday."

"After his workout yesterday Mr. Raines came to see me concerning resolutions of his NFL contracts."

"Where was this?"

"My office in Manhattan Beach. I'd say from eleven-thirty until about two. And given the distance, I'd say he couldn't have killed her and made it to my office even if the coroner can establish that it was closer to eleven than noon when Ms. Orlean was strangled."

Fahrar was about to speak, but she held up a black-nailed hand. "He used my private entrance, some of my clients are high profile."

Homeboy looked like a man chewing lemon rinds. "Okay, Superstar – for now." He waded out of the joint, adjusting his hat as he went.

"Thanks," I said to Wilma. "You sure took a chance."

"Not really. I've had actors and supermodels in my office, and the front staff hasn't seen them. I do have a private entrance. And there's so much traffic in and out of the parking garage, the attendants aren't reliable witnesses." She whipped her pretty smile on me and walked on up the stairs.

At the top, Nap greeted her and they walked off toward his office. Was the big switch-hitter banging her too? He'd told me this was boy month, but maybe he did that so I wouldn't mack her. But then why did she alibi me?

I got back to the pad around three-thirty in the morning and was stripping off my shirt when the phone rang. Immediately I assumed it was Terri hoping to catch me in.

"Zelmont," a familiar female voice purred through the answering machine. "Please pick up, this is Wilma."

Of course I picked up.

"Come on out to the office," she said. "That way if that cop asks you, you can describe it in detail."

Normally, I don't come running 'cause some fine hammer tells me to. But this one was different. This one had my nose open, and maybe my freedom in her hands. And sure enough, three quarters of an hour later, she had my balls in those hands too.

We were in her gold bronze Chrysler Phaeton on the open-air roof of her office building. A few other lonely cars were up there with us. She'd unzipped my fly and sprinkled some crank on my johnson, then licked the powder and me. I was about to lose the top of my head. She moaned and I was getting ready to bust when she stopped.

"You tryin' to give me a heart attack, girl?"

"Wanted to get your attention." She straightened up, smiling. "You honestly think Weems is going to let you play ball again?" This chick knew how to finagle a dude's head. "He's gotta give me a shot, Wilma." I sounded more needy than I wanted to.

"No he doesn't, Zelmont. He can't legally stop you from trying out, but he can exert a lot of pressure on Stadanko, and on Coach Cannon, not to sign you. Weems is a smart prick. He's got some cold shit on a lot of people. What do you think his Truth Squad is for?"

"To make the league look like Boy Scouts," I answered, squirming uncomfortably. I snorted some more blow to take the edge off. "What the fuck you want from me, Wilma?"

"To make you mine." She finished what she'd started.

Afterward, I must have dozed off 'cause I came to with her staring into my face.

"Sorry," I mumbled.

She got on top of me. I was laying back, the front seat having been let down. Her pants were off, her blouse open, and I was hard again. The beauty of crank. She had on blue lacy panties and was about to slip them off.

"Leave 'em on," I told her. She got a condom on me and I maneuvered around the material to enter her. It felt like a million pinwheel stars were exploding behind my eyes.

As we did it, she talked business. "You want to make some money, don't you, Zelmont?"

"It wouldn't hurt," I grunted.

"That's right." She rocked on me as I held onto her sides tight. She bent forward and I tickled her nipples with the end of my tongue.

"You want to get over, don't you, Zelmont?" She breathed hot air all over me.

I could barely put words together, I was so wrapped up in the pleasure. "Uh, yeah," I said in a husky voice.

She did a move my grandma could feel down in Arkansas. This chick was too much. "Wha, what are you sayin', Wilma?" I managed to stammer.

I lifted my butt and she hit her head on the headliner of the Phaeton. She grabbed my shoulders, digging her strong fingers into the muscle as she grinded on top of me.

"You're chasing old glories, Zelmont," she said between gritting her teeth. "You got to be real." She moaned loud as she worked her good thang on my rod.

I pulled her close, biting her ear and slobbering on her neck. "I'm a player, baby." I put a hand in the middle of her back and went to it like I knew I could. She matched me stroke for stroke.

"You're a former marquee name, Zelmont," she said softly, "but I can show you how to be set."

We kept banging, my crank-powered endurance making it seem like I could go all night. "I've been workin' out every goddamn day." We kissed, our tongues locking and separating with force.

"Even if you could get a slot, Weems will block any attempt you make to ever play ball again." She reared back as we both began to sweat. She came forward again, burying my head between her breasts. She must have taken hold of the latch, because the seat's back flipped up as she pulled me into a sitting position, rearing back again.

The windows were clouded over and we kept at it. I wondered if some square was spying on us outside, and it made me more excited. Soon I came and shuddered to a halt. She stayed on me, which I hate. But I figured this was the first time, I could be gracious. I was exhausted, like after that game against the Dolphins in 105 degree heat and matching humidity.

"Who else do you know that has money, real money, that if it goes missing he can't report it to the police?" She squirmed and reached her hand down between us.

"Woman, you got to stop talkin' crazy." I didn't know what this broad was up to, but it made something tickle in the back of my head.

"Shit," she snorted, getting off me. "You're scared."

"I think you been hangin' around Stadanko so long, you think you can be like him. He's straight gangster, you understand. We fuck with him, his buddies with the funny names will chop off our fingers and make us watch as they feed them to their pit bulls."

She wasn't listening to me. She was busy with her finger inside her panties. I watched as she wiggled and moaned and got herself off. Then she put her finger on my lips. "Be brave."

"Be cool, Wilma." I knocked her hand away, getting heated from anger, not from sex. "Just 'cause you alibied me don't mean you can clown me."

"You're clownin' yourself, Zelmont. You won't admit you're not going to get back into pro ball. And no club will let you coach for them either. It's in front of your eyes, but you refuse to see." She sat up, looking at me directly. "I'm talking about millions, Zelmont. Untraceable millions in cash."

I started putting on my clothes. "We gonna knock over Stadanko's safe in his office, Wilma? Or maybe he keeps the ducats at his pad out there in the Palisades. Then what? Keep running for the rest of our lives?"

"You're used to running," she cracked in a nasty tone.

"You got a mouth on you." I got my pants zipped up.

"I got eyes too, Zelmont. Stadanko hired my firm because he knew Brad, our senior partner. He brought in Brad a few years back when he was in trouble over campaign financing. After we negotiated the Barons deal Stadanko was going to cut us loose, but I convinced him having a woman of color as the team's lawyer would be good for his image and deflect criticisms."

I had to get out of there. "History was always boring to me, Wilma."

"Stop thinking small, Zelmont." She talked to me like I was a child. "We can do it so the U.S. Attorney General comes down on that goof Stadanko while we make off with his goods. And Chekka and his Little Hand punks will run and hide if the feds show up."

I couldn't get what she was talking about. How in the hell were we going to rip off Stadanko? "He keep all his millions laying around, huh?"

She got impatient again and popped my bare chest with the back of her hand. "Of course not. But it won't be hard to figure out where he hides it. He's a peasant at heart."

"Stadanko may have a hands off, excuse the pun, relationship with his cousin, but as you'd say, he must know where the benjamins are kept." Her top lip curled back like a wolf's and I got a tingling in my spine.

"We got to be cool," I said.

"No, you be cool. Go home and soak your hip in liniment so you can get up tomorrow and do your road work, old man."

I gave her a little shove to let her know I was nobody's chump. I shook a finger at her. "Ease up, Wilma."

"Ooh, so tough. That how it got out of hand with Davida? She challenge your bad boy 'tude one time too often? That why you had to choke her and you snapped." She laughed, but not happy like.

"Whatever it is your sellin', you're crazy if – "

"Get the fuck out of my car," she said, cutting me off.

"When I'm ready, bitch."

"Get out, or your little mixed-race pal will hear how you threatened me with rape and murder. It won't take much for him to believe that about you."

I felt like knocking her ass around for giving me that belittling stare of hers. Sitting there only in her panties, she still seemed like she was queen of the city. But I kept my hands to myself 'cause she was a lawyer, and was about as tame as a shark on a leash. I got my shit and booked for my vehicle several floors down.

Back at the pad I had some V.S.O.P. and tried to put what she said out of my head. I was going to make a comeback. I was going to sacrifice, work hard, and earn a spot on the Barons. I'd been playing football one way or the other since I was nine and my uncle slapped me for crying after I got tackled for the first time in Pop Warner. Uncle Gene was an asshole, but he taught me one thing – if you wanted something, ain't nobody going to get it for you unless you get it yourself. And once you got it, make goddamn sure you hold onto it.

*a*ll morning I'd been ducking the call. She'd left a message waiting for me when I'd got back, but I knew I wasn't going to return it too soon. Before I was up she'd called again around seven and again after eight as I rolled over. My head was pounding and my muscles ached. The hip, though, felt good. I got my workout gear on, including a rubber top to bring on the sweat. I went over to the Canyon, and after warming up with some calve extensions I hit the hill. By the time I got to the top, my hangover was damn near burned off, and the hip only throbbed a little.

As I stood getting my breath, in my head I could hear the first message Davida's mother left on my machine. Her English had never been too good, and it was worse now 'cause she was all broken up.

"Zelmont," she'd said, and I could tell she'd been crying, "Zelmont, tell me what has happened to my favorecida, Zelmont," she pleaded, "Diga me."

Her favorite, Davida had told me. Alicia, her mother, had four kids, three husbands. Two were boys and had been in trouble from day one growing up in the Pico Aliso projects in East Los. Mario was a glue-sniffing punk who'd been kicked out after she caught him bungholing his boyfriend in a maintenance shed when he was in high school. Though she'd since gotten used to his ways. The other one, Rey, for Reymundo, was a stone knucklehead who ran with some gang, a bunch of vatos under the protection of La Eme, the Mexican Mafia. Right now he was doing a dime in Corcoran for some bullshit or another.

The sister Isabel, who knew how to fill out a dress as well, had been the only one to turn out normal. Davida may have been nothing more than a glorified pom-pom girl, but by her mother's standards she'd done something with her life.

Moms initially wasn't too crazy about her going around with a brother, especially one with my record, but she figured I was better than some of the others her daughter had been with.

Alicia had had to settle for not much her whole life. But Davida had put it in her mom's head she'd get her out of the projects once she got that Top 40 hit. Hell, she believed it too.

There was a mist hanging on the hills, and I couldn't see my house. Like the fog was a wall, a warning that if I didn't get some real money soon, the house would always be lost to me. I jogged down the hill, my upper body sweating inside the rubber top. For some reason, I still felt a chill.

Back home, the red number on the answering machine told me Alicia had called two more times. I peeled off the top, wiping myself down with a towel. I got some orange juice, sat down, and grabbed the phone. I figured best to get this over with.

"Hola," she said.

"It's me, T." 'T' was what I had taken to calling her.

"Zelmont," she cried, then ran off a string of words in Spanish.

"T, you gotta relax, okay? Davida would want you to keep it together." In the background I could hear other voices, no doubt her neighbors.

"What happened?"

"I don't know, T. The first I knew of it is this cop who came to see me last night."

"Yes, the chino Negro," she said. "Oh, I don't mean – "

"No problem. What'd he say to you?"

"That he wanted to know about her friends, people she knew in the record business. He asked me about you and her." She lost it and started to cry. "Zelmont, what will happen now?"

"The cops will look for her killer, T. They'll probably find him." I didn't really think so, but I needed to tell her something so she'd let me alone.

She didn't say anything, and it was making me nervous. I knew what she wanted to ask me but couldn't. "Is there anything you tell the police, Zelmont? Anything that will help them find who did this bad thing to our Davida."

"I'm helping them anyway I can, Alicia, you know that."

"Yes, yes, of course. Mario will be here this afternoon. Will you come by?"

"I may not make it today, T. I've got some legal things I need to take care of, you know, football stuff. Important. But you say hi to Mario for me, and I'll be by soon, okay?"

"All right, I understand." She then told me she'd call back with the funeral time and I hung up. I guess I shouldn't have been lying like that to a woman who just lost her daughter, but going over there, sitting around crying and carrying on, lighting candles to the Virgin of Guadalupe.... Jesus.

I showered, going over what Wilma had said. She was smart and she did have the inside dope on Stadanko. But was she so greedy she wasn't thinking straight? Did she really believe it would be that easy to steal money from a wheel like him? Or maybe it was the crank talking and she always went on like that when she was high.

No sense waiting until this evening, I thought, and drove over to talk to Nap. She had talked to him at the club the other night about something. If he was in on this thing, it would give me more reason to consider the doing. Nap wasn't nobody's joke, and he did have reason to want to move on Stadanko. About fifteen minutes later, I pulled to the curb of his Mount Olympus pad on Cyclops Road.

There were tall cypress trees in a half circle in front of the house, and he'd repainted the joint recently in a orange-brown with dark green trim. The house was built in what Nap had told me was called Greco-Roman with touches of Assyrian. Whatever the hell that meant. It did have these large columns and looked like it should be in one of those funky old Steve Reeves Hercules movies.

Like I figured, his maroon Lincoln town car with its gold wire rims was in the driveway. Unless he had to be somewhere, the big man wasn't an early riser. I knocked but there was no answer. I figured he was probably in there pipin' his boyfriend Pablo, the color consultant. On the lawn was the morning paper.

Maybe Davida got some fame at last and her murder was mentioned in the *California* section.

"Nap," I yelled, looking up toward the second-floor bedroom. Nothing. I listened closely but didn't hear any moaning or groaning or little Pablo squealing with joy.

"Nap," I called out again. Still no answer. In the back of the house was a pool and a guesthouse which used to be maid's rooms in the old days. I wasn't so broken down I couldn't manage to get over the iron gate. I got your old man, Wilma. Yeah, she was a hard-ass bitch, but there was something about her. I landed on the other side expecting Hugo, Nap's bull mastiff, to come running. The dog knew me so I wasn't worried about him taking a nip. Only the dog wasn't around.

I tried the back door and it was locked. I knocked loudly but got no answer. The curtain was closed behind the sliding glass door and I knocked there too in case the lover boys had fallen asleep in the rumpus room. Then I turned and walked over to the guesthouse. The door was open. Inside, chairs and a table had been tossed around, and the pictures were hanging lopsided on the walls.

Danny Deuce was in his Nike sweats, no shirt, no shoes. He was laying with his head against the wall and bent to one side.

Over his legs was a dude in a suit, a gun in his hand and a gash in the side of his skull. His blood had splattered on the back of his coat and the cream carpet.

The metal rod in Danny's hand had the cat's blood on it, I guessed. I pulled the man off. His eyes had that vacant look, telling me that the renter was gone. Danny was breathing and I didn't see any holes in him, though there was one in the wall near him.

"Ugh," he said after I got him stretched out on the couch and slapped him awake.

"That one of Chekka's boys you wasted?"

"Motherfuckahs come bustin' in this mornin' while I was sitting on the stool, man." Danny sat up, rubbing the back of his head.

"The other day upset 'em, huh?"

He finally focused on me, blinking. "Yeah, Nap said you and him had to set these fools straight at the club. They rolled up and I could hear them arguing in the front." He pointed toward his brother's house. I guess they didn't know I was staying here and I jumped them." He looked around. "My piece is around here somewhere."

"Where's Nap?"

"He ain't here?"

Danny had keys to the main house and we looked all over it. No Nap.

"Aw, snap," Danny said as we stood in the kitchen. He hit the table with his fist. I noticed the phone had been ripped out of the wall next to him. "When we was tusslin', I think one of them said something about takin' Nap to the dump." He looked at me, panic on his face. "You got any idea where they're talking about?"

I didn't, but I knew who did. I made a call on my celly.

"Okay, yeah, I am grateful, is that what you wanted to hear?" This woman was gonna kill me yet.

"I apologize for giving you a hard time before, Zelmont," Wilma said sweetly on the other end of the line. "You sure you don't want me to call the police?"

"Naw, that'll just bring more attention than we need right now. Me and Danny should be able to do this." The youngster was all up on me, breathing his stale breath in my face.

"Call me when you get back, darling."

"What she say, man?" Danny blurted, grabbing on my arm. I tried to ignore him. I figured she was playing me, but it seemed to be worth the ride, at least for now. "I will." I disconnected. "Wilma says Stadanko's Shindar Enterprises uses the landfill out at the Sunshine Canyon dump in the Valley. She thinks they have a facility there too."

Danny had found his gun, one of those sleek plastic numbers with about a hundred bullets in the clip. Legally, civilians could only buy a sixteen-round magazine in California, but Danny's pieces were always off-market, untraceable, and street lethal. He was holding it tenderly, like it was his girl's tit.

"You know where this place is?"

"Yeah." I didn't tell him that I knew where a lot of the garbage dumps were around Los Angeles, or why I knew. My father had been a garbage man for the city. The father who never was around much, never came to my games or got on the phone to tell me he liked what I'd done.

When I was a teenager, I'd go to the city depot where the garbage trucks were, trying to catch a glimpse of him. But the trucks were always out real early in the morning, and by the time I'd get there after school and practice, he'd be gone. A few times I'd cut class and take the buses for hours to the various dumps, hoping to see him when they came to drop off their loads. It took me a while to realize each truck didn't always go to the dumps, that some of them unloaded into larger trash-hauling trucks that drove out to the sites.

The one thing I did get from my dad was a talent for womanizing. Though it wasn't like he taught me that at his at his knee. I only heard about him and his women from my fucked-up Uncle Gene when he was sipping on some Canadian Club, eating up my moms grub.

The two of us went downstairs. We had to do something with the body of the chump Danny had killed. After all, he was dressed and ready for burial.

"Man, we got to bounce," Danny screamed, "we got to save Nap."

"Be cool, Danny, we don't want to raise no ruckus right now. We just lucky y'all's play period didn't get the cops swoopin' down here. They ain't gonna kill Nap right off. They want him alive, they want to teach him a lesson."

"Why you say that?"

"Chekka needs the club."

"He can get some refugee Polack motherfuckah to run the joint."

"No he won't. That would be too obvious. Come on, we got to move the body." I wasn't sure I was telling the truth, but I needed Danny to be on point and not trippin'. Last thing I needed now was hauling around this dead white boy in my car with homeboy looking to bust a cap on the next mother from Herzegovina he thought might have snatched his big brah.

There was no choice but to stick the corpse in the back of my Explorer. Good thing the rear side and hatch windows were tinted. I backed down the driveway as Danny unlocked the gate.

Inside the guesthouse we sandwiched the dude in some blue plastic tarp I found in the tool shed. Then I wrapped a couple of oily rags and some duct tape from the shed around his head. Good thing it was a weekday so most people were off to work. We carried the dude into my ride, me hoping to hell this sucker didn't leak on my carpet.

I pulled out. Danny locked up the house and gate.

Everything looked normal enough on the outside. I got to the 101 freeway, taking it north over the hill. Danny was on pins in the seat next to me, his gun under the front seat. I made him put it there, otherwise he was gonna keep it in his waistband. I swear, these young punks don't know anything but the shit they see on TV and movies. He'd 'a blown his nuts off before we got to North Hollywood.

I took Hollywood Way and kept going north. Every once in a while, I'd look back to see if our passenger was bleeding.

Wouldn't you know it, just as I was heading past the Burbank Airport, a cop car pulled in behind me.

"Damn," Danny said, reaching down to mess with the piece.

"Keep your goddamn hands in your goddamn lap. Don't do anything to make them pull us over. Especially no mad doggin.'"

"Ain't got to do anything 'cept DWB."

"We got a dead man in here, remember?"

I kept below the speed limit and the cops pulled alongside us at a stop light. The one riding shotgun pointed for me to roll down my window. Danny was mumbling but I didn't want to listen to his jive.

"Zelmont Raines, right?" He was older than the one at the wheel.

"Yeah," I said grinning like I was one of the goofy Wayans brothers. "How's it going?"

"You were playing overseas, weren't you?"

"That's right," praying for the light to change. "Had to come back and try my luck with the Barons, you know how it is."

Danny said something under his breath again, and I wanted to sock him to be quiet. The cop was nodding as if that covered anything else he might want to ask. The light turned green and I waited for the blues to take off. But of course this dude had to have something to tell his pals back at the station.

Finally he said, "Would you mind signing an autograph? My boy is playing ball in high school."

He asked it the way cops always do, with that tone that said, 'Look, asswipe, I can make it hard for you if you don't volunteer and do this.' Just like a coach.

"Sure." What the fuck could I do?

Danny looked like he was going to have a fit, but I chilled him with a stone stare. I pulled to the curb, the cruiser slipping in behind me. Cars and trucks went by us like it was any other day. I got out, smiling for the cameras.

"I really appreciate this." He had his notepad opened to a blank page. For a second, I freaked, thinking maybe this was a trap 'cause I hadn't paid my child support. As if having a dead body less than ten feet from a member of the LAPD wasn't enough to get shitless about. "Make it to Jeremy, okay?"

"Hey, I'm just glad somebody remembers me." Like I knew he would, he couldn't help but give my ride the once-over while I struggled to spell his kid's name. "Two 'E's, right?"

"Yes."

It seemed like he looked at the tinted windows a little too long. What if like in one of those horror films the dude we assumed was dead suddenly gurgled? We were standing near the front windows, and he naturally settled on Danny, a young brother whose profile he's probably seen in one bulletin or another.

"There you go." I was going to offer an explanation on where we were going but decided that would sound wrong.

He tapped the pad against his open palm, like he was trying to decide something. I might be able to hit him, take his piece, then what? Have the law chase my sorry ass down the freeway, covered live from a news 'copter. Only they'd shoot me rather than waste time catching and beating me.

He looked narrow-eyed at the rear of the truck, then back at his partner, who held his fingers up from the steering wheel as if to say, well?

"Thanks for the autograph." He stuck out his hand.

I shook it and grinned like a thief making off with the farmer's prize rooster. I climbed back into the ride and could feel Danny's hostility. That boy was wound too goddamn tight and it was gonna be a problem sooner rather than later. But the cops went on their way and so did we. As I recalled, there was a side street before you got onto the rise to Verdugo Mountain Park. I took it and there was no mistaking where we were.

"Aw, motherfuck," Danny swore. "This is some rank shit, man."

"It's a county dump, what'd you expect?" A few big haulers were going up a hill off to the right. A couple of Stadanko's blue and silver Shindar trucks were among them.

"He must have some kind of plant or something around here," I said out loud.

"Yeah?" Danny said, bringing his T-shirt up over his nose.

"Yeah, this is a garbage dump. Stadanko hauls solid waste, toxic shit, and lard here from restaurants. He would have to have a place where they pump that crap out and it's converted – 'rendered,' I think they call it."

"You a garbage-studyin' motherfuckah, ain't you?" He pointed. "On the other side of the hill is where they dump the garbage?"

"Yeah, biggest pit of nothing you'll ever see." I saw a side road to my left and took that. The path led down to an area where there were a couple of regular garbage trucks and some cars parked around several low buildings. Nearby, I could hear cars racing by on the Golden State Freeway.

"Did you see the car they were driving?"

"Naw, I was kinda busy bustin' 'em up."

I couldn't tell if he was being smart or what. Then I saw something I recognized. We had cut down another pathway and had come to a part of the yard not seen from the front. The silver Prowler with the cobalt rims was parked parallel to a building with a door, windows, and no name on it. Behind that building were some tall round towers with pipes running to and around them.

"This is it." No sooner had I said it than he was scrambling out the door. I grabbed his arm. "Slow down, we gotta scope the scene out first."

"Get up off me, man." He snatched his arm back, his piece in his other hand. "We got to go save Nap."

"We will, Danny, only we got to think, okay? You want to go

charging in there not knowing what to expect? Maybe somebody gets hot and pops your brother before we're through the door."

He didn't say squat, his gun half on his lap, that prison yard blank on his mug.

I backed up and parked away from the building.

Then we got out and crept over. I couldn't hear anything so we went around to the rear. There were metal parts from machines and pieces of wood scattered back there next to a concrete wall that was about seven feet tall. A window up high in the building was open. We stopped to listen for a few seconds and heard some shady sounds.

Me and Danny looked at each other, the kid getting sick. The back door, which was near a corner, was locked, and I had to keep him from shooting the lock off. The sound of men laughing, enjoying their work, could be heard through the open window.

I looked through the hunks of metal and found a bar I could use to pry the door open. We got it in position and tugged. The door came loose and we went inside fast. Now we were in an office. There was a door on the other side, which flew open as me and Danny got close. Standing there was a cat with an automatic, and I hit him dead in the face with the iron bar before he had a chance to blast.

He said something in Serbian, or at least that's what I figured he was saying it in. I hit him again, grabbing the heater from his limp hand as he went down, blood gushing from his forehead. Danny was already past me.

"Cut him loose, bitch," Danny hollered at one of the thugs, putting his gun in the boy's face. The guy had the sleeves of his dress shirt rolled up, the skin on the knuckles of his right fist torn and bloody. There was another one looking at us, his jaw all down around his ankles. He'd been sitting eating some chow in fish sauce, one end of a plastic milk crate filling in for a table. His dinner show was Nap's torment. A glass of wine had been knocked over next to the plate. I recognized him from the red wound on one side of his forehead. He was the punk I'd hit with the ashtray the other day.

They'd bound up Nap pretty creatively. A chain was looped over a steel beam running down the center of the pointed roof. The end of the chain was wound around Nap's wrists, his arms up over his head.

A big lock kept the links together. He was standing spread eagle, chains locked around each ankle. The end of each one of these was connected to some piece of machinery, pulled tight as hell. His shirt was off, his pants and underwear pulled down. A small lead pipe was on the ground near his feet. It was dark on one end. He had a handkerchief tied around his mouth and duct tape wrapped over that. His face was pulped up with welts and bruises. Pure hate was in his eyes.

"Sick motherfuckahs." Danny hit the one he had the gun on in the face. As the dude wilted, he jumped on him and began pistol-whipping the fool. I had to get him focused before we had more bodies to get rid of than Dr. Kevorkian.

"Danny, come on, we got to get Nap out of here and to a doctor." I was grabbing for him with one hand and trying to keep my gun on ashtray head with the other. The dude he was wailing on with his automatic was swearing up a blue storm in that language of theirs. "Goddammit, Danny, you got to control yourself."

"They wasn't workin' your brother over." Now he started kicking the dude.

I was gonna point out that Nap wasn't a stranger to this particular form of rear-end action but skipped it. "He's down, Danny, he ain't moving anymore, understand?"

Danny stopped, breathing hard from exertion.

The other chump, the one that had been grubbin', smiled and I walked over to him. "Keep it up and I'll let Danny start in on your war criminal ass."

"This is just business, Zelmont."

"We ain't on a first-name basis, son. Turn him loose."

He hesitated like he was gonna make a move, but the fact I was still hefting the piece of metal made him reconsider. "Of course, we weren't going to kill him."

"Uh-huh, just a little negotiating of the terms of the new contract."

He unlocked Nap, then we made him get the big man's pants on. The Little Hand gangster and Danny walked him to the wall, where they let him slide down and lie with his back against it.

Danny was nodding his head. "Okay." Fast as all hell, he spun and backhanded the cat with the butt of his gun in the middle of his face. He went down and out like Buster Douglas used to in every fight.

"Sure glad you made it." Nap managed a smile. Damn.

"Can you walk?" I asked him. "We gotta get you looked at." Though I didn't want to, I glanced at the pipe. It made me queasy.

"Give me a couple of minutes, will you?" He put his head back and closed his eyes, gathering strength.

"Come on, Danny, we got to take care of this other thing."

"What?"

No wonder gangbangers were always doing drive-bys on the wrong mark, or getting their simple selves busted 'cause they forgot to take the surveillance tape out of the camera. All that kronik must mess with their memory retention. "Follow me. We'll be right back, Nap."

At my directions, we snuck back around the building. There were some dudes in overalls walking nearby, and we had to wait for them to move on before I went back to my ride. I drove it closer to the building and parked. Moving as quick as we could, we got the body out and brought it inside. I hoped to Jesus no one saw us.

I turned to Danny after we plopped the body down in the room where they'd tortured Nap a few minutes ago. "Wipe down your piece and leave it."

"Fuck that," Danny argued.

"Don't be simple, fool. Is the piece registered to you?"

He cocked his head. "You know better than that, dog."

"So like I said, drop your heater here. If it can't be traced to you, then there's nothing to sweat. But you keep walking around with it, then the cops got a match for these holes in this boy you done."

"It was self-defense," he whined.

"We ain't got all day for this shit, Danny."

"Do like Zelmont says, Danny," Nap said. "He's right."

Danny finally wiped off the gun and set it down, his bottom lip sticking out the whole time like the spoiled knucklehead he was. We got Nap into the Explorer and I drove back around the building. Except this time I got smart and had swathed some mud on the plates in case anyone was paying attention. Not that I thought Rudy Chekka would be complaining to the law.

I guess I was too wound up and went down a one way road. I turned back and was trying to figure out how to get out of the dump when a Shindar garbage truck rumbled past us on the road I'd turned off of.

"I wish we had time," Danny began, "cause I'd like to deep six some more of those Little Hand bastards."

"Let's just concentrate on getting your brother out of here," I said. "We ain't got time to follow all their trucks around."

"Follow that one," a voice I didn't recognize for a hot second said.

I turned to look at Nap, his eyes were fluttering and he was breathing heavily. "Why?"

"Just follow it," he repeated in a whisper, "they talked a lot while they were having fun with me." Then his eyes closed shut.

So I followed behind the Shindar truck, and got the tingle as we went down a narrow road. The instincts that used to put me among the top five receivers in the NFL, that feeling that used to tell me where the defender was without me looking, kicked in like a mother.

"Why you fallin' back?" Danny said, pissed. "We got to get this done so we can get Nap out of here."

"We will, little brother, we will."

"Don't call me that," he said in a tone that told me he wasn't bullshitting. I let the truck get farther ahead, then I went down the path. It was dirt, so I kicked up a lot of it just like the truck had. I was betting the driver hadn't noticed me. We went along, then I stopped and backed up. There was another tiny road leading downhill. I followed it.

"Goddamn, this'll not only do Nap in, but us too."

Danny was right for once. The stench from the garbage pit was strong enough to make the Hulk weep. I figured the road must wind around it on one side. I stopped the car.

"What the fuck is wrong with you? Back the fuck up."

"Stay put," I ordered.

"Man." He shook in his seat. Nap was whimpering.

I got out and walked down the path, walls of dirt rising up to my right and left. Suddenly I came to a driveway. It led upward and was bordered on one side by a concrete wall about my height. I walked up and stopped at the corner of the wall and peeked around. At the top of the driveway was a building with a satellite dish on the roof. The truck was parked in front of this building. My eyes were watering and my stomach was starting to roll from the overpowering odor.

The two who'd been in the truck were out. They had on rubber suits and gas masks like I'd seen on *X-Files* re-runs. What they were doing made me forget for a few minutes the sick feeling coming over me. They had the big doors on the rear of the garbage truck open. Both of them crawled into the garbage. They came out, holding onto some packages. Pieces of rotten fruit and who-knew-what was dripping off of them. One went back into the garbage and the other one walked around the truck out of sight. I was fuckin' fascinated.

I kept watching the garbage diver. He put some of his packages on the ground. This cat was unloading bundles of money wrapped with brown paper and wire, a few bills sticking out. The other one returned with a flat cart and they stacked the packages on the thing.

I wanted to stay and watch as they carried the shit inside the building. One of them keyed an electronic combination lock, and the door to the joint swung open on hydraulic hinges. My eyes were better than anybody's, despite all my years of abusing my body. But even my 20/15s couldn't see the numbers he'd punched in from the distance I was at. Plus the smell and fumes had gotten the best of me so I hurried back to my ride.

"What the fuck you been doin'?" Danny was pacing beside the Explorer. He didn't know what to do with his hands since he didn't have his piece.

"You'll find out." I could barely turn my SUV around, but managed to do it. Mainly I hoped those studs down the way didn't hear us, 'cause I was sure they were packing serious heat and we'd get blazed on. I found the main road out. There were a couple of guards standing around, and they looked at us as we got closer. I waved like I belonged there and kept going. For once Danny was on point and didn't try that prison yard stare on the gun toters.

We got back on the regular street and I took the 170 south to the Magnolia exit, then drove down side streets until I was in North Hollywood.

"Wake him up," I told Danny.

"Why?" Anything to argue with me.

"'Cause I can't remember the street the clinic is on. And before you ask, it's a place entertainers and sports stars like your brother go when they need to, you know, recharge." I didn't say anything about how I'd been there more than once, but had always been on my back in a controlled substance haze.

"Come on," I said with frost in my voice.

He glared at me in the rear-view mirror, but without his gun, he knew if he tried to bitch-slap me, Nap's brother or not, I'd knock his lightweight self out. "Nap," he shook his brother's shoulder gently. "Nap," he shook him again.

A couple of middle-aged Valley chicks with butts tight from working out on treadmills strolled by on the sidewalk. One of them had a hairy rat dog on a leash. He looked happy.

"Yeah," the big bruiser mumbled.

"What's the name of the street Burroughs' Seven Souls clinic is on?"

"Banyon. There's a Shell station at the corner of that and Riverside."

"Right." I got us there in five minutes, and we helped Nap inside. The ol' cut-up Burroughs cam lurching out of a back room. He was a tall reed stalk of a white man who always walked with a stoop. Burroughs had a hook nose, and what was left of his thin hair was greased on one side of his large head. He had a voice that never changed expression, and the whites of his eyes were always red like he'd just finished smoking a blunt. Which was often true.

"Ah, Mr. Raines and Mr. Graham." He touched Nap's bruises. "Another encounter with the Mistress Dandelion?"

"Yeah, doc, things got a little out of hand and we figured it best to get him over to see you." Me and Danny got Nap into a wheelchair. I went over close to Burroughs. He smelled like toothpaste. "There's a little problem in the end zone, if you catch my meaning," I whispered.

The old degenerate smiled with teeth belonging to a young girl. "Oh yes, I know the kind of care brother Graham requires. I'll see to it. Sign him in, will you?"

I started to walk off to the front desk when he called to me. "How's your recovery coming, Mr. Raines?"

"Clean and sober." I'm sure it gave him a chuckle to know I was lying. I got Nap settled in, and me and Danny headed back over the hill to L.A. His mind was on his brother. Mine should have been on my tryout the next week. Instead it was on what them two had been unloading in that hidden away building. That's how I should have left it, just me knowing I'd seen where Stadanko brought his dough before he parceled it out for laundering. Yeah, I damn sure should have kept it to myself.

*t*ommy Earl blew off Ward Pruitt and one-handed the ball thrown by "Hack" Hassendorn. He skated past the goal line, the ball tucked under his arm like a stuffed goose. Even I had to admit he looked good. We'd been given the Barons' uniforms to do our scrimmage in that morning. They were deep blue and green teal; Davida had called the color. The practice field in El Segundo had been some kind of missile and plane place back in the day of us sweatin' about the Russians. For the first time in a long while I couldn't get to sleep the night before, I was so worked.

Around four in the morning I was desperate to bring my anxiety down and was about to have a little crank I had left from my date with Wilma, but for once I practiced self-control. I did some cals and went jogging before the sun was up. I felt good by the time I rolled up to the field, even though there'd been another message from Davida's mother telling me when the funeral was. Why did she have to mess with the focus I was trying to bring on? Can't people think of more than just themselves?

I got past Jon Grainger, my hands up for the ball. We'd been trading off on offense and defense since early afternoon.

The ball stung as I started to bring it down and turn my head toward the goal line. Then the hip decided to act up and I dropped the ball, overcompensating from the sudden pain jabbing at my fibula.

Don Cannon, the head coach, leaned over to say something to Nolan Blake, the offensive coach. Blake shook his head like a doctor about to give you the bad news. I walked with my hands on my hips like I was winded, but I was really trying to massage the upper thigh.

"Nice try," Tommy Earl said as I walked past him. He didn't try to keep the arrogant look off his face.

We ran more one-on-ones, then scrimmaged from the I formation. I went out, cut across two defenders' zone, and Hassendorn planted that pill just right. I stepped and came up on the side of my right foot, the hip responding like it should, my legs pumping. Antoine Palupo, the 310-pound, six-foot-five mobile as hell linebacker they'd drafted from Penn State filled the slot I was trying to make it through. I went over on my side, holding onto that ball like it was my first paycheck.

"Not bad, old man." He pushed himself off me, giving me a hand up.

Cannon blew his whistle. "How's the hip, Zelmont?" Him and Blake came onto the field.

"Ain't nothing." I tossed the ball to Palupo.

"You seemed to be favoring it this afternoon." Cannon stood close to me. He was a robust dude with heavy arms that swung back and forth while he walked. He had black glasses, flat feet, and a brown-gray beard he was forever scratching at. "Everything's cool, baby." "Yeah?" He did that thing he does, looking at me over the top of his glasses. He then looked at Blake, who was looking at me.

"You been going to support groups or something like that?" Blake worked something around inside his mouth.

"You want me to pee in a bottle after practice?"

"What if I said yes?" Blake was gonna be on my jock.

"Show me the way." I hoped the big vein in my neck wasn't pulsing.

"Get ready to run the R-9 play I went over with you." Blake walked over to talk with Earl.

"I guess I don't need to tell you those days of chasing pussy and partying till all hours are supposed to remain ancient history, Zelmont." Cannon was making notes on his clipboard as he spoke, and didn't look up.

"I'm cleaner than a skeeter's peter, coach."

"Get ready to run the play." He still hadn't looked up.

They put Earl at safety and me at tailback. I came up, then shot through the gap Gilman and Travers opened. I made the block for Earl and he got seven yards. The next down we reversed the positions and I veered right off Earl's block but didn't get two steps when the cornerman Langdon slowed me up, then Malcolm Washington got me around the waist and took me down. I landed right on the hip. But I couldn't show it, I just couldn't show the pain, goddammit.

I jumped up, playing the hit off. I trotted over to the sideline. Grainger was redoing the tape around his calve.

"You don't look like you lost too much, Zelmont." He finished wrapping the tape, checking out his work.

"You got something in front of you, youngster." I lifted my helmet and chugged down some Gatorade. "I got to be on it 'cause I ain't got nothin' but the past creepin' up."

He picked up his helmet, holding it gladiator style against his leg and wrist. "This ain't nothing but a game, Zelmont."

I drank some more. He put on his helmet and went in to run his series. I didn't want to face it, but he looked all right. Grainger didn't have what you'd call steady speed, but he made up for it in his ability to drive on tacklers like Barry Sanders used to do.

Cannon signaled me to get ready. I snapped my helmet back into place, snuggling the mouth guard between my teeth. I chewed on the plastic, the old feelings swooping over me. In the stands I pretended there were thousands who'd skipped mowing the lawn or doing the wash, fixing that fence for Aunt Sarah, or changing the oil in the station wagon. It was live time, and I couldn't let the fans down.

I went in and did a simple pattern toward the flat, then broke right. Trevor Grier, the cornerback, stayed with me. The ball went over both our hands. He gave me a shove and I went down.

"Punk." I got back up, walking away from him.

"Your mama."

"At least my mama washes under her arms. Yours got a garden growin' there." He was a born-again Christian who once, before he saw the light, got caught giving it to a nineteen-year-old beauty contestant in the men's bathroom of the Dallas airport. Damn hypocrite.

The second play was for Blake to see how their $20 million running back out of Texas A&M, Orlando Matthews, was doing. He got six yards before coughing up the ball. But he recovered, then looked nervously over at the sidelines. Blake had his arms folded, making his jaw work like he was tasting rotten meat.

On third and three, I beat Grier on a stutter step, turned my upper body, and easily caught the throw from Dillworth, the second-string QB. By then Grier had turned, and him and free safety Leroy Collier – the only white boy I knew named Leroy – were coming for me. I faked left, but Grier was too quick. He got me, and tried to spin me around to throw me to the ground. I put my shoulder pads into his chest as Collier's arms locked around my legs. I went down on top of Grier, trying my best to make it as painful as possible for him.

"Back off." He slapped the side of my helmet.

Collier rolled off my legs. I laughed and gave Grier a jab with my elbow, close and tight. "That's what you get for being a pussy." I got up and trotted back to the huddle. I was on my J and everybody knew it. We had first down, and Blake and Cannon decided to keep the ball on the ground. On third and nine, Sistrunk, in for the regular center, hiked. I pivoted left and went into motion, but before I could get fifteen yards, Grier came charging and upended me.

"Motherfuckah," I hollered. Cannon was blowing his whistle as I hit the turf. I jumped up, throwing off my helmet. Grier stood there like he was bad. I swooped on him and we started trading blows. Hands were on both of us, people yelling at us to stop.

As Grier was being pulled back I got a punch in under his chin-strap. His head jerked back like he'd gotten whiplashed.

Then Cannon got in my face.

"This isn't how I run my team, Raines."

"Tell him, he made the illegal tackle."

"Don't tell me how to deal with my men, Raines. You haven't earned your spot yet." His chest was rising and falling rapidly, and he was snorting air through his nose. "Go sit down."

"Hey, look – "

"Go sit down." He pointed toward the bench. I was gonna argue, but I was in a weak position.

Blake was talking to Grier, who was glaring at me like I tripped his grandma going to the store. Walking over to the bench, I could see

Stadanko had come out onto the field. He was tall
with his back to me. I knew that funny hat.

Fahrar.

I got close to them to show him he couldn't get
with my flow. Be like Swingin' Dick Clinton and den
cop shook hands with Stadanko and started to wal
like I wasn't there. I was about to call him but controlled myself. I sat
down, stretching out my right leg. It seemed to be okay as long as I
was moving, but once I rested, I didn't trust it not to lock up.

When scrimmage ended we ran some laps and hit the weight
room. Cannon called me into his office.

"You've got some convincing to do with me, Raines." He sat behind
one of those executive desks, the playbook open on it.

"I looked good, didn't I?"

"Attitude is a big part of how I see a team coming together."

In the old days I'd have made a crack, then walked out and found
some honey to curl up with for a few hours while the front office
argued about how much they had to pay me and how I was worth
the hassle. Then some college boy would mention how much gate I
brought in, how I delivered on clutch plays, and they'd shake their
heads and get on with how'd they have to put up with me 'cause I put
butts in the seats. But those days were behind me.

"I realize that, coach." I hoped that satisfied him.

"You realize what?"

"That it's your team and your rules." Like your ass can't get replaced
anytime Stadanko thinks you're dragging his profits down, clown.

"You don't sound sincere to me." He put his hands together, leaning
his elbows and hairy arms on the desk. He bored in on me, waiting
for the right response.

"I'm for real about wanting to play ball again." Take it or shove me
off, there's only so much ass I can stand to kiss.

Cannon pulled his big frame back from the desk, measuring me.
"Go on and get your gym time in. We'll talk again in the next few
days."

"Okay."

After my two full sets of weights and a whirlpool – with me and keeping arm's length but glaring at each other like we molested somebody in the other's family – I headed out into the parking lot. Grainger came up beside me.

"So what do you think, man?"

I wanted some crack was what was on my mind. "We'll see," I said.

"You was haulin' out there today."

I figured I was supposed to give him props. "You looked good too, Grainger. Take it slow or any way you can get it."

"I'll see you tomorrow."

"Yeah." I got in my ride and away from that Cub Scout.

Dude was all worked about being sportsman-like. That wasn't my trip. You come on the field, it's dog eat motherfuckin' dog.

You gotta do for yourself and get your thing in order. Only thing I was concentrating on was how bad I was gonna make Grier look when we hit the field again in the morning.

As I pulled out of the parking lot, Wilma's Phaeton was about to pull in. I almost drove past her, but she'd stopped and let down her window.

"'Zup?"

"You." She was wearing deep red lipstick, and when she smiled I got that feeling you know where. "How'd it go today?"

"All right."

"I spoke to Napoleon today, he's doing better."

So she and Nap were talking to each other. Could they be bangin' a girlfriend or boyfriend together? Maybe that halo consultant queen Pablo. "He's too tough to stay down long." A car pulled behind me and honked. I didn't glance back.

"That's what I figure about you, Zelmont." She gave me a look to make a man forget his own name. "I'm sorry about what I said." She put her car back in gear. "But not about what I want to do." She drove into the lot as the car behind me went around. It was Grainger, and he looked pissed.

All the way to the pad I should have been reviewing the plays I was gonna have to run again tomorrow. Or maybe wondering about Fahrar talking to Stadanko. Instead, I couldn't get Wilma Wells off my brain. Damn.

By the next day I really was back in the groove. Even Stadanko had to nod as he stood on the sidelines, trying to be all that. I zagged on Grier, and though Pruitt was ten years younger than me, I got past him too. If I didn't at least make the exhibition season then God didn't make nipple rings.

"How you like me now," I capped. Grier stood there, hands on his hips, tucking in his bottom lip. He had a four-year, $20 million package plus shoe and gear endorsements. I knew his agent had probably been texting him yesterday soon as he heard about our set to let him know he had way more to lose than me if he wanted to act out.

Especially since that asshole Weems had his spies all over the place. Talk was Coach Blake was one of his brown nosers, had been forced into it. Weems was supposed to have fag files on the secret booty bandits in pro ball. Nap had told me about playmates of his who'd spotted Blake tipping out to his share of gay spots.

Either 'cause of his agent or Weems' jive, Grier played it cool this time. He didn't say anything much the rest of practice 'cept grunt now and then when we bumped.

My hip was twinging and moving in and out a little, but I did my best not to show any sign of pain. Cannon was the one I was worried about. He was watching me like a homeless dog eyeing a crippled cat, waiting for me to slip. I leaned against the wall leading to the gym after our sprints.

"Out of gas, old timer?" Grainger put a hand on my shoulder.

"I'm all right." I shook loose, straightening up and heading off to the gym.

"If you say so." He walked past me, his cleats blending in with the rest of the men stamping on the concrete.

I went easy on the leg lifts so as not to aggravate the hip. By the time I got in the shower, everything was smooth. I soaped up, trying to remember when Davida's funeral was.

Tomorrow? Or was it Friday? I should have written it down when her moms told me the other day.

I was dressed and on my way out when I spotted that big bruiser Trace loitering around. That had to mean Weems was talking to Stadanko. I tried not to think if it was about me.

The flaming cross on the bodyguard's cheek looked funny in daylight. He was standing near the entrance to the locker room, tossing a football to himself in the air. He had hands like a lineman – kept dropping the pill.

Just to mess with him I said, "How come you ain't out there tryin' out, Trace?" He caught the ball this time, then frowned at me as his tiny brain kicked in. "The question is, what are you doing here."

"I belong here, baby. But you still ain't answered my question. You're young and in shape."

"I have more serious work to pursue."

Posing nude for Weems, I imagined. "What's that?" Grier floated past, making like he had some place important to get to.

"You and these others have a responsibility, Raines. Children in the ghettos and barrios, and out in the suburbs, follow what you do. They buy the obscenely overpriced shoes you sell for athletic companies. These sheep cut and shoot each other over these shoes or jackets with your signature on them."

"Them clothes and shoes are a reward for those kids, man. Ain't nobody spendin' the rent money on them things."

"Really, Raines, is that so?" He twirled the ball in his mitt-sized hands.

Enough of this chump. "You just happy being Weems' strong-arm."

"It serves a purpose."

He tossed the ball to me, thinking he'd catch me off-guard.

I snatched it out of the air with one hand. "Then it must be righteous." I heard footsteps and turned to see Blake coming out of a door down the side of the building. He started to walk toward us, then changed his mind, taking off in the other direction.

Trace scratched at his cross with the back of his nails, not looking in Blake's direction.

"Raines, I'd like you to step in here." It was Cannon.

He'd come out of a room down the hallway. I knew what was up.

I went over to where he stood holding the door open. Inside he had me pee into a bottle, and some dude with latex gloves on drew some of my blood.

"I'm not going to be surprised, am I?" Cannon fooled with his glasses, moving 'em this way and that on his large face.

"Nothing to be surprised about, coach. Only how good I'm doing."

He folded his arms but didn't say squat.

Afterward, driving home, I got that old urge for a controlled substance boost. I guess it was something about my wiring that made me want to go out and get high right after taking a drug test. For more than a minute, I considered going all the way east back to the 'hood to score some rock.

Instead I smiled at myself and got my ass back to the pad.

There were two messages on the machine.

"You better had sent some money, Zelmont." Terri was all class. Then she put some sugar in her voice. "Why don't you come down here and spend some time with me and your son? You should make an effort." I was. I was trying to get my career going again.

The other message was from Alicia, Davida's mother. "Don't be late for mi hija's funeral, Zelmont. It's at St. Benedict's at ten this Saturday. Don't forget, okay?"

I sank into the couch, sipping on a jolt of V.S.O.P., and nodded off. I woke to some knocking and got up slow, my hip having stiffened. I opened the door to see Fahrar's silly mug.

"Why don't you go roust some hos on Spring Street?"

"There's always more fun at Zelmont's pad." He made to enter, but I didn't move out of the way. "May I come in?"

"You think you like Dracula, don't you? Ask some moron to let you in and that way you say later in court you was just talkin' to me, like I voluntarily asked you inside my house."

I'd had enough dealing with the law to know what was what. "If you ain't here to arrest me, then you best get to steppin'."

He fooled with his hat. "Why'd you bring up court, you got something you need to tell me?"

"Tell you like you deaf, home. I got shit I got to do."

"Like work on your alibi?"

"Work on my chill. See ya." I closed the door and sat down again. He was letting me know he was gonna stay on my jock like a bad

81

rash. But there wasn't nothing he could really do to me. He didn't have anything 'cept his own hard-on about me being a player and him not.

I took a long drink of my brandy and put my head back. On the ceiling, a daddy long legs made his way across, looking for grub. Being that size, the world must have seemed like this endless place. But if he found an ant or fly, he was the man.

That spider would show 'em who was the eater and who the eaten.

I knew exactly how he felt. It was feast time.

*t*here was more water flowing at Davida's funeral than in a busted shower. Mostly it was Alicia, her sister Isabel, and more cousins than any one family should have. The way the priest said his eulogy, you'd have thought she'd been giving out food and candy to kids in the streets. The picture they put on the front of the program book was one of the few from her portfolio where she hadn't turned on the sex. The photographer must have told her to go for the innocent look. That turns a lot of dudes on.

Like I figured, there were a couple of news crews there too. It wasn't California front-page stuff, but there had been one item in the paper about her murder, with me linked to her life. That's how them jokers at *The Times* put it, so you could read between the lines, nodding your head over morning coffee. "Yeah," they'd be saying, "we know that nigger did it." Uh huh.

"Zelmont, isn't it strange that this happens after your return to Los Angeles." It was that uptight skank Lisa Choo from Channel 5.

"I think it's a tragedy." I was using the lines from the second episode of that show I did for a hot minute for syndication. The one where my best friend from the old neighborhood is killed. "I really hope the police find who did this."

"You have any ideas?"

Jam that mike up your drawn-up ass. "No, but of course I'll do everything in my power to see that Davida's death is answered for." That sounded pretty good. Her sister was looking at me, dabbing at her red eyes.

Afterward, we gathered at Isabel's swank pad in Montebello.

There were hip-hoppers, cholos from the old 'hood, other chicks like Davida who had booty but little talent. They were all yappin' at each other, mixing English and Spanish. I stepped out on the patio to get some air. I'd done my duty, been seen in public at the funeral to stall out speculation and finger pointing.

There were people out in the yard too, holding onto paper plates with food or sipping on soda and juice. Isabel had a golden retriever romping around, wagging its tail and barking to get your attention.

"I was kinda surprised to see you at the funeral." Isabel had come up beside me so quiet, I hadn't heard the sliding glass door open.

"What are you talking about, girl?" She was looking good.

Women in black dresses and nylons always got me charged.

She flicked her head to one side. "You didn't love her."

"I didn't hate her."

"You played rough." She gave me that fake innocent look her sister had on the cover of the funeral program.

"How would you know?" I got closer.

Before I could get an answer, Alicia stepped outside.

Her daughter put on the right face and placed her arms around her mother's waist. "It's okay, mama, it's going to be okay."

Alicia used a soggy Kleenex to tap at her eyes. "It's just so wrong, isn't it, Zelmont?"

"Yes it is." I tried to keep from looking at Isabel's legs.

"I think it was one of those crazy rappers she was hanging around with," her mother went on. "All the time singing about killing policeman and doing terrible things to women." Her whole body shook. "I told the detective that, too."

I was surprised Fahrar hadn't come to the funeral, hoping I'd break down crying and make a confession at the graveside.

"He's steady on the case, he'll find out who did this."

She reached out a hand and I had to take it. The three of us stood there like we were in one of Nap's self-realization meetings. I looked over Alicia's head at Isabel. She just stared at me, making me work to get inside her head.

I stayed around a little while more, then split. I didn't get a chance to say much else to Isabel, but she gave me her business card, the home phone number written on the back. I drove out to the Valley to see how Nap was getting on.

"Mr. Raines, Mr. Raines." Burroughs came up to me, his boat end of a face yellow colored from whatever narcotics he was currently popping. "Your smile is your umbrella today, isn't it." He used his boney fingers to feel the material of my sleeve. "Dark hues become you."

"Where's Nap, doc? You got him hooked up to one of your joy juice IVs?"

He leaned back, holding his hands in front of his long body. "Such a mordant wit."

He was too much. Burroughs buttoned up his sport coat. He rolled his tongue around in his mouth like he was looking for a taste he couldn't get enough of. "Nap's out jogging. Should be back in a few ticks, I believe you'd say." He turned away, and a dude I recognized from one of those hot sheet soap operas they got on at night came shuffling out of a side hall. He was in a silk bathrobe and ratty-ass slippers with an old school small- brim hat on his head. He went up to the doc all lost dog like.

"I'm paying premium dollars for you to take care of me." He played a spoiled rich boy on the show, and now I could see it wasn't much of a stretch for him. Burroughs leaned into him, putting his arm around his waist like he was a hottie. He planted that skull's smile on the dude's face, his eyes glittering like I'd seen psychotic linemen get after taking a running back's head off.

"Yes, of course, young sir, Doctor Burroughs is only here to accommodate you. Yes, of course."

The kid bobbed his head up and down like that's the way it was supposed to be. Burroughs put an arm on his shoulder and walked him down the hall. He looked back at me, a nothing emotion on his face. Then the doc followed the young actor into his room.

I found Nap doing cool-down stretches on the side of the clinic, in a kind of garden area with orange and purple flowers.

The only thing I knew the name of was the cactus. There was a lot of cactus.

"You back on it, huh?"

"Getting there. Wilma told me your tryouts have been going good."

He left words hanging off the end of what he'd said. "Looks like I'll get to the exhibition games, then should be gettin' my slot on the regular."

Nap rotated his big shoulders and crossed his legs at the ankles. He bent over, his palms flat to the ground. "What about Rudy?"

"What about him? Danny only zapped one of his boys. You said yourself it was just business. Well, now he understands we can't be punked."

Nap straightened up. "We?"

"I get on the Barons, I got bread. I got scratch, I'm a partner, right?"

Nap rubbed the back of his neck with his hand. "Zelmont, Stadanko is the controlling owner of the Barons, and I'm into him large."

"Yeah?"

"So why in hell would he let you on his team when he's in bed with his cousin? Neither one is gonna turn around and let you buttfuck 'em."

"It's not the Locker Room they're after is it?" I asked. "Isn't it money the two of them greedy fucks want?"

Nap started walking, his hands on his hips. I kept up. "I'm not sure, Zee. It would make sense for them to want the club, it's a happening venue and washing money through it would be easy. Plus the joint gives them an excuse to rub up on all kinds of people Chekka can get his hooks into." He worked his jaw muscles. "I originally assumed Rudy had me snatched on his own – "

"Yeah," I blurted, interrupting him. "The way Wilma broke it down to me, Rudy's the real deal gangster and Stadanko's just a prop."

The big man was quiet, then, "Stadanko may have more to do with his cousin's business than Wilma thinks. And anyway, after y'all rescued me I was considering closing the place down, but realized that would be a mistake. I can't show weakness to Stadanko or Chekka. But I need to lay low for a while to get back in peak form and set things up for the job."

We'd stopped in front of a window with the blinds shut inside. Suddenly Burroughs looked out through a slat, his eyes roving over us. He winked and shut the blinds again.

I tugged on Nap's buffed arm, pulling him away from the window and the doc's big ears. "You and Wilma gonna try and rip homeboy off?"

Nap let the band holding his dreadlocks – they were sky-blue today – loose. He shook his head and those rascals whipped around like insect feelers. "It'll work, Zee. The way she's put it together, we take his money, put the feds onto him, and Chekka goes running too." He stopped, putting a hand on each of my shoulders, his face close to mine.

"I got no choice on this, man. These business talks of his are going to escalate, you dig? Bodies gonna start droppin', and I don't intend it to be me or Danny." He showed his gums and teeth. "Plus, I got an inside straight that's a thriller-diller." He threw back his head and laughed. We started walking again.

"This is my time, Nap," I said, excited. "I been lookin' good out there, man. My shit is back and I'm not going to fuck it up this go-round. I can't, this is my last chance, you know that. Stadanko don't give a fuck we bopped his cousin's boys. What's-his-face, the one that was grubbin' while they were working you over, said it was just business. No harm, no foul in our world, right?"

"You trying to convince me or yourself, Zee?"

I felt like running away from him and this whole crazy thing sucking me in. "You gonna bust this move during the season?"

"Best time to do it, champ. Stadanko does want a winner, he'll be into the games. That's the best time to hit him."

"Fuck." Even if I wasn't involved, Stadanko was naturally gonna think I had a hand in this mess. And Nap knew I sure wasn't gonna call him up and tell him about this foolishness. At least I hope he believed that.

"You gonna have the club knee deep in Danny's Victoria Avenue Rolling Daltons? That ain't good for pullin' in the public."

"Only temporarily," he said coldly.

"I'm out of this, Nap, you understand?" I yelled. "I'm the fuck out of this and y'all on your own on this shit."

"That's a mistake, Zee," he said calmly.

I stomped off, my hands and arms in the air like I could wave it all away. "You and Wilma do what you're gonna do, I'll do what's right for me. We don't know each other, dig?"

I booked from the Seven Souls Clinic in a hurry. Zooming along the Hollywood Freeway, I couldn't shake the feeling that no matter how fast I drove, I'd never get far enough away.

*t*hree weeks later I was in top shape and had passed every goddamn random drug test they used to trap me. The first one that afternoon during the walk-on period had me worried. But not having tried too much of Wilma's crank that past night, and burning it off in my system, was the smartest thing I could have done. Plus I'd drank lots of water and taken a whole mess of vitamin C for absorption, and some B2 to make sure my urine was lemony yellow. Them lab geeks get suspicious if your pee is too clear. The water helps dilute the shit in your system along with sweating it off. Good thing crank burns off cleaner than boo.

The physical was another matter.

The fibula had been giving me a little trouble, but it worked great the day I had to get on the treadmill. In the old days teams had one pill roller and maybe his assistant. If you and he were on the same wavelength, certain things could be forgiven. Especially if you were a multi-million dollar stroker and were bringin' in the ducats, including the sawbone's salary bumps.

The new thing was a roomful of these sports medicine types, women too. They had their machines, their electronic scopes, and their charts and graphs and clipboards telling me how and what a muscle should do and when. They'd X-rayed and MRI'd my leg and hip from different angles, slapping electrodes on different parts of my leg when they'd done it.

Their results only told Coach Cannon what he must have learned from the Barcelona Dragons' medical exam.

"Zelmont, this tendon strain on your hip is exacerbated by

contact, and you know that." Cannon scratched at his chest with one of his big hairy hands.

"Stress on the abdominal musculature, too," I said, having memorized the words. "The ligaments are strained in my thigh and the fibula has bone chips. I know all that, coach. Your docs told you all that, too. But there are days I'm duckin' and dodgin' like ten years ago. You seen me out there, you know."

Me and Cannon were standing near the locker room, the sounds of the men getting dressed for practice coming from inside. "They say if you keep this up, osteoarthritis will surely be the result before you're fifty, Zelmont."

"That's more than fifteen years away, man. You want to bring a Super Bowl trophy back to this city after more than twenty years, or you want to be a missionary? I'm a grown man, I know what's what."

Stadanko, who'd been around each day but I had avoided, came around a corner. His old lady was with him. He was dressed in casual clothes, expensive Mezlan loafers on his feet. Ysanya had on a colorful poncho, white jeans, and cowboy boots. She'd done her hair different than the last time I'd seen her at the party. Now it was brown and orange shag with streaks of purple. I guess Pablo had advised her she could tune in Venus that way.

"Zelmont's damaged goods, Don?" Stadanko didn't bother to look in my direction.

"He ain't no kid, and he's got battle injuries."

"He blew off our number three draft pick yesterday in practice."

"You looked real good, Zelmont."

"Thank you ma'am." Stadanko jingled some coins in his pocket, still only looking at Cannon.

"That he did. But we have to consider how productive he can be in the long term." Cannon folded his beefy arms, touching his glasses like he always did as if they were ready to fall off.

"Long term doesn't always apply to everybody." He kept jingling.

Was Stadanko trying to play me? Get me thinking he means something else?

Ysanya smiled at me. "Well, I'm sure Zelmont hopes to have a good year, make enough to maybe retire, huh, Zelmont?"

"I just want to play." Damn, what cornball bullshit.

Cannon looked at me sideways behind his glasses. "He says he's ready, he's clean, and he's on time."

"Then what more can we expect?" Stadanko spread his arms wide, grinning with no feeling behind the smile. "I'll leave you to your tasks, coach." He split, his old lady sauntering along, humming to herself. Maybe she was getting signals from them planets after all.

Cannon pointed toward the locker room. "Get busy, lucky boy."

"Sure you right."

Walking into the locker room, who but coach's grown son Tommy breezed past me. He had that look that told me he'd come up short again at the racetrack.

"Hey, you're back, huh?" He stopped and glanced back at me, blinking.

"Can't keep a God-fearing man like me down."

He laughed real loud and went on to look for his dad and a loan.

Later that day I got a call from Martin Lowe, which didn't surprise me much. He was the junior flip to the big dick boys in the sports agents firm that said not more than a year ago I wasn't worth their effort to rep. We had a late lunch at a restaurant near the water in Redondo Beach, not too far from Wilma's office.

"Uh-huh, no…I'm on that now, I kid you not. Yeah, this is like done already." He tapped his iPhone's screen, moving his runner's shoulders inside his baby soft leather coat. "Hey, what you gonna have, Zee?" Lowe couldn't have been more than twenty-six. He was tanned and wore a ring on each index finger. One had a black stone, the other a red one.

Usually if a cat don't know me, I don't dig 'em talking to me like we're familiar. But I needed his young sure self, so I nixed the comeback. "Somethin' light, want to be hustlin' when I hit the field on Saturday for the exhibition against the Browns."

"Natch." His phone buzzed again, and he put it to his ear eagerly like Captain Kirk getting a message from Spock. He jabbered some more, then signed off, lifting his shoulders. We finally ordered and got down to it.

"You know you're coming out of a rough patch there, Zee."

Lowe had some of his imported mineral water. "The money isn't like it would be in the old days. And there's the salary caps, the free agent finagling and so forth."

"What you figure your fifteen percent comes to?" I crossed my legs.

He chuckled in his throat. "Stadanko will go seven small this year. And if you perform the way we know you will, then two large next year will not be crazy to consider. Plus, I have a couple of possible endorsers considering."

Considering I don't get busted with anything up my nose or my zipper down when the video is rolling. "I was hoping we could do better."

The waiter brought our salads. "Zee, you were making minimum wage with the Dragons. This isn't bad." He pierced a cherry tomato with his fork.

No, it wasn't. Seven hundred grand would keep a lot of shit from rainin' down on me. But I was expected to moan and he was expected to promise me all kinds of perks. We ate and did the back and forth – what if I asked for this, maybe he could get that. Afterward, we shook hands. He would get a contract to me tomorrow. And he picked up the tab. That hadn't happened in a long time.

I wondered what Wilma would say if I dropped in on her at the office, but good sense told me not to go by. No reason making it seem like I wanted anything to do with their scam when all I really wanted was another taste of that educated trim of hers. Better to get my mind on straight and keep it there.

I pulled into my driveway and Fahrar parked right behind me. I knew it was him before he got out of his tired Toronado. The half Landautop was old and cracked like alligator skin, and the tires were mismatched like his eyes. Damn car was ancient.

"I can't believe they let you drive that piece of crap. Don't the LAPD have standards?"

"My lieutenant likes us to blend in." He came out to the car wearing his hat. His light-colored eye looked wet. "You've been all the rage on the sports radio this morning."

"What is it, Fahrar? You gonna keep your weak-ass Colombo routine goin' until I break down and cry like a bitch? You ain't got shit and you never will. Know why? You ain't competent, that's why."

"Big word for you to use, isn't it, Zelmont?"

I shoulda popped him upside the head with the equipment bag I was holding. But that's what the little punk wanted. He was gonna keep needlin' me until he had an excuse to haul me in.

"What you got, cop?"

Fahrar shoved his hat down on his head. He pulled in his lips, then said, "I got a murdered girl slaughtered by a thrill killer. A young woman who only wanted what all of us want, Raines, a chance, one goddamn chance, for a piece of that silver hope. You've had hope to spare and shat on it each time."

I threw down my bag. "That it, Fahrar? You the Specter, that white ghost with the green gloves in the comic books? You been sent to deal justice, officer? Or is it something more, Fahrar? You get a look under Davida's dress when she was on the slab and can't get it out of your fantasies?"

He rushed me, pushing me back against the carport's post. "Stop it, stop talking like that."

"Or what, porker?" I backhanded his hat off. "What you gonna do?" I looked down at him, his hands latched onto the front of my clothes. "Go on, get bad, chump." We were both pumped, our chests rising and falling. "You want to be the superhero, don't you?"

Fahrar pushed off me, jabbing his finger at my face. "You had everything handed to you and you don't give two fucks. Don't you understand what an opportunity you were allowed and what you could have done with it?"

"I earned every goddamn thing I ever got out of pro ball, Fahrar."

"Yeah, the jail and rehab time too."

"I started, man, I been in the lights and seen the smiles when Zelmont Raines brings the ball down out of the air like Houdini, baby. I ain't no role model, but I never pretended to be one either. See I'm honest, I don't come on Ellen goin' aw shucks, I didn't know about them fucked-up conditions in that Asian shoe factory. Damn, I guess I'll have to get the company to do something about it. Meanwhile, I keep pocketing the endorsement dough, cryin' to hide my greed.

"I know them shoes I used to pimp to kids in Compton and

wherever is made by poor little bastards in Chinese labor camps or Indonesia someplace. So what? They makin' a wage, ain't they? It ain't like they got a good system like us where a man can make what he can with what he got. I think about them like they think about me, not too often. You got to go for what you know in this world, son. 'Cause it don't last long."

I turned to go.

"Don't you walk away." Fahrar grabbed my arm.

I stopped, counting down to myself like I do to keep a clear head. A right head. "Better ease up, fool. I'm startin' to lose my good graces."

He got around in front again. "You ain't walking on water around here, Zelmont."

"That's what kills you, ain't it, Fahrar? You can't figure out why I got it and you don't. You with all your heart seepin' out of your pores, and me, just waltzin' in and snatchin' balls and fame out of the air." My eyes got wide as I shoved him back against my Explorer.

I was spitting out my words quickly I was so excited. "Get used to it, Fahrar. I've been playin' football longer than you been a cop. I see the lines on the field when I'm bustin' a nut or snoozin' in my bed. I hear the crack of the pads when I'm out in the streets and smell the locker room when I got a big steak oozing on my plate. Don't preach to me 'cause you wear a badge and think Jesus himself pinned it on you. Fuck you, Fahrar. You can't come to my house and talk down to me. You ain't my mama, and I don't let her do that either.

"Now if you want a couple of tickets to the exhibition on Saturday, I got 'em for you. You want a date with a Baroness so you can get over Davida, I'll see what I can do for you, 'cause I can see you're lonely."

He was getting red around the jaw but stared at me with his goofy eyes. "Watch me on the field, Fahrar, watch me and see if I ain't got the touch of the wind. Then sit back in your broke-down easy chair sippin' your beer, and ask yourself, if I was guilty, why am I so good?"

I picked up my bag and went toward the front door. I looked at Candy and Dandy keeping silent guard, then went inside.

...

I caught five passes shooting between their zone D, fumbled once, and racked up ninety-two yards in the game against Cleveland. Listening to the crowd in the Coliseum, their voices bouncing off the dome's ceiling, was stronger than any jolt of crack or coke I ever had. The place was maybe half full, but what did it matter? They were paying to see the Barons, and I was one of the team. Even Cannon gave me a smile when I came off the field.

We clapped each other on the backs and swatted towels at brown and white butts. There was slapping and yelling and dancing in the aisles. We'd lost by two points, but that was only after Cannon, Blake, and Pat Warren, the defensive coach, had put the pine riders in to see how they'd do.

"How's it feel to be back in the regular leagues, Zelmont?"

Cindy Havers, sports announcer, had her cameraman cram his lens near my face.

"Like it was meant to be."

"How's the leg? In the third after the hit by Tractor Bradshaw you were limping."

"So would you, Cindy, if a flying slab of 350 pounds came slammin' into you." I didn't limp long, anyway. Bradshaw's tackle had traumatized my thigh, and I had to be taken out and have it massaged as it spasmed. But it calmed down and I ran two plays in the fourth until they brought in the scrubs.

Walking out of the locker room, Grainger caught up to me.

"I heard they're making choices this coming week."

"There's four more games in exhibition, man, calm down. You gonna do all right." Every day he needed me to hold his hand. Rookie.

"Grier was smoking today too," Grainger said.

He was. He was gonna take Grainger's slot, not 'cause he was that much better but because he was that much hungrier. "I'll see you on Monday, Grainger."

"Yeah," he said, like an eight-year-old who'd learned Santa wasn't real.

I split, and after chilling and changing at the pad I went to an after-party Duck Shannon, the center, was throwing at the Locker Room. I was curious to see how things were working out with Danny as the straw boss.

"Zelmont." Danny Deuce nodded at me as I entered. He and his Daltons crew were in sport coats and slacks. Seems Nap had insisted they follow a dress code. Of course, you can take a thug off the corner, but you can't take the corner out of the thug. These brothers all looked like they'd as soon beat you down as walk past you.

"Nap around?" I asked one of the junior gangsters.

"Who you?" he said in that tone they all learned in juvie lockup.

I sighed and went off to find him, but he wasn't around.

And Danny wouldn't tell me squat. I knew Nap had moved out of his Mount Olympus pad, but didn't know where. That made me kinda mad, like maybe he didn't trust me to keep quiet. I ordered another drink, then left without waiting for it.

Who was I foolin'? Like I could go to the Locker Room and pretend I hadn't said what I'd said to him a few weeks ago at the Seven Souls. Like we could go on being friends with Stadanko hangin' between us. For once I went to bed early, by myself, and happy to do so.

Monday I was bending into my locker taking my pads off after practice when this hand landed on my shoulder. I turned, but it wasn't Coach Cannon. "What do you want? This ain't play hour, Trace."

"Man wants to see you." He was crowding me in front of my teammates like I was a punk.

"Back the fuck up." I got in his face, breathing on his flaming cross.

"You can talk like a man in a room full of your other hedonists, but what does it matter?" He grinned, and we sneered at each other until he pointed at the exit. "He's waiting, and now I've already told you twice."

"Maybe you slow, Trace, maybe you hearin' hymn music too much in your bean head, but I got to get somewhere, understand?"

"Understand I'm not telling you another time." He stepped back, touching the tattoo on his cheek like it was a lucky charm. "Go on, find out."

The evilness of his smile made me kinda sick. I pulled on a T-Shirt and walked out in my practice pants and socks. Julian Weems was in the hallway, his hands in his pockets. Two more of his holy-rolling squares were with him. He was in a crème-colored suit and pearl black shoes, his skin the same shade as his off-white shirt.

"Mr. Raines, you're off the team."

He didn't even let me get close. He practically yelled it so it could be heard in the locker room. "I passed your drug tests, Moses. You ain't got no reason to bounce me."

"I know you beat the screening somehow, but that's irrelevant to me." He swatted his hand through the air. "I am exercising my prerogative and removing you from the roster before it's finalized."

I made for Weems, but the beefy boys were prepared for that action. They moved in front of him, ready to rack me in a New York minute. I could sense Trace itchin' to slap me down from behind. "You can't do that, that ain't right."

Weems returned, his hands in his pockets, the slabs flanking him again. "Yes, well, so be it. The indisputable fact remains we will not have your kind in the NFL."

I couldn't get any words out of my mouth.

Feeling bold, Weems stepped from around his protection.

"You don't have a contract yet, you are here only at the pleasure of the owners."

"And you ain't one of them," was the only lame thing I could say.

"I'm the Commissioner, Raines. And though I'm sure you never bothered to read what is the purview of my office, I can assure you I exercise a fair amount of leverage with the owners."

I wasn't sure, but it sounded like he had the goods on Stadanko and was flexing to prove it. "I haven't done anything, Weems."

"But you will. You will get in a fight at a rock concert, or have an assignation with a married woman, or hit a policeman as you did in Atlanta and Denver. You will do something to make a mockery of what we are attempting to do in this league, and I will not suffer it. I simply won't. You are gone."

A twitch jerked one side of his lip. Then he walked away, his dog pound trotting after him. Trace said, "You better find honest work, my man. The devil has betrayed you."

I got on my celly and screamed at my new agent, Lowe. "Why didn't you know about this?" Players went past me into the parking lot. Cannon must have gone out another way. The coward wouldn't face me.

"Calm down, Zee. Don't you know I'll get on this like last week? They can't get away with this kind of shit. What's Stadanko's position?"

"Prone, his ass in the air and puckered up so he can get reamed easier by his lord and master King Julian." I threw the phone against the wall, breaking it. I got my street shoes on and drove off in my football pants. I stopped at a liquor store near the airport on Century and marched inside. I got stared at but they took my money for the fifth of Cutty. I'd finished a good part of the bottle by the time I rolled home. Too bad Davida was dead, she could really ease my tension right now. Drunk and mad enough to kill, I broke the rest of the scotch against Candy's skull. "Put that goddamn tongue back in your head," I told her. I stumbled inside and called Isabel at her work. She was a clothes buyer for Bloomingdale's or Macy's or whatever the hell it's called.

"Busy?"

"Workin' a couple of buyers. You sound down."

"Got fired."

Nothing for a bit. "Look, I have to close this deal, alright? How 'bout you come by tonight 'round seven?"

"Sure." I hung up and got my cognac out. I juiced up the stereo, a Paris CD jammin' on it as I sipped and plotted and sipped some more. I fell asleep and woke up a little after five. If Lowe had called, I'd been lost in snooze land. I still had a edgy high on. I showered and had something to eat. By then I was in a half sober way, together enough to manage the freeways at the end of rush hour to get into East L.A. and Isabel's pad.

I knocked and she answered the door.

"You look real professional," I said, noticing her business suit.

"You look wore out."

"I ain't that wore out."

She let me in and we made small talk about how messed up it was that Weems did what he did to me, how she had a lawyer I could talk to, and so forth. Pretty soon we let the feeling that'd been building between us since the funeral take over and I had her dress up, panty hose and panties down, and was doing her doggie style on the couch.

"Zelmont," she said between moans, her hands on the back of the sofa cushions. "You didn't kill my sister, did you?"

"Of course not." I kept on keeping on.

"Good," she said, "it wouldn't be right making love to you if you did."

"Yeah, that'd be sick."

Afterward, we sat slouched down on the couch, watching the 10 o'clock news, our legs over each other. She was in an old man's bathrobe and I was in my bikini draws.

"What are you going to do?" We were watching this story about a kid who went into a burning apartment to save a three-legged cat belonging to this crippled 70-year-old woman.

"I don't know," I said. I was scared of what was bubblin' inside my head. I didn't want to fix on it, but the idea wouldn't go away.

She snuggled her head on my chest. "I don't cook breakfast."

One of these days I was gonna catch me a domesticated chick who did. "Ain't no thang, Isabel. I didn't come here to get my eggs scrambled."

"You sure about that?" She started kissing me and we got busy again.

Later, in her bed, I woke up sometime in the early hours. I couldn't remember what I'd been dreaming, but it had given me the chills. One of the bedroom windows was open, the humid air of the night spilling into the room. I lay there, my hand on my chest, wondering how many beats my heart had missed.

"*f*uck." I slammed the phone down and kicked the coffee table, knocking some magazines onto the floor. Wouldn't you know the one I could make out the best was the cover I'd made of *Sports Illustrated* right after the Super Bowl. I picked up the magazine and tore it to pieces, cursing and wishing I could get my hands around Weems' chicken bone neck.

Lowe had been on the horn telling me how hopeless it was.

If Weems said I was out, I was out. He also told me if Stadanko had put up a stink, the situation might be different. Stadanko was fronting $370 million, and since I hadn't broken no league rules, Weems really didn't have a legal right to ban me if it got to court. But Stadanko hadn't said squat.

"Goddamn," I got mad again, and looked for something to break. The phone rang again, and I was surprised it was still on the hook.

"Yeah." I was in a mood to tear whoever was on the other end a new one.

"I'm sorry."

It was Wilma. "You sittin' in the front office, why didn't you tell me?"

"Get real, Zelmont. I have my own office, and Stadanko doesn't need to tell me about something like this. His exposure is minimal, since, let's be honest, you don't have the money to fight him. And Cannon can be squeezed to say you were a medical risk. You're in a tough position."

"But you know the way I should turn." I guess I wanted her to make me do it. I guess I wanted her to have me lust after her and the promise of money. In the end, I knew I wanted to do it for myself. I wanted to get back at Stadanko and Chekka and everyone of 'em. Then I'd figure out something special for Weems.

She didn't say anything, but I could almost feel her and smell her through the phone. "Well?"

"You going to be home around four?"

"I suppose." What the hell was I gonna do? I didn't feel like working out, it wouldn't burn off this hurt I had.

"Good." She hung up and I waited. I didn't drink, although I felt like it. Didn't take a toke of nothing either. Instead, I watched some shit on cable, infomercials and such. There was one about a device that let you count cards and coins, and with a simple attachment it became a fan. This English dude with a pink face was very excited about the silly-ass gadget, how wonderful a time saver it would be around the house.

I was imagining other uses of the coin counter when the doorbell rang. It was a motorcycle messenger Wilma had sent. He handed me an envelope and I didn't tip him. Man, I had to watch my ducats. Inside was a note written in Wilma's perfect schoolgirl handwriting. "The Encounter, 8:00, burn this," it said. I did, and got over there at the right time.

The restaurant was inside the building at the airport that looked like it belonged in *The Jetsons*. There were curves coming out of the round upstairs part, making it look like a concrete spider. I'd heard somewhere that a black architect had designed the place. Wonder what ma and pa flying in from Iowa might think about that if they knew.

"What the hell is this?" Danny Deuce had gotten used to his new style. He was dressed in a Hugo Boss blue serge number with a maroon shirt and a tie that looked like somebody spilled paint on it. You could tell he liked being the boss while his big brother laid low.

"Duck fajitas," Nap said. He'd cut off his dreads and looked like he'd lost some weight after his stay at Burroughs' little hideaway. His biceps were loose in the sleeves of his Prada sport coat. He scooped meat and onions and guacamole onto his plate. "It'll expand your palate."

I didn't think Danny knew what the word meant but no sense getting him worked. Not now, at least. "So let's do this thing." I had more of my Maker's Mark.

"Yeah, let's get the money," Danny said like a kid getting to go on the scary rides at Magic Mountain for the first time.

"This is not going to be some gangsta smash and grab," Wilma said. "We know where the money is taken to be housed for transfer," she tipped her head toward me. "But there's much more we have to learn and set in motion before we strike."

"Like what?" Danny said, stuffing fajitas and pieces of tortilla into his mouth. "This shit's aw'right."

Wilma's eyes were slitted, hiding the look she must have been giving Danny. "Stadanko is on a precipice. Coming at him is the Justice Department on one side and the Armenians on the other."

"What in the fuck are you talking about?" Danny had more food. Nap wasn't grubbin' like he normally did, just eating a nibble here and there. Outside, a plane zoomed by, making the windows shake.

"Through a college friend who's now in the major crimes section of the DOJ, I've learned that local vice cops placed an illegal tap on the Pink Cavern strip club in Brooklyn two and half years ago."

Danny kept eating as Wilma talked. I drank and listened. Nap worked on a piece of bell pepper.

"The cops were following a trail of Tijuana-issued heroin. Supposedly, the border cartel boys were looking to expand business to the east. The strip club was owned by a Puerto Rican-American named Octavio Colon who had ties to these guys.

"If it was illegal, then how were they going to use anything they got off the tap?" I asked.

"Cops do it all the time," Wilma answered. "They do the tap, find out something that puts them in a certain direction, and claim later they got the new goods through an informant or a piece from another bust. Anyway, who should be dating one of the strippers but Yagos Ondanian."

"I know him, right?" Danny said.

"He's been to the Locker Room once or twice," Nap told his brother.

"Ondanian is part of an Armenian group muscling in on some of the Russian mob's action along the Eastern seaboard. Well, anyway, the tap picks up him and his girlfriend hinting around about the heroin delivery."

"I'm getting lost here." Danny kept chowin' down.

"The point is," Wilma went on, "Ondanian had turned one of Stadanko's Russian mafia connections. This guy now works for Ondanian."

Danny looked blank and Nap seemed bored. Maybe I was the only one who got it. "That's when Little Hand decided there were virgin pastures in L.A."

"Right. At the same time there was this big push by electeds to bring a new franchise to town, and Stadanko was in the middle of it. Thus a perfect opportunity for his cousin. A lot of money floats around the league, what with insane TV and cable revenues. How better to hide the origins of your money than through Hollywood-style bookkeeping? They brought in some others, all of them bent to some degree or another. You can't make millions of dollars by always playing fair. And the NFL was anxious to have a team back in the number two media market in the U.S., so it was destined to happen." Wilma had some of her wine. She licked her bottom lip and I kinda forgot what we were there for.

"And Ondanian followed Stadanko out west?" Nap was finally eating like I was used to seeing him do.

"There's supposed to be a detente between the two mobs. But it's Ondanian that Justice has been keeping watch on since that night. The vice cops made sure the info leaked up so they'd have favors with DOJ down the road."

"But these Justice scrubs would be happy to nab Stadanko too," I said.

"Yes," Wilma said. A look I couldn't figure out suddenly came across her face, then left just as fast. "You do pay attention when you want to."

"You think I learned all them complicated plays by just running around?"

"I can see you didn't, baby." The way she said that word got me twitchy in the right places.

"So why in the fuck did you tell us that?" Danny spit out some food.

"Please," his brother said, holding up his cloth napkin.

Danny swatted it away, but the two smiled at each other.

Wilma didn't hide what she was thinking about Danny this time. It was there for all to see. "Because as I learned long ago in law school, we need to know our target before we move. And therefore we need to do our research."

Danny slumped in his seat like the little nitwit he was.

"Yeah, whatever."

"Anyway, we have another in on Stadanko." Wilma toasted Nap with her wine glass.

"Huh?" Danny said.

"Pablo's sweet on your brother," I said. "And Pablo is scamming Ysanya."

Nap smiled for the first time. "There you go, brah. And on the QT, that's where your participation in the preparation of this scheme comes in." He wiggled his eyebrows like I'd seen Groucho do on AMC. It made me jumpy.

"Look here, Nap, if you think I'm gonna make the fag dreams of your swishy boyfriend come true with a threesome, think again, pardner. A'right?" Another jet took off and Wilma's wine glass shook.

"Don't worry, it won't be an unnatural act for you." Nap ate more.

I drank whiskey but didn't taste anything. Wilma was giggling and Danny was practically falling out of his chair.

"Zelmont, we gonna rig up a video and sell that shit to all the bungholers from West Hollywood to London. Shit." He laughed so loud, other people in the restaurant turned to look at us.

"You motherfuckahs better be kiddin' or we're gonna need a new goddamn plan, and now."

"Zee," Nap clapped me on the shoulder, "don't even think twice about it. You ain't gonna be doin' no plumbin', at least not on a man." He squeezed my shoulder like that was supposed to make me feel okay. It didn't.

Later, sitting in Wilma's pad in Westchester, I had that and another matter knocking around inside my head.

"Why you in this, girl?" We were in the living room of her pad overlooking the marina. Outside one of her windows was a view of the Loyola campus in the flatlands.

"I got your girl." She had on her glasses and was reading one of her legal magazines, *California Lawyer* or something. I was playing John Madden's NFL Extreme on the Xbox I'd hooked up to her flatscreen. I'd picked the Packers against the Barons. The Pack was losing.

"My bad," I said. "But you're still duckin' the question. Why you down for rippin' off Stadanko? You got a gravy contract representing the team and other high-priced corporate clients. Why risk all that on this thieves' enterprise?"

She took her head out of the magazine. "You can be quite poetic when you want to be."

"You can learn a lot in locker rooms."

"Apparently." She tossed the magazine on a small table next to the chair where she sat. "I intend for this to be a smooth operation." She put her hands together and raised her index fingers. She touched her lips to the fingers. "I'm in this because, sooner or later, some of the nasty shit chasing Stadanko is going to catch him, and the Barons franchise will come down around him. There goes my fat contract. I'm a woman who demands, Zelmont." She got up, gliding over to where I sat.

"What's wrong with wanting more than a paycheck?"

She stood over me and took the controller out of my hand, letting it slip to the floor. "You feel threatened by a ruthless woman, Zelmont?"

I would have bet the house on that. But she turned me on every time she called my name. That couldn't be good.

She had her shoe in my crotch, digging in softly with the heel. Wilma took my hand and tugged me off the chair. We walked to her bedroom door, our arms around each other. She had her hand on the knob as she turned her head and kissed me. Then she leaned against the door, thrusting her butt out at me. I stood close behind, grinding her through the pants she wore, my hand rubbing between her legs.

Eventually we made it to the sack.

In the morning when I got up, Wilma was already in the shower. I was surprised to see the walls of her bedroom were empty except for one painting. It was the kind I hate, all squiggly lines and explosions. Why anyone would spend good bread for something like that was beyond me. I guess it was expected if you ran in certain circles.

"I think it would be a good idea if you and Nap started showing yourself at the club." Wilma was naked, drying her hair. I watched her breasts jiggle. She threw the towel at me.

"Pay attention, you horny roughneck."

"Sure, coach. I'll sit here and imagine Cannon naked so I can keep myself focused."

Now she was making a thing of bending down and looking in her dresser. She slowly slipped on her panties, playing with me. I faked like I was interested in the morning newspaper. I never read the paper except maybe sports, and the business section back when I had money. I gave that up and enjoyed watching her get dressed. She sat on the bed and had me help hook her bra. Like she really needed me to do that.

She snuggled into pantyhose, and from her long closet she got out a matching skirt and jacket.

"What you got planned today," I asked. She was zipping up the side of her skirt.

"We have a meeting with Stadanko and the principal owners. We have to start going over the players' salaries and perks."

A stab of jealousy tightened my gut. "Grainger in the mix?"

"I think so." She was brushing her hair, looking into a mirror over a makeup table.

"He's too nice," I said. "All the time askin' how you doin', how you feelin'. Boy got to get in the right frame if he wants to get somewhere in this league." I knew I sounded like Terri, my son's mother, and I didn't care.

"They can't all be hard like you, Zelmont." Wilma patted my cheek. "I'll see you later." She gave me a peck and left.

I sat there for a while then finally got my ass out of bed.

I went home and got into my sweats. No sense letting myself slip when, if nothing else, I knew I'd have to depend on my body for the job.

As I pushed against the creaking in my fibula, it occurred to me I might even call Terri and see about the baby. Now why all of a sudden was I starting to worry about that knothead kid?

"on't need you, Zelmont." Danny sipped on a tall glass with a dolphin stirrer in it. Several of his boys marched around, looking for something to do as the afternoon came on.

"You don't own this place, Danny. You just the caretaker until your brother comes back."

"Then maybe you should talk to Nap." He tilted his head like he was hoping I'd start something. "But he left me in charge, and really, you ain't necessary to this operation."

"This ain't no army base, this is a nightclub."

"One you ain't needed at 'less you standing in line and payin' at the front door." He stood there, daring me to pop his full-of-himself ass. If I did, one of his clique was gonna bust a few caps in my dome, crying while he did it.

I split. Now I was back in the unemployment line until the job went down. Which meant my stupid grandstanding play of sending money to Terri was just that, stupid. Then wouldn't you fuckin' know I got the call when I rolled home.

"Zelmont, no more delays," my attorney Barry Kleinhardt warned. A few hours later I was sitting near the links at the Wilshire Country Club.

"Ah hell, Barry, ain't I been on the fair and goddamn square? Didn't I make an offer to her parents to further the little ho's education?"

Kleinhardt rubbed at what was left of his disappearing hair. He threw his pen on the glass table and scooted his chair back on the patio, then put the bottom of his golf shoe against the table's metal edge. "She's in a wheelchair, Zelmont. It doesn't matter that you say she came on to you, or that she was sixteen at the time and she showed you a fake ID stating she was twenty."

A wrinkled white man, his gut hanging over his belt buckle, walked past us. He had one of those old-fashioned thick mustaches and he looked at me like he expected me to get up and start serving drinks to him. I opened my mouth and gave him the ghetto glare. He picked up the pace and went into the clubhouse.

I hadn't checked her ID. But it was a good defense Kleinhardt had tried, as he'd found out she did have the bunk driver's license.

"You gave her wine and then showed her the magic torpedo, and baby, you should be thankful for the four and a half years I've been fighting this charge."

"Four years and three hundred and fifty grand," I said too loud. A few of the golfers at other tables on the patio looked over their shoulders at us. I leaned in under the umbrella.

"Let 'em wheel that connivin' bitch into court, Barry. Your investigator got testimony from them boys on the wrestling team she blew. Don't that show the chick's a freak?"

"I'll grant you it shows a pattern, Zelmont. But we've only found guys who are willing to testify about the last year or so, after her 18th birthday. Young men who are in her appropriate age range."

"And race."

Kleinhardt held up his hands and sat straight in his chair again. "If you'd signed with the Barons it'd be a different story. A couple hundred thousand more and her family would be satisfied."

"Family." Her father showed up once he smelled money coming out of my black ass. He hadn't been around for years before that. And her frizzed-hair mama. A couple of times it seemed if I'd given her a turn with my sweet thing she'd have got her daughter to back off.

Kleinhardt bit his bottom lip on one side. "Zelmont, we have photos of her made up, and she looks older. Her friends that brought her to your house that night have been deposed and said she wanted to meet you in the worst way. Her girlfriend Becky said the two of them talked about what it would be like with you."

"Isn't that good enough?"

"No," he said. Kleinhardt looked off at the green as if an answer might rise up from the ninth hole. "We drew Judge Kodama, and she don't play around when it comes to adults and minors, especially with guys like you. Even though her old man is black."

I drank my iced tea as if I was tasting it for the very first time, or the last.

"Even the best case means you'll still have to do five to seven. That's if I can get it reduced to consensual sex with an underaged minor with extenuating circumstances, as opposed to sodomy and statutory rape."

I felt like finding that old fuck who'd been giving me the "what's the native doing here?" look and swatting him. "I don't know what to say."

"Peep this," Kleinhardt leaned closer. "Either way you'll have to register as a sex offender."

My head was swimming. "I'd rather do twenty years getting reamed by the Aryan Nation brothers every day. Zelmont Raines may have dropped down some, man, but I can't be goin' 'round and have people pointin' at me like I was some kind of child molester. You know I ain't that. What would my mother think?"

"Judges get elected just like D.A.'s, Zelmont. Even if she's inclined to be lenient in her sentencing, which she won't be, this is one guideline she can't waver from." Kleinhardt reached for his Reuben sandwich, but only looked at it. "If there was any other way."

"There is, Barry." I grabbed at my head like it was coming unscrewed. I looked over at him. "You go to that beauty school drop-out mama of hers and see if she won't hold out her hand when I offer the dough."

"What do you mean?" Out on the links, a dude got a nice birdie.

"Watch," I said.

Four days later I was on Fox Shoppers World, hawking my Super Bowl ring. I could almost hear Grier sitting at home, calling his homies and laughing at me. Fuck him and the lawyers and the judges and especially that crippled tramp and her no armpit shaving mother. They'd run an ad in the sports section in the morning, plus some radio coverage, so the viewers were primed when I got on air.

I put up with some bullshit from the slick dude who worked as one of the hosts of their Collector's Showcase about how big and shiny the ring was, and what a great piece of history it was since it was the first and last time the Falcons had won a Super Bowl, yakkaty and blah. I just sat there, grinning like Stepin Fetchit mumbling one lame excuse after another as a bunch of assholes called in to belittle me or remark how low I'd fallen, how ashamed I should be, and so on.

Finally, though, the numbers started coming up, and the ring sold for $350,000 to, of course, a Japanese businessman who'd made a killing after electricity was deregulated last year.

What with the admin fees Fox got and the percentage I'd worked out with Lowe for setting up the deal, I'd take home a little over three large. That was before settling with the crip and my bill with Kleinhardt. Goddamn, I needed a fuckin' break, and in a hurry.

A day later it was set.

"One hundred forty it is," Kleinhardt said to me. He clicked off his cell. "Mother and the daughter's lawyer are convinced of your sincerity, Zelmont. And they acknowledge there may have been some slight innocent, unconscious enticement on the young woman's part, being not wise in the ways of the world. But that's in the past. They all want to move forward with their lives."

"Especially since they figure they'd only be beatin' a dead horse to hold out for more." We were standing in the waiting room of a foreign car repair place on the Miracle Mile.

Kleinhardt was having some work done on his sharp ride, an emerald green Beamer sedan.

I didn't have much to say so I stood there, hands in my pockets.

"What's on deck for you now, Zelmont?"

Kleinhardt said it like I had a future mapped out. More and more, there was only one direction I was heading. Sitting in the restaurant the other day at the airport, I was kinda in, kinda not. Like how I've been pretty much with every woman of mine. In the mix, but sorta standing outside of it too, watching stuff go down around me even though I was involved.

Yet here I was, looking silly like any other middle class square. Kleinhardt was on the phone again, happy with himself for keeping me out of jail. Shit, I was the one that came up with the idea. What'd

I get? Money out of my pocket and then some. Not much of the ring money was mine to keep, and I had a hefty mortgage to meet. One of the mechanics was working underneath a Jag, back toward the muffler. He was probably in a better financial situation than me. That didn't make me sad, just determined.

"I'll see you, Barry."

He waved at me and continued gabbing on the phone. I was already played, as far as he was concerned – my big paydays behind me. Wouldn't be no calls to get in nine holes like there used to be from him when I was raking in the green. I was trying to stay afloat in the shark tank. And if I wasn't careful, I might be their food real quick.

The garage opened out on an alley and I took that and turned at the corner where the car repair place was. I crossed Wilshire at an angle and went into the Electric Bongo. It was a big building near the corner of Detroit painted a slate blue. Years ago the club had once been a Jack LaLane's gym and sauna. I heard some actors and others had invested some dough and turned it into a salsa joint. There was a big bongo drum hanging on chains from the edge of the roof.

At the bar I had a Maker's Mark, then another one. The bartender, a decent-looking chick in black pants and matching vest and white shirt, eyed me twice but didn't say anything. The TV was on and Weems was talking.

"As I've said, I'm not insensitive to how this might appear to our fans. They are the only reason we want to bring them the kind of football we know they want and deserve."

Trace and a couple of other flat-shouldered boys were flanking the comish like what he had to say was important.

Weems tried to smile but knew it looked too fake. "It was no easy task informing the team owners that certain men wouldn't be allowed to play, but we must have standards. We must adhere to the new course we've taken if we're to restore the integrity of football. It must be made clean and good and strong like it was when we all first became fans."

One of the reporters asked him about playing fast and loose with the rights of free trade and so forth, but I was into my second whiskey and couldn't care less what the fool had to say.

Apparently, though, he'd bounced me and five other sorry bastards out without so much as a blink or a nod. Cold, cold motherfuckah.

I weaved outside after my third drink. Kleinhardt shot past in his BMW heading west and didn't even see me. Or at least he made like he didn't. I got in my ride and went home. Nothing else to do but chill with my buzz on.

Back at the pad there was a message waiting for me from Isabel. I called her, but she was out. I needed something to do, I was wound up tight and had to release it somehow. The phone rang and I grabbed the thing.

"Yes," I said, trying to sound relaxed.

"We're on for tomorrow, stud."

It was Nap. "What?"

"One-thirty on the t-i-t, and you might want to stock up on your Cialis before you get over there."

"Negro, what you goin' on about?" I sure wished Isabel had called me back.

"Service with a smile, homebrew."

Then it sunk in. "Oh damn."

The next day I headed out to Stadanko's pad, following the directions Nap had given me. As I neared the place, I started to get more edgy. I was worried it had to be a trap that Chekka had set to get back at us. After all, Ysanya was one of them, from Nagomo-Karabakh, Kosovo or some such place where fools until recently were still lighting each other up over who killed who in what century. But Nap said everything was on the positive tip, plus this was an important part of the plan. I was sure this sneaking around was really just part of the freak game him and missus were into playing. Me being in the middle didn't make me feel too easy.

I got lost a couple of times but found my way onto the right street in Palos Verdes Estates. The joint was huge like I'd expected, and there was a gate attached to a high brick wall around it. I pulled up to a call box on a post beside the entrance. I sat there looking at the box, not knowing what to do. Sweat was making the top of my lip wet.

"Come on in, Zee," Nap said over the intercom.

One side of the gate opened quietly. I drove in and followed the drive to the front door. The house – mansion, I guess you'd really call it – was three floors and had balconies and vines crawling all over it. It wasn't a modern look. No, Stadanko's pad reminded me of the kind of cribs I'd seen in old flicks from the '40s where the crazy widow hangs out and the stranger rolls up to throw her life off balance.

But I was the one off-balance right now. Nap's car was there and I parked near him. I didn't see any other ride, but that didn't ease my nerves. There were big dragon heads on both sides of the double wooden doors. Before I reached the heads, one side opened and I froze like a high schooler caught in a double team.

"Sir." A heavy woman wearing jeans and a work shirt was standing at the door with her hand on the knob.

I considered spinning around and bolting, but she'd already seen me, so that would have done no good. I went on in.

The woman didn't say anything else as she shut the door behind me. She just smiled and pointed up the stairs. She then walked off through a doorway to my right. I hit the stairs and went up past some photos hanging along the wall. One was Stadanko and Chekka in younger days. The two punks had their arms around each other, standing in front of a bar with foreign letters in the window.

I could hear voices and followed them down a bend in the hall to a set of doors with old-fashioned glass knobs. I went in and found myself standing in a room with colored light coming in from above. There was a skylight made of stained glass cut in the ceiling. The walls were painted a girly shade of pink, the bottom half of them made of dark wood. Normally, I wouldn't pay attention like some gay decorator to stuff like that, but I'd learned from past incidents involving me and my johnson, that it was best to know as many details as possible.

There were paintings on those walls, modern jive that for some reason I kinda liked. Off to one side was a desk with a computer. The curtains were open to those French windows houses like this always have. A long telescope was pointing out the window to the ocean.

Ysanya and Nap were sitting on a love seat in another part of the room. Nap was naked, the old lady in a fancy get-up like in a *Penthouse* layout, not sleazy like a *Hustler* chick. Though she did have his rod in her hand, strokin' that bad rascal nice and slow. In the other hand she was tokin' on a joint.

"Hello, Zelmont. Would you like a drink? There's a bar in the next room. And there's more dope too." She said it like we were standing around at a dinner party.

I got a drink at a bar made to look like the Titanic. The thing split apart, the racks of booze inside. On a side shelf were the joints, but I decided against the kronik. I wanted my mind on right. I had a Scotch and went back into the other room. Ysanya and Nap were feelin' on each other fiercely. I drank and looked at the paintings. I'd been in threesomes, but it had been me and two chicks, not me, a woman, and another man. Standards, you got to have standards, man.

I hoped Nap wasn't expecting me to do no Marv Albert shit. Like one of us bunghole the other while she watched. If that was the plan, motherfuckah better get a new playbook, and I mean like yesterday.

There was a table done up like an altar, with crystals, a couple of the demon statues like in Nap's office, and other mystical crap on it. There were also some candles burning in twisty kind of holders. Next to that was a stereo unit. I turned it on. Anything to help cut the tension rising in me. I was so paranoid, I didn't know if I could get it up when the time was right. Yeah, and when would that be?

A CD was on and it took me a couple of moments before I recognized Dean Martin's voice. Dino was singing "Let Me Go, Lover" as the two of them got up and trotted off through a door way behind the love seat. Nap looked back at me, making a sign for me to follow. I finished the Scotch and went in, getting the knots out of my shoulders by working them up and down, back and forth.

There was a fancy bed high off the floor made of carved wood that I swore I'd seen in a Christopher Lee Dracula movie. Nap and the lady of the house were going at it like teenagers. I stripped down and suddenly got another fear. Pablo wasn't going to show up all of sudden grinning like a possum in a grain factory, was he?

I looked around but didn't see no other clothes so I figured everything was cool. But I wouldn't put it past these two to have a faggot orgy planned and not let my naive ass know about it until it was too late.

The drink and Dino had helped my mood, and pretty soon me and Nap were turning Ysanya every which way but loose. I was between her legs doing some scuba diving, and she was rubbing my head and moaning.

From down below I heard Nap asked the question point blank: "Say, baby, where exactly does your old man and his cousin conduct their business?"

I stopped, damn near choking.

"You know he doesn't tell me, Nap, honey." Ysanya squeezed her thighs against the sides of my head. "You're not stopping now, are you, Zelmont?"

"No, ma'am." I went back to work.

"Why you want to know that, sweetie?" I could hear them kissing, and she moaned even louder.

"We gonna take down your old man."

I just about fainted. I brought my head up in a hurry.

"Look here, have you not heard of subtlety?"

Ysanya stared first at him, then me, and I knew she was going to start hollering or some shit and Trace and his acolytes would show up from nowhere and blow us away. Instead she took a drag on the joint she'd been holding and started laughing like Nap had told her the funniest joke of the week.

Then she turned to kiss the muscle-bound boy, her big butt wiggling with pleasure. "Can we do it, baby? Can we take that bastard for all he's got and more? Then you and I can go away and leave this place of ruination."

"Only with your help, honey." Nap put an arm around her and pulled her on top of him. They clearly didn't need me at the moment so I got up and went into the can. Afterward I came out and found Nap laid back on the love seat, still smoking maryjane.

Ysanya was bending down before the altar, gesturing with her hands and swaying side to side. Her eyes sparkled like I'd seen rookie linemen's after getting their first pro sack. She scared the shit out of me.

"This is destiny," she mumbled. "My beautiful black knight will deliver me from hell into a brighter future."

I looked at her black knight. He was lit up like a fuckin' Christmas tree. What had I got myself into?

Nap tipped the spliff toward me. I shook my head no. Then he asked Ysanya. "You ever have to call your husband out at the place where they meet?" He took a long drag and told me, "Cell phone reception is spotty out there, so they use a landline she says."

"He's a sly pig, he is. He changes the number each month for security reasons even though it's a swept line." Ysanya rubbed a few crystals over her bare top. "But he also doesn't fully trust his cousin either. So he's circumspect about telling me where they meet, but he also wants to leave some clue in case he doesn't make it back from one of their pow-wows." She got up and went to sit next to her boyfriend.

Nap played with her dyed blonde hair. She didn't dye down below. "When do they meet next?"

"It has to be soon because I came in the other day to his office, the day we saw you, Zelmont. Anyway, I walked in and he and Rudy were yelling in Serbo-Croat to each other. Mine has fallen off, but I caught enough of it to know they were pissed at you two for what happened at the garbage dump."

"Mad enough to whack us?" Nap asked.

She frowned. "I don't know, others have done worse to them and they've all wound up being in business together."

"But they weren't black," I added. I needed another drink and went to get one.

"Well yes," Ysanya said as I walked past her. "But they're also worried about Weems."

That stopped me. "Yeah?"

She put a hand on my thigh, kneading the muscle. "He and Weems hate each other. But what can Weems do? The owners took a vote and let my husband and his backers into the league. There's no hard evidence against him, but that's why the Commissioner moved out to L.A. His pet project is to screw Ellison."

"Wonderful." I went and got another Scotch.

"I know the cabin," I heard her tell Nap. "Actually it's a good-sized lodge on several acres of land with stables and a heated pool. It's somewhere in Ridgecrest."

"How do you know that?"

"I'm not stupid, Nap, I find out things."

"Oh, I know, darling, I know."

We talked about what would happen once she got the new number. Then we showered, me by myself, them two together.

After that, me and Nap were let out by the woman who'd let me in. She just smiled, and I figured she must know plenty of secrets. Maybe she and Ysanya had a thing going on for all I knew.

We drove over to the Locker Room in our separate cars and went up to his office. Danny had set up headquarters in another room, so Nap's area was untouched.

"You really gonna hat up with her when this is over? It's gonna be hard enough laying your large self low, let alone dragging around a chick more than ten years older than you who's used to popping over to Rodeo Drive or Newport Beach."

Nap was leaning on his desk, his forearms and triceps bunching and releasing. "I know, man. But once we play this hand I just can't leave her to take the heat. That wouldn't be right."

"If her old man gets a hint of what's up, you think for a hot minute miss freaky-deaky won't go screaming to her crystals and give you and me up? Get our asses shipped off to Bosnia where hunting down niggas is something to do in between killing each other."

"She's better than that, man."

"Are you in love with her?" 'Cause love can make a motherfuckah slip, and slipping is not an option."

"Understood," he said, his eyes beaming straight into mine.

"A'right." I made to go but then stopped. I didn't want to ask, but I had to. "I realize Danny and his posse have the club covered, Nap. And I know you got to be cool with him, but I was wondering…" I couldn't make myself finish it.

Nap didn't say anything. He walked to the stone head, did his sequence touching, and got some scratch from behind the curtain. "Three is going to have to do, Zelmont. I've got to watch my expenses myself."

My hand was out. Under my breath I said, "'Preciate this, Nap. You know I'd do the same for you."

"We boys, right?" He slapped the hundreds in my palm.

"Yeah, man. Just folding money, you know?" I couldn't raise my head and went out into the parking lot. It must have started to rain or something even though the sun was out because my cheek was wet. The devil is beating his wife, moms used to say when it showered with the sun shining. I got in the Explorer and drove over to the High Hat bar on Crenshaw.

"Naw, he ain't been here," the beefy girl in the tight red dress and green eye shadow growled at me. She went to wipe down the bar on the other end.

"Sonny Sticks is always around here," I said, following her.

"He ain't here now." She stopped moving her rag. "Ain't you supposed to be somebody?"

"The dude who's looking for the dude who owes me money, that's who I am." Like Zorro, I wrote my initial on a coaster.

"Tell him I was here and that next time he better be too." I flipped the coaster toward her.

"Oh sure." She looked at it, then went over to speak to a older cat in a ratty turtleneck and plaid knit coat sitting on a corner stool. I drove around for a while, half looking for a couple of other Gs who owed me some dough. As the sun went down, I wound up in Watts, dropping by Kelrue Cumming's grandmother's house on 107th near Santa Ana. When he didn't want to be found, that's where he'd go. He'd have heard of me getting the ax again and would know I'd want another ring or two to tide me over.

"Not now, Mr. Zelmont," his granny said through a crack in the doorway of her shack, "Kelrue hasn't been around much, you see?"

"Can I leave him a note?" Did I sound innocent enough?

"I'm not so old I can't remember, Mr. Zelmont." Granny's voice cracked. Kelrue was probably crouching down in a back room.

Putting some weight on the door, I said, "This won't take but a minute."

"Please, we don't want no trouble. But I got me what they call a panic button inside the door here, Mr. Zelmont. The City Council done gave 'em out to us senior citizens in a safe streets program, yes sir."

Fuck. I could get the door open and knock her down before she could reach that button. If there was one. I pushed my weight against the door some more. "It'll be over before you know it, grandma. Kelrue has a contract he has to honor."

"Good Jesus."

I was almost inside when a pair of high beams suddenly flashed on, catching me in the glare. The car had driven up quick across the lawn. A door opened and slammed. I didn't need to be John Shaft to know who it was.

"Prone out on the lawn, Zelmont." Fahrar stood to one side of the car, the lights barely outlining his form. I was sure he had his gun leveled, firing range steady on me.

"This ain't none of your concern, cop."

"You gone simple? Do what I tell you and step away from the citizen."

Grandma made a face at me. "Serves you right for being so evil."

I could have popped her but that would give Fahrar an excuse to shoot me. "Don't you and your fat grandson get too cozy, old lady. I'm coming back."

That took some of the vinegar out of her. Fahrar was close, his nine pointed at my head. "Do as I told you." He grabbed me, pulling on my arm. Then he pushed the muzzle of the automatic against my cheek, digging it in hard. "Let's go."

He manhandled me down onto the grass, kicking at the back of my legs with his feet. I got down on my knees and he thumped me in the middle of my back with the butt of his gun. "Prone, motherfuckah."

I turned my head and saw those crazy eyes of his were full of anger. I went face down, and he patted me all over. Then he made me put my hands behind my back and he cuffed them.

"Get up."

I did. Granny and a couple of her neighbors were watching the show. Then Fahrar marched me to his car and told me to sit in the passenger side. He got in on the driver's side. There was a prisoner bar on the dash and he clinked the short chain on it to the cuffs. He reversed the car and we took off.

"You ain't got nothing, Fahrar. I didn't touch the old lady and she didn't squawk." He wasn't heading down 108th where the station was. But come to think of it, Fahrar didn't work the Watts Division.

"How'd you find me?"

His fucked-up hat was pressed tight against his head. "When I heard you got cut, I knew you'd be desperate for money. I'd developed a list of the losers who owe you dough." He grinned at me, his yellow eye giving me a shiver.

"You done lost your mind, son."

"Your mama lost hers having you, Zelmont."

He pulled his Toronado under where the 105 and 110 freeways crossed, near Figueroa and 111th. Overhead the cars and trucks went by. Down where we were there was nothing but dark shadows and the smell of gas and trash. Fahrar got out, leaving me chained to the bar. He came around the back of the car and opened the passenger door. Fahrar stuck the gun against my nose.

"You bad now?"

"You better – "

"Shut up," he yelled, slapping me with the gun.

"Fuck you, punk. Let me loose and let's see how hard you are."

His answer was to poke the side of my face with his nine again. "I could run you in on assault for harassing the old lady."

"I didn't assault anybody, clown. You the one doing the assaulting."

He backed up, the gun still out toward me. "You're going to own up for once, Zelmont."

I screamed, "You gonna shoot me, Fahrar? You didn't even know Davida."

"It's not about her, asshole." He reached in and hit me with the gat again. I could feel blood on the side of my nose.

The end of that gun was the only thing in my world. I didn't hear the cars going by above us or my own breathing. It was just the gun and nothing else. He undid the chain and pulled me out, throwing me to my knees in the dirt.

"Your time's coming." He walked a wide circle around me, keeping out of reach. Then he got back in his car and took off, leaving me handcuffed and dirty.

"Let me loose, you high yella bitch," I hollered into the cloud of dust his wheels kicked up in my face. His taillights disappeared into the darkness. I got to my feet, one of my knees skinned. Like an idiot I strained against the handcuffs, knowing they weren't going to break apart.

It was getting cold, and with only a shirt and no jacket I needed to get moving just to stay warm. I walked around under the freeway looking for something to get myself loose. Off to one side there was a lumpy shape. I walked over there. It was a homeless man sleeping on a ragged bunch of towels, his shopping cart near him. It was hard, but I did my best to dig through his junk in the cart. I wasn't in no mood to be delicate, and the noise woke him up.

"Say, man, you better get away." He sat up, stink coming off him like a backed-up toilet.

"Sit down." I kicked him in the chest – not too hard, but just enough so he got the message.

"I'll cut you."

"You best sit the fuck down." I kept moving his junk around, trying to watch him too in case he wasn't bullshitting about having a blade. But all he had in the cart was broken plastic toys, pieces of faucets, used pens, hunks of Styrofoam, and other crap. There was nothing of use to me, or anybody else for that matter.

I left the chump and his sad life and went out on the sidewalk. I was shivering and probably looked like a nut to anybody passing by. I had to walk with my arms down in front of me to try and hide the cuffs. A Spanish broad with a basket of laundry on her head was coming at me from the other direction.

She must have seen the cuffs 'cause she cut across the street in a hurry, almost getting run over by a pick-up truck.

At Imperial and Flower there was a filling station with a working pay phone on the east end of the lot. I managed to turn my pocket inside out, spilling out some coins. A lowered Chevy Caprice rolled by, the ballers inside scoping me out. They must have figured me for a mark, a drunk mark. I was down on my knees picking up the silver. The car came onto the lot, a 50 Cent number thumpin' on the car's speakers.

I got the phone off the hook and managed to get a quarter in the slot. But I dropped the other quarter. I bent down to pick it up, knowing that the hawks in the car were sizing me up. I couldn't see their faces, but I could read their minds. If things had gone different, if I hadn't had that scholarship and been picked ninth round in the draft, maybe I'd be in the car, looking to push up on a fool as well.

I got the coins in the slot and punched her inside line. The thing rang on the other end, me holding the phone to my ear with my shoulder and two hands clinked together. I watched the car.

"Hello," Wilma said.

"I need you to pick me up at the corner of Imperial and Flower, it's a Exxon Station."

"Zelmont, what's – "

"Now, okay?"

"Alright."

I let the phone dangle and walked to the lights shining down on the gas pumps. If them boys in the ride flexed, then so be it. I'd get these cuffs around the neck of one of those studs and take him with me to wherever the hell it was we went after this bullshit.

I stood under the lights waiting for Wilma. A couple of people who pulled in for gas seemed surprised when I didn't ask to fill their cars up like I was any other motherfuckah beggin' for spare change.

After a while, the punks in the Caprice got bored and drove off. When Wilma got there, I was moving back and forth, trying not to freeze.

"What happened," she said, getting out of her Phaeton.

"I'll tell you when I'm warm." I managed to open the door and got inside.

Wilma pointed at the cuffs. "One of your chicks get too rough for you?"

I put the stare on her. "Can you get these off me?"

"Sure, Zee," she giggled. She called Nap on her cell phone and drove me to where he was staying in the Valley in Panorama City. It was a funky-looking apartment building near the Anheuser-Busch plant.

Nap worked on cutting the cuffs with a heavy-duty hacksaw he borrowed from the manager. After he got them off, I told them what happened.

"So we have to be careful," Nap said, looking at the cuffs.

"With this cop having a big stick up his ass about you, he's going to make it his mission to fuck with your life until he can bust you for Davida's murder."

Nobody said anything for a few ticks, but I knew the gears were turning in Wilma's head. "Does Fahrar know Weems?"

"That's being overly paranoid, Zelmont." Wilma walked over to the refrigerator and opened the door. "You have any beer?"

"Rolling Rock," Nap said.

"Really?" I said, walking around. "Then why don't you check, Wilma? Weems has a hard-on for law and order, ain't that right, Nap?"

"Hell yeah. It's a known fact some of the members of his Internal Truth Squad are ex-cops."

"I know that," she said.

"Then check," I said. "We have to know what we got lining up against us."

She didn't like being ordered around. But she also didn't like being caught from behind. I waited while she sipped her beer.

"Fine."

I laughed. "Big spoiled baby."

"Shut up." She sat on the couch.

"Got anything stronger than that pale-ass brew?"

"In the cupboard." Nap pointed with the hand holding the cuffs.

I got down a bottle of gin. "Ysanya know you're here?"

"Why you want to know?"

"We got enough to worry about without that dizzy bitch spilling the goods, that's why."

Nap came toward me. "I said she's cool, Zee. You worry about your end of things."

"I am, that's why I want to know." The bottle was on the counter, my hand on the neck.

His shoulders hitched.

"She's unreliable, man."

"You should know about being unreliable." He was breathing in my face. Now I'd find out how long I'd last before Nap beat me into the ground.

Wilma got between us. "Alright, let's not fall apart until we're millionaires, okay? You two are supposed to be tight. Don't let a woman come between you."

She put her arm around my waist. "Grab the bottle and let's go. Everything's going to be all ours." She pulled me to her. "Then we can get out of here and start over, make it good."

"You and me?" It sounded natural when I said the words.

"Yeah, you and me."

We tongued, and later at her pad we got down. Not like was the usual for me, being the macker and bangin' the coochie, or getting off on rough sex like with Davida. We were tender with each other, held on to each other and touched the other one's body with our fingertips. That was something, really something.

"e got it," the note from Wilma read. "Meet me at the Townhouse, 9:30 tonight."

I'd been out running the hills. I wondered if that asshole Fahrar was watching my house and had seen her drop by.

The note was in an envelope, so maybe that fuck would think I was being served with a new suit or something. Maybe he'd found out that I'd put the crib on the auction block this morning, short on bread like I was. Whatever. As Wilma had pointed out, we couldn't be slippin' and use e-mails or some such that left a trail.

Even though the job was coming up, I needed cash to cover living expenses. My NFL pension was nothing, and the house note was just too big a nut each goddamn month. I didn't see anything for selling my ring, and Terri had got her lawyer daddy to get an injunction on me so now they were going after what was left in my bank account. What a fuckin' fool I was to have sent her money like Weems was gonna let me play and I was gonna be able to make regular payments.

There were other envelopes in the mailbox and one was from Terri. Her letter was on pink paper and there were photos of her and the baby. She'd put on weight but was still into wearing them form-fitting dresses over her packed ass. The kid looked cool, though. He had his mother's wide eyes and a cute kinda Mohawk look. She'd insisted on naming him Cody 'cause that's the name her favorite TV star, Kathie Lee Gifford, had given one of her kids. I tried telling her that any black kid named Cody was gonna catch a hard time, but she didn't listen.

I sat there, his picture in one hand, the note from Wilma in the other. I picked up the phone and called.

"Is Terri there?" I asked after some man said hello.

"Who's this?" The dude put bass in his voice.

"The father of her baby."

"Yeah, so?"

"So put her on the phone if she's there."

"Yo, man, you don't call over here and bark orders, you ain't my daddy."

"And you don't own the phone you're talkin' on, chump. Put Terri on the line."

"She ain't here." The sissy hung up in my ear.

No matter. I figured he'd tell Terri I called 'cause he'd want to show off to her about how he'd put me in my place. Then she'd call back, and I knew I could sweet talk her into getting her father to back off. But even so, it was only a delayed hit.

The fucked-up truth was the house was too big a drain on my income. Particularly since I didn't have an income.

With that in mind, I'd gone over to a real estate office on the Strip and talked with a chick, a botoxed cougar, who said she'd start things in motion.

"Making some changes? Wish to go up market?" She must have been pushing sixty, but she worked out, so the young outfit she was wearing looked okay on her. The dye job on her hair wasn't as good as Ysanya's, and I had to catch myself from thinking about what color her snatch was.

"Something like that."

One of the dudes in the office, a cat in suspenders, recognized me, and that got her more excited about how she could move the property. Seems like my past was the only thing of value I had going. She got the paperwork underway and said she'd be by tomorrow to take a look at the house.

"I'm done, Mr. Raines," my cleaning woman Adrianna said, packing up her bucket of brushes.

"Thanks." I gave her some dough and a tip.

"Thank you," she said, looking at the money. "Everything okay with you now?"

"Like butter, baby."

She smiled. I hadn't told her this was probably the last time she'd be cleaning up this house, at least for me.

I showered and messed around with this and that, mostly chillin' and listening to some music. I didn't have any new stuff, but last year's cuts did me fine. I burned Wilma's letter and went over to the Townhouse on La Tijera at the right time. As usual, the place was bumping with booty house music, and the babes to go with it. I found the two of them at one of those tall circle-type tables you stand around.

Nap's chest was out 'cause he was feeling proud. "Ysanya called with the number yesterday, Zee."

"I back-traced it through a contact I have in the phone company. It's a stationary phone all right," Wilma said.

"I have the address in Ridgecrest."

I was going to ask who her contact in the phone company was. Probably some middle management dude who had his nose wide open for her. I shouldn't have been dwelling on it, but I was. "Now what?"

A waitress came over. "Can I get you something, sir?"

I gave her my order and she slipped off.

"Stadanko and Chekka have a meeting coming up there," Wilma said.

"How do you know that?"

"He's made plans to fly down to Miami for an owners' meeting this Tuesday." She tasted her drink. "The meeting is only scheduled for two days, but he doesn't get back for a week."

"Maybe he's got something on the side he's gonna see about tightening up," I said, not understanding why Wilma was so sure Stadanko and his hoodlum cousin had this confab planned.

Wilma leaned closer to us over the table. "Look, here's the deal. Chekka came by the office yesterday. I was there for a meeting on the broadcast rights for cable and Fox. Anyway, he's hitting on me – "

"He do that on the regular?"

The waitress came back with my whiskey. I paid her, counting out ones.

"Relax," Nap laughed.

"Rudy says he wants me to meet him in Palm Springs on Sunday."

"Like I asked, this a new thing he's got for you?" A shortie in platforms bumped against me and mumbled something, then stepped off with her girlfriends.

"He's always sniffing after money or pussy, Zelmont. He's hit on every girl in that office." She drank her drank, eyeing me over the rim of the glass.

"This is about third and goal, Zee," Nap reminded me.

He was right, but that didn't change what I wanted to know.

"So you two are on your way to Palm Springs and grinnin' watermelon eatin' grins."

Wilma made a sound with her tongue. "I strung him along, Zelmont. Yes, he's tired to get his hands up my dress once or twice, and that's it, understand? But it was important that I teased him a little to find out what I could." She knocked off half her drink. "Like you haven't played anyone, right?"

I let that go by. "So?"

"So Rudy hints he's got big things doing and has to be at the hideaway – that's what he called it – at a certain time because he and Stadanko have some business to take care of. He likes to hear himself talk and make himself look important."

She leaned back. "Stadanko comes around the corner – we were talking outside of the conference room – and Rudy shuts up. He's full of himself, but he's not crazy. I don't say anything and the two of them marched off."

"So me and Zee get up there now?" Nap asked.

"No, it should be me and Zelmont," she answered.

I looked at Nap. "Why?"

"Because there might be some computer files to hack into. Can either of you do that?"

Nap and me didn't have jack to say.

"Okay, then, we go up early tomorrow morning. I have to be in New York to finish these broadcast negotiations on Friday, and I know the haggling will take me over to the following week. So once I get back, I don't want to raise any speculation should I then turn around and go out of town again. The season is almost on us, and I'll need to account for my time."

I was about to talk when the square came over and tried to join our set. "Man, you is the bomb, home." He was pushing past me, shoving a drink toward Nap's face. "'Member that game where you knocked the shit out of Brett Farve and the ball flew up and you snatched it back down and went on in for the touchdown?"

Nap put his eyebrows up. "Sure do, I – "

"Yeah," he shook a finger all excited at Nap, "and that time you blew past Drake and White and got the one-hand tackle on Young? It must have been twenty below."

"He's your number one fan, Nap." Wilma winked.

The dude didn't take the hint. "You got that right, baby. Ain't nothing about football I don't know, and certainly ain't nothing about the big man here I'm not up on. Like that Super Bowl game where he got six unassisted tackles."

The same Super Bowl where I made my spin and a half and caught the game-winning pass. I knew he was gonna slobber all over me any second.

"Let me buy you a drink." He got all in front of me, leaning on the table like he owned the joint.

"I'm cool, my man. Me and my friends are discussing a little business, okay?" Nap said calmly. "How about I catch you a little later?"

"Aw man," the fool cackled like one of them sisters in a bingo game. He moved closer, splashing some of his drink on my sleeve but not noticing. "You ain't gonna high hand me like that, is you? Got my girl over there I want you to meet."

I looked over to where he was jerking his Jheri juice head. The chick he was pointing to had a big ass, a tight dress, and a bad weave you could tell was gank even in this light. "Nap, sign a napkin for this fool and send him on his way."

He put his drunk eyes on me. "Who the fuck is you, his motherfuckin' secretary?" He jabbed me in the chest with two fingers. "You ain't nobody but a hanger-on, ain't that right?"

"Yeah, that's right." I was getting real hot so I wasn't breathing right.

"Then skip your ass over to Office Depot and get a pad of paper for him to sign."

I was about to jack the chump when Nap put his arm around the dude. "Look here, brah, let's go over and meet your fine lady friend."

He looked up at Nap like he was a kid about to ride a merry-go-round for the first time. "Oh, that's great, man, great."

Nap took him away. Wilma touched my hand. "We have to be circumspect from here on out, Zelmont. No untoward business that will give Fahrar an excuse to jam you or any of us up."

I was barely paying attention to what she said. I couldn't believe that gin-soaked punk didn't recognize me. I just couldn't believe it.

...

The drive up to Ridgecrest took over three hours, me at the wheel of the Explorer. Wilma wasn't much for rap so it was a steady diet of the CDs she'd brought along. Her taste was okay, but along with stuff like classic Led Zeppelin she had a weird-ass album by some band called the Squirrel Nut Zippers. Their music was like listening to old radio recordings, and I was glad when she slipped on Otis Redding.

"I can't remember the last time I've been out this way," Wilma said. The sun was now up and we had the windows cracked. The cool morning air felt good on my skin, and it smelled sweet outside. I usually didn't notice shit like that, but riding along with Wilma half-dozing on the seat beside me it seemed natural. Almost made me forget we had a job to do.

On the side of the road were those tall spiky trees with white flowers at the top. "What do you call those again?" I asked.

She didn't have to look. "Joshua trees, baby."

Ridgecrest was much more built up than I had expected. If I didn't know where we were, I might have thought it was some part of the Valley, except it looked clean – like Disneyland does 'cause they always got them schlubs walking around with their brooms and dustbins picking up trash and horseshit. And every night they're scrubbing down the streets and scraping up gum before it gets ground in.

"Can we stop and get breakfast?" she asked.

"How many black people they got up here, Wilma?"

She turned her head at me. "We're not going to get jumped."

"We don't need to call attention to ourselves."

"Yeah, one of these ol' boys might recognize you. I guess we better find the cabin."

Maybe she was just saying that to make me feel better, but it did. I was starting to sweat so I rolled up the windows and put on the air conditioner. We drove, using the map Wilma had drawn after she got the address for the cabin. The houses we passed were out of a Spielberg movie about the 'burbs, the lawns very green and no cracks in the sidewalks.

Eventually we were back in the countryside again. "Do you know where we are?" I checked the gas gauge. Off to the right were some mountains that had shaved-off tops and funny angles.

"What the hell are those called?"

"The Trona Pinnacles, I believe," Wilma answered. "Part of the charm of this area. And yes," she said, studying her handmade map, "I do have an idea where we are. We should be heading toward Indian Wells."

We passed the turnoff we were supposed to take, but Wilma caught it and we doubled back. I drove downhill through all kinds of shrub on a gravel road barely wide enough for my vehicle. We hooked right and came to a flat area where there was a lot of bamboo growing in front of a tall stone wall. In the middle of this was a large, showy iron gate.

"Let's scope this out first." I turned off the ignition.

"Why? Let's drive in," she said, pointing toward the gate.

"I think it'd be better if we go in on foot."

"So you can bust a move?"

"We should be careful, Wilma." A jackrabbit scooted past us, then back into the greenery.

She looked like she was gonna argue but let it go. "Fine."

We got out and stretched. She got her purse from the car, then we walked inside the gate. I was surprised it was unlocked. There was a mess of plants and the same weird, stick-like cactus that grew on either side of the roadway we'd come in on. Wilma was already marching past me and up toward where the cabin must be. I grabbed her arm.

"We ain't in that big a rush, are we?"

"There's nobody here."

"How do you know?"

"They only use this place for their meetings." She took off again.

"But you said he kept his files here too. Otherwise what are we doing here?"

"You're right. Okay." She slowed down, waiting for me to catch up.

We went up the walk, different kinds of plants and cactus and yellow and purple flowers all about us. Any second, I just knew a bad breath Rottweiler with nasty teeth was gonna come running out of nowhere and snack on my leg.

In a few more ticks, we were facing the cabin. Well, it was about as much a cabin as a classic Jaguar is just a car. The joint was big, two stories and a deck, with a triangle for a roof. There was as much glass as there was wood and stone to the place. A satellite dish was on one part of the roof, and some kind of other antenna was sticking up beside that. It looked like a small radio tower.

"How the hell are we gonna get inside this place? He's got to have this thing rigged with fancy burglar alarms. I know we're in the middle of zero, but Stadanko ain't no clown." How come her or Nap didn't bring that up before?

Wilma had her hands on her hips. "Do me a favor, Zelmont. Check around on the side over there, okay? I think there's some kind of work shed."

"Your boy Rudy tell you that?"

She came up and put her arms around my waist. "When I tracked down the address, I checked out the property specs. There's an additional piece of property listed, all right?" We kissed, and she grinded against me. I went off to do like she asked.

Coming around a corner of the cabin I found a box of a place with some of the plants and cactus grown up around it. As I walked I noticed a door in the side of the building. I could also see the area behind the house. There was a nice-ass pool and deck chairs laid out, and I went to check it out. The pool was done in the shape of a football, with a large painting of one on the bottom. Good thing I was staring at the design 'cause I caught the reflection moving behind me and whipped around just in time.

"Trace," I said as I tackled the corn-fed chump. That caught him by surprise and together we fell back on some of the chairs, scattering them all over the place. I landed a blow on him but he was buffed so it didn't do much damage. His knee came up and I twisted to get away from being groined.

We were holding onto each other, struggling to stand up.

"Defiler," he growled, his dog teeth clamped together. He hit me across the face and I'm not too proud to say the faggot hurt me.

Motherfuckah was strong. But I'd been knocked around by the dirty boys in my day and knew how to hang with some serious pain.

"That's all you got, bitch?" I went low and sunk one into his middle, then immediately followed with a elbow to his jaw.

That got some respect. We circled each other hunched over, hands out like a couple beefheads on the WWE.

"How do you want me to hurt you, Raines?" The flaming cross on his cheek twitched. It seemed bigger than what I remembered.

I lunged but he was ready. He caught me dead on the side of my face, dazing me. I fell against some kind of statue of a honey with four arms and a snake crawling around her. It tumbled over but didn't break. Off balance, Trace rammed a fist into my side, making stars pop behind my eyes. Fuck. I sank down to one knee.

"You're going to be my woman, Raines." He kicked me in the shoulder, knocking me over. I tried to focus my sight, and from the angle I was at I could see some tools leaning against the shed. Knowing he was going to kick me again, I rolled to one side. My shoulder still burned like a mother. I got up and ran for the shed. I could yell for Wilma, but what good would that do. Anyway, what kind of man would I be if I did?

"Come on, Zelmont, I want to play," the big punk laughed. "Don't go home yet, your mama will let you stay out a little longer."

I dove through the plants, cutting myself on cactus thorns and what all. I scrambled up faster than I had in any drill I'd ever done and was about to latch onto a handle of a shovel when a fist socked my hard in the kidney. I fell against the shed, damn near crying from the pain. Hands grabbed me and turned me around. It was another

Internal Truth Squad sack of shit. His cross had a purple kind of flame dancing from it. He hauled me out of the shrubs and dumped me on the deck like I was wet clothes.

Trace, standing next to his God-fearing pal, looked down at me with a sick smile. "Meet one of my good friends, Zelmont. Randy, meet Zelmont."

I was trying to rise when Randy said, "Mr. Raines," and hit me across the back of my head, knocking my face back onto the tiles. Trace stepped closer.

"What business do you have out here, Zelmont?" He put his hands in his pockets, relaxed, enjoying seeing me crawling like a prison sissy at his feet.

I looked up. "Your sister asked me up here 'cause she wanted some new dick to suck 'sides yours." That got me a heel aimed at my mouth like I hoped. I grabbed his foot, and with all I had I lifted and shoved him backward. Trace went over. Randy was already on me and had his iron-hard arms around my chest from behind. He had a knee in my back and was pulling the top of my body back too. I felt like I was going to pass out.

"I like dark meat, Mr. Raines." He started biting the mess that was my face and I screamed, the blood warm against my sweaty skin. I got a hand behind me and latched onto his johnson. I squeezed it like I was trying to get the last drop out of a toothpaste tube.

"Oh Lord, grant me strength," Randy cried, his jaw letting go of my face. Trace was running forward. I shifted, Randy's weight on his knee having let up some. We fell over, Trace getting tangled up too. This was worse than games where I was half doped on painkillers and my hip was doing weird tricks in its socket. But fuck it, this was no game.

I had my hand on flesh and bone. It was a neck, Randy's thick neck. Punches were landing on me and I didn't care. I squeezed that neck like I was wringing out a rag. Trace had his arms around my waist, trying to pull me loose. But I wasn't going to let go, ever. I got a foot under Trace's jaw, using his solid body to wedge myself against him and Randy. I got my elbow up, then came down hard with it, ramming Trace's partner in the Adam's apple.

Trace yanked me clear. I slid into the statue. I got up, operating only on reflex. Randy was also on his feet, gulping hard, his eyes bugged out at me.

"Curse of Ham," he slobbered, coming at me like Lon Chaney Jr. in one of those old Wolfman movies. Trace moved at me from the side. Just then one of Randy's bug eyes came flying from his head. His body kept stumbling forward and landed hard on the statue, breaking it into sharp chunks.

Both of us stared at him and then at each other. I looked past Trace to see Wilma standing at the edge of the pool. She had a gun in her hand, and obviously knew how to use the thing. Trace rammed past me, jumping into the bushes and plants.

"Get him," Wilma yelled.

I was already moving. I ran past the shed, catching something out of the corner of my eye in the way I spotted a lineman angling at me. The shovel was missing. My face hurt like hell from Randy's chewing and my body was stinging from all the blows, but I kept going. If Trace got away, I knew it wouldn't be good. No good at all. I got to a sandy patch of ground. All around were them Joshua trees Wilma had told me about. I stopped, waiting and listening. Why run? Trace would want to finish the fight.

I yelled, "Thought you was gonna make me put my hand in your back pocket. You ain't punkin' out, are you, homeboy?"

I crept up near a part of the trees and heard him moving somewhere nearby, hidden from me. I went into the trees, ducking low and moving as quiet as I could. My hip started to act up but there was nothing I could do. I had to show Wilma I could take care of business. Off to my left, in front of where I was, I heard him moving again. He was trying to figure out where I was, too.

I started to move in a circle, and a plant cracked behind me. I froze, crouching down. Trace stopped too, listening for me. I took off again, moving like a dog on my hands and feet. The hip was grinding in the socket and I wanted to stand something fierce, but I kept moving. At any moment I knew I was going to run out of gas, my second wind all played out.

There, to the right. I shot forward, bumping against a tree. Trace turned and swung the shovel at me and I dove out of the way. Its blade edge sunk into the tree, and he yanked on it to get it loose. I was already up, absolute fear blocking the pain. I latched on to Trace and hit him with the top of my head under his jaw. He stumbled back, letting go of the shovel.

He'd almost got the tool free so it was loose. I grabbed the handle and did and swung it, tripping him up as he tried to run off. My second swing caught the shovel flat in his face, knocking him back to the ground. He was still awake so I hit him again, this time dead in the nose. He went over on his side, his grill splattered with blood.

I leaned over, holding myself up with the shovel's handle, the business end planted in the ground. My lips tasted salty and I stayed like that for a while, getting myself together. "Wilma," I shouted. I was so goddamn tired. I shouted some more and she finally trotted into the open sandy space.

"Keep your voice down, there are other properties around here."

"Like they didn't hear that gunshot?"

"People are always target practicing out here."

"You got an answer for everything, don't you?" I said as I dragged Trace into the opening by his heels. I sat down.

Wilma stood over him, a concerned look on her face. I knew it wasn't 'cause I'd broken his nose and he looked like shit. She was wondering like me what Weems' right-hand man was doing here, and what that meant in terms of the holier-than-thou commissioner's involvement.

"Well, he's breathing, that means he can answer questions."

"You should have been a cop with that kinda attitude."

Wilma bent down, slapping Trace on the side of his face with her gun. It was a good-sized heater. Pistols weren't my thing, but it was clear homegirl knew something about them.

Trace's eyes fluttered like I'd seen wideouts do after getting their head rung.

"Why did Weems send you?" She stood back, the gun on him.

"You have broken a commandment," he said.

"Let me worry about my soul." She waved the gun, a shiny automatic of some kind. "You need to focus on the issue at hand, Trace."

He grinned. "And who is he that will harm you if ye be followers of that which is good?"

I shook the end of the shovel in front of him. "How 'bout I bust you upside the head again and see if that harms your Bible-spoutin' ass?"

"The defiler can never know the ways of the righteous."

Wilma kicked him in the leg. "Cut the sanctimonious bullshit. How much does Weems know about Stadanko? Or were you and your dead pal up here on some kind of fishing expedition?"

Trace lifted his large shoulders and let them come back down. "I am but a vessel. Thou therefore endure hardness as a good soldier of Jesus Christ."

I sank the handle end of the shovel hard into his gut. He didn't flinch much, but I could see the hate work around in his true believer glare. "He's just going to keep this bullshit up. We're wasting time."

Wilma put on her lawyer face. She walked in small circles as she talked. "It doesn't seem likely Weems would send these two to hide out and wait around for Stadanko and the rest to get here this weekend." She had one hand on her hip, the gun loose at her side in the other.

"Maybe they came here to look for the files like us."

"That's more delicate work than I'd send Trace to do."

"That why you didn't want me and Nap doing it?"

She came over to me, touching my wound. "Now, baby."

Trace made a move and I tripped him with the shovel's handle. The bastard hit the deck, his hands out before him. I kicked him in the middle and this time he felt it. He held his ribs.

"Your day is fast approaching, defiler."

Wilma pointed the gun at him. Much as I didn't like the asshole, killing somebody like that made me jumpy. I guess it shouldn't have, but it did. "You're gonna dust him? That's two goddamn bodies we gotta deal with, Wilma."

"This is so he'll behave." She jerked the gun. "Give him the shovel."

"Are you – "

"Please, Zee," she said sweetly, "I know what I'm doing."

I didn't dig it that I wasn't in control, didn't know the rules for this kind of play. Wilma did, or at least that gun and what she did with it made it seem so. I threw the shovel over to Trace. He was on his feet again, rubbing his ribs, sizing me up for another rumble.

"You're going to bury your friend." Wilma got an angle on him for a good, clean shot.

He touched his flaming cross. "I will not."

Wilma shot past his head, the bullet sinking into the wall of the shed in a puff of plaster.

Me and Trace stood there with our mouths open. She didn't say anything else and Trace picked up the shovel. We walked over to the area behind the shed where there were Joshua trees and cactus and other shit I couldn't name. We stopped at a patch of earth and Wilma pointed at the ground. Trace got a funny look on his face and I tensed. But he got busy digging. He didn't talk, didn't take off his coat. He kept working, stopping now and then to get his breath. Eventually he'd dug a hole big enough for Randy. The space wasn't too long but was deep.

"Put down the shovel and let's get your boyfriend."

"You will be punished." He was breathing heavy, sweat pouring off him like rain. His suit was dirty and wet.

"No, that's not going to happen," Wilma said.

"Zelmont, search the body just in case they found anything," Wilma said.

I did and only found a pocket edition of the Old Testament and two pens. Then we placed the body in the hole. The dead man was tall so his body didn't really fit lengthwise. He laid there, his knees bent like he was resting, his eyes open and focused on nothing. It gave me the goddamn willies.

Again without a word, Trace got busy, filling the hole with the dirt he'd just dug out. When he was finished, he broke off two small branches from a Joshua tree. He fastened them together with his shoe-laces to make a cross and stuck it over the place Randy's head was. He bowed his own head and mumbled a prayer. All the while I didn't take my eyes off him. I was waiting for him to try and get slick.

"And now, Mary Magdalene?" he said.

She came up on him, the gun level. Trace was gonna get to be with Jesus faster than he might want to, his cap pealed in the bargain. Wilma patted him down, looking like she enjoyed what she was doing. Trace did not.

She then told him, "Get in the car you came in and go back to Los Angeles. Tell Weems what happened, don't spare the details, you hear?"

Trace finally took off his coat. He put it over his arm and went off, walking directly through the bushes and what not.

"Uh, what the fuck are you doing?" I pointed after him.

Wilma was walking toward the shed. "What can Weems do, Zelmont? He sent those two up here for something, but it's definitely off the books, right?" She tried the door but it was locked.

"Yeah," I said, not really sure what she meant. I stepped up and leaned on the door.

"We have to make it seem like we were never here," she said.

"I know." The door caved in after a few knocks with my shoulder. It wasn't too busted up, so it would look pretty normal when we shut it back, I figured. Wilma figured to leave the broken statue as is, figuring Stadanko would chalk it up to a coyote prowling around and knocked it over

She went inside. Sunlight came in through the dirty windows. Wilma found a switch and put on the light. "Weems is up to something," she said, sensing I was still confused about her sending Trace off like she did. "If he reports Randy's death, then he has to explain what those two were doing here. And he doesn't want that."

After a few seconds, I said, "Stadanko can't call the law since they're after him, and big-stick-up-his-ass Weems can't 'cause his slippery shit will come out."

Wilma was looking around. "Exactly. Ironic, isn't it?"

"Very."

The shed contained what you'd expect to find. There was a power drill, a rake, ladder and so forth, and a big table with those little drawers built in with a long rack above it. A vice was lying on the table next to different kinds of parts. Standing there I felt kinda sad. It was like the workplace I'd always imagined my dad would have when I was a kid. Like we'd be together in it while Moms cooked dinner, working on a model car. Or he'd be showing me how to fix a faucet – family shit like that.

"Damn," I said quietly.

Wilma wasn't paying attention. She was looking around very carefully. If she picked something up she was sure to place it back just where it had been. I did the same.

"Wouldn't his records be in the house?" I opened a big rollaway toolbox. The thing was filled with shiny socket wrenches and all kinds of stuff. None of them look liked they'd ever been used.

"I know how his mind works, Zelmont. He thinks he's much more clever than he really is."

I worked on trying to figure out what she meant as I searched around. We kept it up for an hour but didn't turn up zip.

"We have to check the house," I said, leaving out "and then book." I didn't want Wilma to think I was scared, but hanging around in a house we broke into with a fresh corpse buried in the yard was not my idea of a good time.

"I already checked it. There's a safe in there in the master bedroom. Weems must have given Trace the combination because its door was laying open. But they must not have found the files inside."

"When'd you find that out?"

"When I went to see how I might get in the house I saw that the alarm had been turned off. I knew something was up so I got out my Sig." She nodded her head at the gun, which was on a stool.

"I went through the house slowly. When I was in the master bedroom, I heard you going at it with the Hardy Boys."

"So they came outside when they heard us coming up?"

"Or," she snapped her fingers, "there was some reason for them to be searching outside."

I followed her out and we stood there next to the shed. She had her hand over her eyes, blocking glare from the sun, scanning the area. "What would make them go outside?" she mumbled.

"Maybe we can find what it is up in the bedroom."

She winked at me and we walked into the cabin through the back door. Upstairs, Stadanko's bedroom was outfitted like I figured the big show-off would have it. There was a bear skin with the head on it on the floor. The bed looked like it had been handmade from logs. There were Indian-type rugs tacked on the raw wood walls. At the foot of the bed was a long black lacquer box about the size of two hope chests put one on top of another. Some kind of stereo unit. He even had deer horns tacked over the bathroom door.

I cracked up. "This is some shit right out of *Bonanza*. Stadanko ain't never been hunting in his life."

I was standing over the spot where the safe was sunk into the floor. The rug had been thrown back and a section of the floor removed, revealing it. Inside the safe were a lot of packets of greenbacks and some other stuff. I crouched down to help myself.

"We're not here for that," Wilma said sharply. "You need to keep focused."

As broke as I was, I still knew she was right. From where I was squatting I could see through the sliding glass door and the balcony's railing. Beyond that was the plants, shrubs, and the shed. There was also an opening off to the right between a bunch of green. Trace probably had good eyesight like mine. I saw what he must have seen. Standing up, the gap in the plants and leaves wasn't that noticeable.

"Come on."

"What?"

"Come on." I was already heading for the door. Back outside we went through the greenery in the direction I saw from upstairs. The bite Randy had given me had stopped hurting and it almost seemed like it happened a long time ago. Almost. We got to the place I'd been looking at.

"What in the hell?" Wilma said.

It was a pumpkin patch. The funny thing was, the area was surrounded by a high fence of barbed wire.

"To keep out coyotes?" Wilma touched the fence.

"It's damn near seven feet high," I said. "That's a pretty big goddamn coyote to keep out." There was a gate in the fence, and it had a heavy lock on it. "I bet he would have put an alarm on except the rabbits and other animals around here would keep setting it off."

She wrinkled up her face. "What are you getting at?"

"I know a little something about Stadanko, too." I walked around the outside of the patch. "See that pumpkin over there?

Ain't there a crack going around the top?" I pointed to the one I meant.

"I don't see anything."

"I do." I went back and got the ladder from the shed. Then I leaned it on a tree near the patch. From the top of the ladder I dove over the fence into the patch, coming up in a roll. We couldn't cut the wire, as that would have tipped our hand to Stadanko.

"How are you going to get back over?" Wilma stood by the barbed wire, a smart-ass look on her lips.

"You'll see." I touched the pumpkin I'd been looking at.

"It's plastic."

"No shit," she said.

I lightly kicked at a few. "Most of these are real, though." I opened up the bogus pumpkin. Nestled inside were a couple of flash drives. Bingo. I took them out. I handed Wilma the drives. "But won't he check on these when he has his meeting this weekend?" I asked.

"We can buy blank replacements. He might look inside the pumpkin, but I'm betting he won't take them out to plug them in."

That sounded right to me. I found more drives in two other fake pumpkins hidden among the real ones. Wilma left and bought the right kind of drives from a Radio Shack at an outlet mall a few miles away. I put those back in place

"Now how are you going to get out of there?" Wilma put her hands on her hips, a little smile on her lips as she blew me a kiss. "You're so smart."

"Take the ladder and turn it sideways between the barbed wire." I pointed to a section low to the ground.

She brought the ladder over and we got it jammed in place.

That created enough room for me to ease through the opening.

"Shit." The barbs had caught me as I went through the opening. A chunk of meat was ripped from my back.

We got the ladder back to the shed and Wilma took me inside again. She had me take off my shirt and told me to lie on Stadanko's bed. What the fuck. I did, and she dabbed at the wound with something on a washcloth she'd gotten from the bathroom. As she took care of me I was looking at this dresser off to the side. On it were a bunch of videotapes and DVDs.

"Stadanko's some kind of movie nut," I said.

"Oh, he's a nut all right." Wilma got on the bed beside me.

She grabbed a remote off the dresser and pressed a button. I heard something whir and turned to see a TV rising out of what I thought had been a stereo unit. She got one of the disks and put it in a slot on the TV.

On screen was a homemade video of some women spanking each other, giggling, and snorting coke. One of them was even doing another with a jet black strap-on dildo. Wilma was watching, fascinated. I was getting turned on knowing she was getting turned on. In one scene Chekka was running around naked in a cowboy hat chasing the chick with the dildo. I could hear Stadanko hollering at him in that language of theirs. Stadanko would put the video camera down now and then and join in.

"This is what happens after they talk business," Wilma said. She unbuttoned her shirt, rubbing her own nipples.

Pretty soon me and her were getting busy on the bed, the partiers on the tape whooping and having a great time too.

Sometime later, laying on my back staring at the ceiling, it crossed my mind how it was she knew what was on the DVDs, unmarked as they were except for a number. Was it just a guess, based on what she'd heard about Stadanko? Or was it some other reason?

At some point, Wilma had put in another session and it was playing as we laid on the bed. She had a leg over my lower legs, asleep. I shifted and looked at the action on TV. This one involved some light S&M, with Stadanko getting his jollies by being spanked with a long flat paddle with holes in it. This big ice blonde was doing him. She was dressed in thigh-high boots, leather mini skirt, and a cap like I'd seen the German officers wearing in *Hogan's Heroes* reruns. She was definitely enjoying her work, and so was Stadanko. The boy was almost crying he dug the pain so much.

I laid back down, my eyes getting heavy too. The sounds on the porn video were my lullaby. "Faster, faster, goddammit," I suddenly heard a voice say. A voice I knew. I shot up, almost waking Wilma. On the TV, Davida was getting banged by Rudy Chekka. She was spread eagle on a couch, her arms and legs tied apart with thick white ropes. Rudy was working hard, sweating and grunting like the animal he was. It didn't help my mood that Davida was really digging it. The ice blonde stood on the side, whacking Chekka's butt with a whip. But she wasn't doing it too hard. I watched the whole goddamn recording, not tired anymore at all.

*t*he next day I had to move out of my crib. I'd been trying not to say anything about this, but Wilma and Nap had to have some way to contact me.

"I didn't realize," Wilma had said on the drive back to L.A. the evening before.

"I'll get it back 'fore it's sold. We got the information now, right?"

She put her hand on my crotch, massaging me. "That's right, baby, everything's going to be ours now."

So here I was watching the movers take my shit out of the pad. I had to get out from under that rock of a mortgage. To save dough, I'd arranged to rent the place out for a couple of months while it was on the market to be sold.

Most of my shit was gonna have to go to storage 'cause there damn sure wasn't enough room to put it in the apartment in Lennox. Maybe I was being too cocky, but what better place to chill before the job than Davida's old pad? I mean, it was empty and Fahrar would have to think harder than his pea brain could muster to look for me there. Plus the landlady knew who I was and had given me a break on the move in costs.

I put my box of trophies in the rear, then closed the back of the Explorer. I fired up the SUV and started to drive off. On the way out, I passed Candy and Dandy, my demon statues.

The men from the prop shop I'd sold them to were digging around the pair's feet, getting to the cement base they were bolted to.

I sure was gonna miss those rascals. If I didn't get over on this job, I was sure to get fucked worse than a prancing sissy in San Quentin.

Wilma was out of town until the weekend dealing with broadcast negotiations. Nap and his color consultant boyfriend Pablo were also getting away for a couple of days. As I got on the 101 heading south, I thought about giving Isabel a call later to see what she was up to. But I nixed that, knowing it wasn't a good idea to get too involved with her, what with Fahrar on my jock. Where was my favorite asshole these days anyway? He'd been laying low, but that only meant he was waiting for me to slip. And now, especially now, I had to be careful. I couldn't let anything happen to blow the operation.

The next few days I was nervous as a long-tailed cat on a porch full of busy rocking chairs. Every goddamn noise had me going like it was Trace and a couple of his holy-rolling buddies come to settle his debt with me. But that didn't happen. I supposed Wilma was right, but I still couldn't see Weems' angle.

Was his Jesus jive all a front? Was he as crooked as the rest of them? Shit. The waiting was eating me up.

Then there was the apartment. I never really paid attention to how fucked up the area was. I mean, I wasn't blind or anything, I knew Lennox wasn't no Newport Beach. What dough she had she'd put into keeping up appearances with that car of hers.

Most of the people who lived around here were Hispanics or Latinos or whatever they call themselves these days. Some of 'em worked in the hotels near the airport, which weren't far away. They also slaved in other hotels in El Segundo and downtown, as well as in restaurants.

The noise was the worst part. Every other goddamn minute it seemed like some jet or another was buzzing by above heading to Hawaii, Montana, Bofunk, Iowa, wherever. The windows would rattle, glasses dancing to the edge of the table. Jesus, how in the hell did she put up with this bullshit? I guess when I was over here I was either figuring what new way we could sex each other down or worn out after doing it, so the goddamn planes weren't big on my mind.

I had to fight the urge to score some crack or coke. I wanted to be as sharp as a motherfuckin' tack when it was time, but I had to cut the edge. I drove back to the Canyon and worked myself as hard as I could. More than halfway up the mountain, my hip started aching like a mother and I had to stop. The fibula had a new twang in it I hadn't experienced before. The fight with Trace and Randy, and me showing off by leaping over that barbed wire fence, had done its job on me. I managed to limp to the top, sweat coming off me by the gallon.

From that spot I looked over at my house, or what used to be my house. Soon another name would be on the title if I couldn't buy her back I bent over, the palms of my hands pressed hard against my lower legs, then went back down the hill. Walking toward the drinking fountain I saw a beat-to-fuck Camry do a U-turn from the curb and head west on Fuller. Fahrar. I was wondering when he was going to show his dead eye again.

The problem was not so much that he'd showed up again. I expected that. What bothered me was I hadn't noticed him. He was smart not to use his own boat 'cause that lame-ass Toronado was too easy to make. But I also had the feeling he wanted me to see him do his turn, wanted me to know he was still on me. I had to be more careful.

That meant no illegal shit. I couldn't give that tight-ass an excuse to run my sorry self in, none whatsoever. Better to stick with the legal highs I enjoyed. I dialed Isabel even though part of me worried I might be bringing bad luck down on me. But I was always weak that way.

"What's up?"

"Hey, good to hear your voice," Isabel said on the other end of the line. I could see the smile on her face in my mind.

"Busy tonight?

"Yeah," she giggled, "you know I have to get this report – "

"How 'bout we go check out Ozomatli at the Locker Room?"

Danny at least threw me a bone after I bugged him. The little punk got my name on the VIP list.

"I shouldn't." She was hesitating, figuring out which way to go. I could sense it more than hear it. "Maybe you're too much for me to handle, Zelmont."

"Oh I think you handle it just right, honey girl."

We had some chow at this Asian fusion joint on 6th, then bopped to the club. We got in with no effort and made our way around, checking out the action. Ozomatli was the kind of band, what with their blend of salsa, rap, and ska, that pulled in all kinds of people. It didn't seem Danny would be cool enough to have anybody but one of his gangsta-rappin' homies play the set. He wasn't. I chuckled upon spotting Nap as we went up the stairs.

"Hey, man, I want you to meet Isabel. Isabel, this is one of the original bad boys, Nap Graham, All-Pro and all right."

Nap, looking fly in a purple suit and black and yellow checked shirt, clicked his heels together like Basil Rathbone in an old-school flick. "Good to meet you." He shook her hand and bent forward.

"Same," she said.

"So the band was your idea?"

"Yes, I've been trying to get these cats to play here for more than a minute."

The band came on stage and everybody gave it up for them.

From where we were standing, next to the rail at the top of the stairs, we had a pretty good view as they went into one of their numbers.

"This is cool, thanks for inviting me." Isabel kissed me quickly and turned back to watch the band.

When I had the chance, I went over to speak to Nap, keeping my voice low. "Negro, I thought you was supposed to be layin' low till we did the do."

"Pablo can be so trying after a while, he's so high maintenance. That and Wilma convinced me it was probably better I started showing my face again. Stadanko and Chekka are out of town anyway, and it would look more natural that I'd come back around like nothing was up."

When did Wilma talk to him, after the trip to Ridgecrest? Did she tell him she calmly killed a man? What I said was, "Say, man, you and me got each other's back, right?"

Nap put his large hands on each of my shoulders. "We down for each other. That's how it's always been."

At that frozen moment in time, I believed him. "Yeah, you got that right."

We stayed for the first set, then left to find a quiet place. It wasn't my idea – I like noise and crowds – but no sense getting into a fracas with her. I was hoping to get a little 'fore the night was over. She guided me to a tequila bar over on North Broadway in Glassell Park.

"That cop came back to see me." She belted down her El Torpedar in a shot glass like it wasn't nothin'.

"I knew he would." I sipped at mine.

She sorta glanced down while still looking at me. The bar was dark, smoky, that Rock en Español they play down in TJ was on the jukebox. On the walls of the long bar were velvet paintings of Mexican wrestlers and boxers. We sat at a small round table in the rear. A couple of hombres gave me the eye, but they didn't flex so neither did I.

"Zelmont, what did you think about my sister?" She turned to the waitress walking past and ordered another jolt of El Torpedar for both of us.

I never really burned brain cells about it, not like she meant. Me and Davida got along good 'cause we didn't expect anything out of the other. Or maybe that's what I kept believing. She had been going on of late about her career. She wasn't getting younger, and that cheerleading shit was getting played. I guess she really wanted to make the music thing happen 'cause it was something she liked and thought could bring in some dough. I damn sure couldn't fault her for that.

"We understood each other, Isabel."

"No talk of long-term commitment?"

"You'd know better than me, baby."

"We didn't talk that much. We weren't that far apart in age, but I guess I was always considered the serious one. She and I both went to St. Mark's High School over in Lincoln Heights." She lifted her shoulders and thanked the waitress, who had brought back the two tequilas.

"Book learning just came natural to me, and I think she could have done as well had she tried. But she was pretty from the get-go and she knew what she did to boys."

"Them nuns let you go to school with boys?" Two dudes at the bar got into a shoving match but quieted down after a couple of their friends jumped in to break it up.

"We didn't live in plastic bubbles, Zelmont. Every once in awhile St. Mark's and Verbum Sapienti, the boys school in Mount Washington, would have dances together. And of course we went to their football games." She smiled at me and drank.

"So that's why you both have a thing for ballplayers," I said. What I was visualizing was her and Davida sitting in the bleachers in their pressed and pleated Catholic school wool skirts, the socks pulled up high on their calves. I had to stop myself otherwise I was gonna let my imagination go too far.

"I guess." She reached for my hand across the table. "You bring a different me out, you know?"

"Sure, baby." I had no fucking idea what she was talking about.

On the way back to her place, Isabel gave me a blowjob while I drove. She was drunk and moaning and going on in Spanish while she polished my knob. I got so worked I damn near flipped the Explorer over whipping around a corner to her pad.

That Sunday, the Barons beat the Raiders in the game opener 23 to 18. The TV had a shot of Stadanko up in his skybox clapping and getting all excited like a kid winning a new bike.

Next to him I could make out Weems and Wilma.

...

"You got back from New York early."

"I sewed up the deal with Fox quicker than I figured."

"What did Weems say to you?"

"Nothing." She took a long hit on the spliff, sucking in and expanding her chest as she came out of the water a bit.

"Take it easy, girl, you gonna pop your eyeballs."

She laughed, a cloud of smoke gushing out of her. "I guess I'm a little keyed up."

"That's only natural, you want that edge, that feeling, 'cause it'll keep you sharp, in the zone." I took the joint, settling back in the Jacuzzi. It was part of the sauna setup Wilma had built in her backyard.

"So you ain't nervous?"

"Yeah, that's what I'm talkin' about. If you don't get them whales swimmin' in your stomach, then you're either a liar or a psycho."

"But it's what you do with the feeling, huh?"

"Just like one of your big trials, right? Anyway, what did Weems seem like when he saw you?"

She got a strawberry out of the bowl sitting on the edge of the Jacuzzi. "I'd been in there since halftime, chatting with Stadanko, Ysanya, and a couple of Hollywood types he was trying to impress."

"That why he trot you out?"

She looked like she was gonna hit me. "I am the team lawyer," she said proudly.

"Damn, I didn't know you was so sensitive about it. I was just bullshittin'." I handed her the blunt.

"Yeah, well." She took another drag. "Weems shows up somewhere in the third, right after Grier ran for 15 yards."

"It ain't him we're talking about."

"Now who's sensitive?"

"Whatever."

"Aw." She came over and patted my cheek. I pinched her nipple.

"Dog. So he comes in – "

"Trace with him?"

"No, he was alone. He nods at me and is introduced. But what was he going to say? Both of us know the other had no business up at the cabin unless we were up to no good."

"But we still don't know what kind of no good he's up to. And you're sure there's no connection between Weems and Fahrar?"

"No, I already told you," she said in that teacher tone of hers. "You got that cop on the brain."

"Somebody oughta."

"Shit." Wilma got out of the Jacuzzi. She only had on bikini bottoms, and I watched her dry herself off with a towel. She knew I was feasting my eyes and took her time, going slow down her legs and rubbing them dry. Then she threw the towel at my head and I chased her out on the grass of her backyard. I pulled down her bikini and we ran around naked like a couple of goofy kids.

*t*wo days later we were in Nap's office going over the plan. His brother came in, one of his homies trailing behind. He was an extra-large, overfed brother who looked like he'd knock his mama in the head if she cracked wise. This dude was carrying a heavy equipment bag that he set down in the middle of the floor.

I looked at Wilma, who was looking at Nap.

"This is private business, you know that," Danny's brother told him.

Danny stood there with his mouth open, a dull look on his dull face. "Yeah, so? Little Tito is my bodyguard."

"What in the fuck you need a bodyguard for?" I raised.

"Why you think, motherfuckah? I got to take care of my business, Zelmont. What you got to take care of, huh, niggah?"

"Before all this is through, you and me is gonna straighten some things out." I didn't even bother to get out of my chair.

Little Tito came over toward me like he was Godzilla and was gonna swat me down as if I was an airplane buzzing him.

Wilma pointed at Danny. "You either have your bodyguard raise or you're out of this altogether."

"You better watch who you steppin' to, bitch," Danny yelled.

"And you better slow your roll, little brother." Nap had gotten up from behind his desk, coming around in front of it. "You knew from jump street what the deal was, and you said you'd follow the program." Nap hunched up his muscled arms. "Now before we get going, you gonna jam up the works?" He looked at Tito.

"Is she giving the orders or is you?" Danny said.

"It's Wilma's plan," Nap answered him. "You either down with that

155

or you ain't. It's four of us 'cause you're my blood. But if it has to be, it'll be three."

Danny wasn't that goddamn stupid. "Go on out and pour yourself a couple of stiff ones," he said to Little Tito.

"Aw man, you know I'm on a fruit juice diet," the big slob whined.

Danny gave him a look and Big Tito left the room, closing the door behind him. I went over and opened it to make sure he wasn't standing there eavesdropping. Satisfied, I shut it again.

"Danny, this has to be a team effort or we're through before we start." Wilma picked up the bag with two hands and put it on Nap's desk. She unzipped it to see what was inside.

"They're clean and untraceable." Danny's bottom lip was sticking out like the spoiled punk he was.

I hefted one of the Remington autos from the bag. There were two more shotguns in the bag and two Glock 16-shot pistols, plus ski masks, duct tape, and some kind of electronic device about the size of a shoebox. Danny got this out too.

"This is used for cloning cell phone numbers," he said.

"It's the latest shit so it works even though them companies got what they think are security measures that can block it." He was smiling so I guess he was happy with his toy.

"As long as it stops them marks from calling out," I said.

Then I opened up the nylon bag I'd brought and removed one of the grenades.

"We don't need to blow up the truck, do we?" Wilma said, pointing at the pineapple I was holding.

"These are flash grenades," I told her. "They'll blind the drivers." I learned about those beauties when I'd done that cop show. There was something else I learned doing that cop show, but I kept it to myself.

"Where'd you get those?" Nap asked me.

"From the prop dude on that TV show I did for a hot minute a few years ago."

"You mean they're fake?" Wilma picked one up.

I took the thing out of her hand. "They're real. This dude is hooked into a lot of outrageous shit – survivalists, NRA nuts, the kind of guys who – "

"Does he know about – " she broke in.

"No, and he don't want to know what I'm gonna use them for," I said, cutting her off like she had me. "We set on the truck?" I asked Nap.

"Ready for Freddy, baby."

"How we got the route they take?" Danny was messing around with one of the pistols, like maybe that was supposed to intimidate me. Like I wouldn't shove the shotgun butt up his rectum 'cause he was Nap's brother. Shit. Nap would help me.

"We got their files," Wilma said. "Ellison Stadanko is very organized and has his shipments worked out months in advance. The truck will be making a run a week from Thursday. A special run, in fact."

"How much?" Danny asked what all of us were thinking.

"Six to seven million if not more."

"Damn," I said. "How come so much?"

"He's got the Justice Department breathing down his neck, and we know Weems is up to some shenanigans too. I think Stadanko is suspicious that the commissioner is nosing around in his business. From what I can interpret in his latest file entry, he wants to move a sizable amount of cash for reserves and cool out that part of his operation for a while until things settle down."

"Then let's get busy," Nap said.

"Yeah," I put in, "we need to practice."

Danny and Wilma looked at me and Nap like we were trippin'.

"Y'all didn't think we could just walk up to Stadanko's boys, put a gun on them, and they'd get all weak in the knees and hand the shit over, did you?" I sat on the edge of the desk, folding my arms. "You don't win because you only go over the opposition's moves. You gotta scrimmage, and then scrimmage some more until the shit is reflex in your muscles."

Nap spoke again. "I've secured a couple trucks for us to use for two days. One is the blocker we'll use in the actual robbery and the other is larger, like the garbage truck."

"Won't that draw attention to us?" Wilma frowned at the grenades in the bag.

"There's a reasonably isolated spot out in the desert past Palmdale we can use," Nap said. "I was out there a couple of times for, shall we say, an activity involving flutes, bonfires, and cavorting naked in the open. And we weren't spotted."

Danny shook his head in disgust.

"Plus," I said, tossing a shotgun at Wilma that she caught, "we all gotta get used to handling the equipment. There's no on-the-job training once we're into it."

That Sunday, the Barons beat the Oilers by one point. They were two-and-zero and on a fucking roll. To make things worse, that goddamn Grier caught two touchdown passes. Meanwhile we were doing our practice runs for the robbery.

Four days later I was sitting next to Danny Deuce in an old '83 Cordoba, which was idling badly. The seats were torn up and there was a particular smell coming from below the dash I didn't want to know why. It was close to sunset but we were hardly relaxed.

The cell phone jamming device was in Wilma's ride, a couple of miles down in the flats where she was waiting as lookout. She was to signal me on a disposable cell when the truck had gone past her.

"What the fuck were you thinking when you got this rig?"

Danny worked his tongue inside his jaw. "How many times you gonna whine about that? It can't be traced so shut the fuck up."

"I'll keep on you until you get it in your malt liquored head this ain't no Western Avenue mom and pop robbery we're pullin', Danny. This is for all your mama's bags of chips."

"I know that." He showed his teeth to me.

"No you don't, Danny." Wouldn't you know it but coming down the goddamn hill we were hiding behind on the side road was a pair on mountain bikes. "Whatever you do, don't look at them," I warned him.

"Man, I'll do as I motherfuckin' please." Of course he looked at the two like he was gonna bust a cap on them as the man and woman came down off the hill right in front of us. There wasn't much around in this end of Chatsworth except hilly area like this and a couple of power stations. Over the rise behind us was a development of tract houses inside a high wall called Rainbow Estates. The place didn't look my idea of paradise.

The bikers were trying to look nonchalant, drinking high-priced water from their designer bottles. But I knew they had to be wondering what in the hell two brothers were doing up here in a broke dick ghetto special ride in the land of the white man near the Ventura County line.

"This is about more money than your brain can count to, Danny," I said under my breath. The couple, dressed in those strange-ass Speedo outfits, were straddling their bikes, having a conversation. They had to be talking about us. I looked at my watch. It was less than three minutes before we had to get the function on. If they didn't get gone in one they were gonna have to be dealt with. I had way too much riding on this to see it go bust. The shotgun was along the side of my seat, down out of view.

Danny was staring straight ahead at them. His Glock was in his lap.

"You think life is gonna be the same for you when you got that kind of green?" Forty seconds.

"Yeah, I'm gonna – "

"I know, spend it on hos, Ferraris, a pad on top of a hill somewhere." He didn't say anything, 'cause I was reading his mind. Those had been my goals too. Thirty seconds.

"Well, you may not want to believe me, young stud, but you better be about puttin' your cut to use for the long term. See, you ain't always gonna be so fly that all the honeys flock to you, or have some scheme come along that'll get you over like a fat rat. This is a one-time thing." Twenty seconds. My hand gently touched the butt of the shotgun like I was pushing up on a titty.

Danny finally looked my way. "I hear you, Zelmont."

We both had a hold of our gats. But like they'd suddenly got ESP, the couple peddled down the incline and went off to the right, out of sight. I had no idea where the police or sheriff's station was and didn't give it much thought. It was two minutes to the biggest game of my life. We eased the guns back into position and waited, saying nothing. Then my cell vibrated.

"It's on," I said.

Like one, we slipped on our ski masks. We already had on our gloves. "Don't forget your goggles," I told him.

I started counting down from ninety as we'd planned. I signaled Danny to put the tranny in gear on twenty-five and he did. Once in drive, wouldn't you know it but the engine smoothed out and the Cordoba ran like a top. We came down and around the hill as the Shindar garbage truck passed by on the main road. The thing was chugging uphill like we knew it would. Nap was coming from the other direction at the top of the rise. The roadway was narrow as hell on these twists and turns.

"Easy, easy," I said. Danny was excited and giving the pedal too much.

"I'm on it." The Cordoba didn't back off enough from the rear of the garbage truck.

Nap got closer, then he brought the bobtail sideways across the double yellow lines. The garbage truck slammed into the side of the other truck. We came up lurching behind, too close, but I was already moving.

"Back this short up," I screamed, tumbling out of the ride.

The garbage truck was moving backward, but I had forward motion.

I blew out the passenger window with some buckshot, tossing a flash grenade at the opening.

"Shit," I yelled in frustration as the grenade bounced off the metal frame of the window. The damn thing went off in mid-air but it didn't matter. I had on protective goggles and jumped on the truck's running board as it crunched into the grill of the Cordoba.

"Back it the fuck up," I hollered again to Danny. The driver of the garbage truck was squinting, so I figured the grenade probably reflected off the windshield. The dude on the passenger side where I was hanging on must have closed his eyes when he saw me throw the grenade, or maybe he'd just been scared shitless and couldn't stand to see it coming.

Whatever, he blasted off a round at me, the bullet going right past my cheek as I batted his arm away.

"You're dead, bastard." He popped off another one, but I spoiled his aim by grabbing his arm. The sound made my ears ring and my right one went out on me. I yanked on the dude hard, lifting him halfway out the window. I was hanging onto his clothes to keep from falling to the ground.

The truck was still going backward. Danny had finally gotten out of the car, having moved it off to one side. The boy was supposed to have done that sooner so he could shoot out the truck's tires. That's why I'd had him get Teflon loads for his piece. But I had other worries at the moment.

The gun was coming up at me and I bit down on the fool's arm like it was Christmas turkey.

"Fuck." I hadn't noticed before, but he had an accent like Stadanko. Figured.

I head-butted the chump, but he had a hard skull and didn't seem to feel it much. He caught me solid with his other hand, stunning me. The truck jerked sideways, skidding. Where the fuck was Nap?

The driver's vision was clearing and he was pulling out a piece too while he slammed on the brakes. Me and the other cat were still wrasslin'. There were some pops, then the truck fishtailed and went backward real fast into the side of the mountain. I grabbed the strap holding the shotgun slung over my back and quickly brought the piece up over my head with one hand.

Danny had finally done what he was supposed to and blown out the truck's tires, but of course he'd done it too late. I got knocked loose, my back scraping against the mountainside as I flew off.

Operating on pure instinct, like I had so many times before, I let loose with the shotgun before I hit the ground. I tagged homeboy in the passenger seat as he was clipping off a couple rounds at me with his piece. The blast took his arm off from the elbow to his gun hand. He was screaming something fiendish as I tried to stand up and run to get around the truck on the front end. But I went right down again on one knee, my hip on fire.

The dude whose arm I'd just blown away was climbing out of the truck, blood spurting from his stump like he was a zombie in a Wes Craven movie. He was trying to pull another gun from inside his jacket, but what with it being on the same side as his good hand, he was having serious trouble. I couldn't get up, my hip was locked. I put the shotgun on him as he lurched forward and cursed at me in his mother tongue.

Fuck me if a bullet from somewhere else didn't drill itself into my chest. If not for the Kevlar body armor I was wearing underneath my sweat top, I woulda been toast. On that show I'd done for a hot minute, the cat that did the explosions and firearms always had this kinda shit around. I'd got the vest from him together with the flash grenades. Now I was damn glad he'd mentioned that if I was gonna do something heavy, I'd better be protected.

As it was, the impact drove me back, knocking the wind out of me. The driver had me cold with his rod, then his head disappeared in a cloud of red. He dropped away and I could see Nap running forward, the Glock in his hand. But the one-and-a-half-armed motherfuckah – what did this boy eat for breakfast? – leaped on me, beating at me with his good hand. He lodged his stump under my neck and damned if he didn't clamp his mouth around my Adam's apple.

"Shit," I screamed, falling on my back. I hit this vampire as hard as I could in the side of his head with the shotgun's butt. His eyes got real wide, then rolled up in his head. Nap and Danny got him off me and helped me to my feet. We all listened for what seemed like forever, but could hear no cop cars or anything else on the lonely stretch of the mountainside.

"We're paid, man," Danny said in a quiet voice.

We still had on our goggles, making us look like Outer Limits rejects. Me and Nap looked at each other, and I knew he was grinning underneath his mask like I was. The three of us made our way to the rear of the truck. Nap carried the gas masks we'd need to use to dive into the garbage.

"Let's get the back open and then see what's what." Using the straps of the gas masks, Nap put them on one of his big arms. Then he started undoing the latch so we could open one side of the large rear double doors.

"Man, that's rank," Danny said. The smell was enough to knock you to your knees.

"For once we agree," I said, putting a hand over my nose and mouth.

"You girls can snivel if you want," Nap joked, "but I smell fortune."

Suddenly the other door got shoved open from the inside.

Gunfire sputtered and Nap tumbled back into the road. The gas masks flew off his arm as he fell back.

"More marks," Danny yelled, gesturing at the three gunmen who'd been laying in wait for us inside the truck's garbage container. They were dressed in rubber suits with built-in gas masks to hide inside the garbage. Stadanko, or more likely his devious cousin Chekka, had planned for an emergency.

I tossed two more flash grenades and went low as one of the stiffs let loose with his chatter gun. The whiteness spurted up around us like fireworks.

"What in hell," one of them yelled.

The shotgun's buckshot caught this cat in his stomach. Parts of his suit and body splattered everywhere as he slammed back into the truck.

I went over the edge of the roadway, using my arm to vault the low rail. The brightness of the grenades was fading. Bullets tore into the rail and the air around me as I dropped down on the side of the rise onto something sticking out from the hill.

Danny had pulled Nap behind the Cordoba. One of the shooters was burying bullets in the car from where he crouched beside the truck.

I stuffed more shells into the Remington from the extras I had tucked away beneath my flak jacket and pumped off a couple at him. Where was number three? I went back down before the shooter turned my way and buzzed off some rounds toward me. He couldn't get us, but we couldn't get him either.

"Hey, how is he?" I yelled at Danny.

"He's breathing." More gunfire popped off.

I was crouching on a large sewer pipe buried in the hillside. There was a grate over the front of the thing. My hip had eased some, and I crawled up the hill on my elbows. The truck was sitting near the top of the roadway. It was starting to get dark. I looked around. Across from where I was on the other side of the valley I saw some kind of power plant. There were large tubes running from this into the hillside. I looked back toward the road again.

I had a bad feeling the third gun was trying to sneak up on us, but

I couldn't see how. There was no way to get to where I was except by coming over the rail. Maybe he was climbing on top of the truck to give himself a better shot. That way he could draw down on Danny too.

"Hey," I hollered again, but stopped. I could hear the garbage truck going into gear and looked through the gap between the railing and the road to see it being turned straight again. The gunman who'd been shooting at us dived into the back, which was still open. The truck smashed into the Cordoba, crunching in the front part. Then the driver shoved the clutch into first and got it churning uphill again. The fool was going to try to get past the bobtail on one side. I went over the rail, holding onto the shotgun.

The driver went to the left of the bobtail where there was some space. He slowed down, then revved up, hitting the bobtail smack on the corner. He was gonna do it like a bank shot on an eight ball. The bobtail's rear end swung toward the mountain, then stopped. The damn thing was too heavy to ram like that. Me and Nap had put sandbags in the cargo part to give it extra weight. I let loose with a round from the shotgun, only hitting the side of the truck.

The driver souped the truck again and shot forward. This time he clipped the bobtail just right with a lot of force. The gunman in the back lost his balance, though, and dropped out on the roadway, landing on his side. As he got to his feet, Danny caught him square in the lower leg and he went down again.

The bobtail had been knocked straight enough to allow the garbage truck almost enough room to pass. The garbage truck spewing smoke from the rear as it chugged upwards Goddammit, stupid-ass Danny must have missed and not have shot out any tires. The garbage truck lurched to the left again, tearing up railing like it was tin foil. Smart motherfuckah.

The one in the roadway tried to get up and run for cover but his wound was too bad. He fell back down, holding onto his gun. I stood up and he drew down on me, but Danny clipped him from the side where he was hiding next to the Cordoba. The cat went over like he was a piece of cardboard in a strong wind.

I took another shot at the truck, running uphill. But a return blast came from the driver had me going flat in the road, rolling to my right. Good thing he was busy trying to get the garbage truck away. He went back at it, the truck half climbing over the rail as it ground the thin metal under its weight. The tires smoked and the gears made loud whining sounds.

The bobtail shook and rattled as the garbage truck bumped against it. I took off the flack jacked, dropped the shotgun, and started booking. They were weighing me down, and I was gonna need all the speed I could stoke. As I started to run up the hill, the driver steered the garbage truck out toward the edge of the roadway. Then he righted it when it looked like it would go over. He swung it back and around the bobtail.

My hip was absolute Jell-O. A hot shiver going up and down my leg. But I had no choice, I had to catch that truck. There was way too much to lose. Much more than I had already lost. The fibula and all that shit in my hip started to grind, but I couldn't take the time to care. A lot of those pretty little green ones was gonna disappear around the top of the rise, and that damn sure couldn't happen. My future was in that garbage truck. The crowd in my head was getting to their feet, cheering and clapping for me. I couldn't let them or me down.

The truck was making its way to the top, garbage spilling out the back. I didn't know if Wilma was coming up from below.

She must have heard the gunplay, but that was expected. We'd decided not to use even the disposable cells more than necessary just in case the DOJ or whoever was doing any monitoring. Maintaining radio silence – that's what they called it on old episodes of Combat. I sure could've used Sergeant Saunders' sweet machine gun right then to drop out of the sky and into my hands.

The truck's clutch wound up and I knew he'd slipped past second and popped it into third, hoping for more speed. A shot ripped out from the driver's side, striking the ground near me. I zigged anyway. The bastard was using one hand to shoot at me while he kept trying to get away. Ain't that some shit? Good thing it threw his aim off.

The truck was gaining speed and I wasn't. Come on, Zelmont, this is it and there ain't no more. No more chicks throwing their twats in my face, no more fine vines and badass rides, no more house in the hills.

Yeah, no more house in the hills. I put to it, knowing my hip was gonna explode any second. The truck had dropped down to low gear 'cause he needed the torque to get that elephant of a machine up the hill.

Let's do it, Zelmont. No time left in the quarter and only one chance. I had the endurance but the hip was weak. No matter, I had to catch this fool. The truck was almost at the top and that would be my last chance. He'd have to slow up 'cause there was a turn and it was too sharp to make it like he was going.

Do it, Zelmont, do it.

I pumped and just as I was closing the gap I got wise.

Rather than run up alongside where the driver was and get ganked, I'd go to his blind side and try that action. Keep going, Zelmont, keep going. I got to the truck just as he was doing the turn. Sure enough, he let loose with gunfire, knowing I was closing in on his trifling self. But I was already latching onto the unlocked rear door. The truck bolted forward, whipping around the curve and down the hill. Below us in the valley the lights were on and the city looked so peaceful, like there would always be tomorrows. I hung onto the door for life as it kept flapping, praying for my hip to keep functioning. If I slowed down I knew it would lock up again. I got going, scooting up the door along its edge. Twice I almost slipped under the wheels of the rig, but somehow I got to the top of the truck. I went flat to rest and plan my next move. Below me I felt a lump, and I knew what to do.

The truck was whipping down the hill, the wind finally opening the ear that had stuffed up. The driver shot rounds into the top of the cab's roof, trying to nail me. But I'd laid back, waiting for him to do that. As we sped along I pulled the tab on the last flash grenade I had, then tossed it inside from the passenger side with the busted-out window. It went off, the driver swearing as it exploded.

The truck swerved, the brakes screeching like crazy. Any second we were gonna tip over and I'd be thrown off the truck and the mountain. I held onto the frame of the passenger window, the little pieces of glass still left cutting into my hand. The truck's rear froze and the damned thing went sideways, tearing up the railing. The garbage truck tipped over like I knew it would, the driver's side pointing down toward the roadway. I held on, my hands numb. I couldn't lose, I just couldn't.

Part of the thing now hung over the side of the hill. The engine was still running. I pried my bloody hands lose, my triceps tight like I'd just done a hundred reps. I waited, listening, but couldn't tell if the driver was moving around or not. I didn't have a gun or any more grenades. I looked back down the road but couldn't see Danny.

All right, do something. I leaped off the truck, landing where the underside was facing out. Suddenly gunfire tore from somewhere and I could hear the windshield explode into a million pieces. I dove flat, covering my head, almost peeing in my pants.

"Come on, hero," he teased me, "are you man enough or not?"

He shot the assault weapon again, but he wasn't moving around. He was popping from inside the truck. I smiled. He must still be blinded from the grenade. I got up, my right leg almost unable to bend. But I couldn't worry about that right now. Whatever I'd done to it, I could use some of my millions to get it fixed.

I latched onto the axel to hoist myself up. My shoulder brushed against the oil pan, and it burned like hell. "Shit," I yelled.

The blind boy in the truck laughed. "Hurt yourself, honey?"

Motherfuckah.

I eased around to the front. Then the damn truck moved and my heart shot into my throat. The fucking truck was rocking on the edge. But there were no other plays to make. The shooter's vision would be clearing up any second and I had to be in motion before that. I peeped around the corner of the front of the truck. The chump was lodged in there, the steering wheel pressed up on him. He was holding the gun, swinging it this way and that.

"Hey," Danny called from below, at least having enough sense not to use my name. "She's monitored the police calls. Somebody called the sheriff, man."

The gun went off again. He was shooting around, hoping to hit me. Obviously he still wasn't seeing good. I moved as fast as I could. The dude was blinking, trying to hear which way I was coming. His gun swung up, left, right, then dead on me. His eyes were looking better. Blood was running from his nose. My hip was oatmeal. I sprinted at him, crying silently in pain, and all but leaped into the truck through what was left of the windshield. I grabbed the barrel of the gun, then landed an elbow on his face.

"Black bastard," he yelled, beating at me with his fist and trying to pull my mask off.

Seems my weight did it 'cause the truck went over the roadway, sliding down the hill. I held on, my arms pulled so tight I was afraid I'd dislocate my shoulders. It was only a few seconds but it seemed a lot longer. The truck stopped, wedged against some rocks and natural ledges poking out of the hill. How long it would stay there I had no idea.

The breath was knocked out of me. I was laying all up in the cab, my arms barely able to move. But I had to keep pushing myself, I had to win. There would be no rematch after today.

The driver was wailing in pain. The steering wheel and dash had collapsed more on him. Using my feet – I couldn't make a fist and my arms couldn't swing – I knocked the shit out of the fool with whatever I had left. Suddenly dust clouds whooshed around us. The truck was starting to slide again.

"Zelmont," Wilma said from further up the road I was so goddamn worn out I was gonna collapse.

"Zelmont," she screamed.

"Get your ass down here and help me. This rascal is about to slide down the mountain with our money." The fool pinned under the wheel groaned and I slapped him upside the head. I'd already thrown his piece out the window.

"Nap's hurt," she said. "Danny is bringing him over."

I stuck my head out the window as the truck wobbled some more. "Wilma, didn't you hear me? You gotta get down here now."

The sirens could barely be heard under our voices. We stared hard at each other. I started easing out of the busted window, but the truck was teetering and tottering so I stopped. Wilma started down.

Danny came hobbling up with Nap. The big man didn't look too good. His face was losing color. His side was red where he'd been shot and so were both of his hands. Danny had tied his sweat top around his brother's torso. But we all could tell it wasn't helping much.

"Come down here and get this cash," I shouted at Danny.

The young buck was looking back, then at Wilma, then at me.

Panic was as plain as zits on the boy's face. "Come on, you and Wilma gotta do it." She looked at me as I pointed at her. "Yeah, miss thing, you gotta get dirty like the rest of us peasants."

Wilma was gonna say something, but didn't. Danny let Nap down on the road.

"Danny, you stay there," I said. "Wilma take the lead to the truck here."

"Where's the money hidden?" she asked.

"In the back, you gotta dive in."

The disgust on her face was enough to make me laugh but I maintained. "Here," I said, holding up the headpiece with it's built-in gas mask. I'd snatched it from inside the cab.

"But – ".

"Hurry up, Wilma," I ordered her.

She scooted down to where I was. She put on the mask, giving me the evil eye with her beautiful browns. I pointed to the rear. "Get busy."

The truck creaked, and at that point I just knew I was a goner. If that wasn't enough, the sirens were getting closer.

But the truck settled. Wilma got to work.

Calling up reserves from who knows where, I got myself loose and crawled over to the rear doors. The shift of weight made the goddamn behemoth move again, then stop. I kept heading toward the back. Luck was with us and both of the doors had been propped open in the crash.

I had to hand it to Wilma though, she kept at it. I guess greed is a great motivator. She hauled out good-sized wire bundles, dollar bills peeking from the edges of the brown paper they were wrapped in. She handed them to me and I handed them up to Danny. We had an assembly line going.

"I think that's it," she said, taking off her mask. Garbage and stink came off her in waves. I sure hoped the cops didn't stop her. "Good thing there was a large bin along one wall underneath the garbage that the bundles were packed in," she said.

I wanted to smile but I was having back spasms. Together with the hip, I could barely move. "Help me up to the road," I asked her, sinking to a knee. Whatever I'd been going on was spent. I put my head down.

When I looked up, Wilma was standing over me. Despite the stains on her clothes and junk hanging off her, she managed to look superior.

"The great Zelmont Raines," she snarled, hands on her hips. She looked over at Danny, who was no doubt loading the bundles into the Mazda van she'd rented. I couldn't see her car from where I was but knew it had to be up there ahead. The engine was purring like a cheetah, all ready to gobble up some pavement. If she was gonna double cross me, this would be the best time to do it.

"Funny how things work out, ain't it?"

"Isn't it though?" Wilma stared down at me.

Danny suddenly reappeared, his Glock in his hand.

"Get Zelmont out of there." Nap had managed to half stand up, but he was damn near out on his feet too. "Do it." He spoke in the tone he used to get us fired up in the fourth quarter.

"Sure, Nap, that's exactly what I was going to do." Wilma grabbed the front of my overalls and got me to my feet. As she did that, the truck crashed down onto the hill, kicking up all kinds of dust and rocks. Me and Wilma just looked at each other.

"If we take Napoleon out of here we're bound to be spotted. The cops are probably going to be stopping all vehicles in this area, and four black people in one is going to attract attention."

I didn't like where she was going, but it did make sense.

"Then you better leave me and Nap since we're both busted up and that will make the po-po suspect."

She shook her head up and down, excited like.

"And the money."

The head shaking stopped awfully quick.

"If you're stopped you're gonna be searched, Matlock. You might argue they ain't got the right, but that won't do you any good once they nab the cash."

"Man, fuck all that," Danny screamed. "I oughta blow a hole in both of you for gettin' my brother in this situation." He was crying and waving the gun around. "Me and Nap take all the loot 'cause you two always think you runnin' the show, and look what it's got him."

"Think, Danny," I said. Nothing worse than a sad and mad gang-banger with a loaded piece. I'd never reach him before he'd bust some holes in me, even if I wasn't wasted like I was.

"He's gotta have a doctor," Danny said, tugging on his brother. The clown was probably doing Nap more bad than good. But I wasn't about to correct him.

"What can we do?" Wilma said, a closed-in look twisting her face into different shapes. "We have to wait until things settle down."

"Settle down like hell." Danny put his gun under Wilma's nose to make his point clear. "My brother goes to a doctor, understand, bitch?"

"That's the second time you've called me that." Wilma pointed at him. "Don't make it a third."

I was impressed. Wilma was one tough broad. "Hey you two, I got an idea. You want to listen or should we have a falling out now and fuck everything up?"

I don't know how, but they bought my plan, leaving me and Nap with the ten neat, nice packages of money in the storm drain I'd been standing on when I'd dived over the rail. The lock on the grate was rusted, and a smash from the butt of the shotgun got the whole thing loose. Maybe the cops would find me and maybe they wouldn't. I was so beat up I didn't even care. Soon I heard cars screeching all over the place and people shouting. A helicopter was up there in the sky too. Nap had passed out, holding onto his side. I fell asleep from exhaustion.

i woke up to somebody moaning steady-like. For a second or two, I was happy, like maybe I was with some fine mama and we were doin' the nasty. But that hope soon left me as it came back to me where I was, in a stank-smelling pipe with my best friend dying beside me.

"You got to keep quiet, Nap." I tried to get my head up off where it was resting against the cold concrete pipe, but there was no energy left for me to tap. It took all my juice just to get my eyes open. Nap was laying on his side, that much I could tell in the darkness.

"Oh, man, ain't this…something…we…aw, God." He rolled onto his back, holding onto himself and moaning again. Only now it was getting to be a wail.

"Nap, you got to shut the fuck up." The fear that was bouncing around inside me gave my battery a charge. I crawled over to him and put my hand over his mouth. "We gonna make it, big man, we are. But you gotta be tippity-toe quiet for sure, baby." I couldn't hear much of what was happening outside up on the road except some cars moving around and that helicopter flying around. I guess that had covered up homeboy's yelling. At least I hoped so.

Nap wasn't focusing on me. As I adjusted to the darkness, I could see his pupils were tight and the whites of his eyes red like he'd been smoking a pound of dank. I wish he had 'cause the boy was getting agitated and he needed to chill. "Yo, home, you got to come to yourself, man. You got to fight through the pain." That was easy for me to say. My vest had stopped the bullet with my name on it. If I'd been tagged like Nap was, I knew good and well I'd be doing the same as him – all out of my head with my guts turning to smashed peas.

Thing was, I did use the vest and it wasn't me who was torn up. You had to play the game the way the breaks went. That's what separated winners from also-rans.

"Nap," I said, leaning over. "Do you know who I am?" His eyes looked all around, and I put my hand over his mouth again, this time with more weight. If he went off there was gonna be more trouble than I could handle. "It's me, Nap, it's Zelmont. You know where you are, right?"

He shook his head. I didn't know if it meant yes or no or it was just the shakes. But I took my hand away. He didn't yell out, he didn't do anything except breath deep and ragged like an old locomotive.

"Zelmont, Zelmont, what have I done?"

"Wilma and your brother went to get that old croaker Burroughs, okay? But they got to wait some hours until the cops clear out of here, man." I looked at the glowing numbers on my watch. We'd been in the pipe for about an hour. A couple of rats were squeaking in the other end.

"Man," he said, worn out. Nap laid back down, barely breathing.

I pulled up the sweat top and his T-shirt underneath. All I could see was grime and slick liquid. What did I expect? I ripped off the wrapping of one of the bundles and put the wadded brown paper over the wound. Using his and my belt I tied the makeshift gauze in place. The wound didn't seem to be bleeding too much now so maybe that would help it.

We waited. Some time passed and I considered poking out of the hole to see if the cops were still scrambling around. I worked around in my mind who could have tipped off Stadanko. It must have been Ysanya. I guess Nap's long dong wasn't enough to make her forget who really was the mack daddy in this situation.

"She didn't, you know."

He was so quiet, at first I wondered if I was losing it and hearing voices in my cabeza. "What you say, man?"

"I know you must be sure Ysanya snitched, but I don't see it that way." He seemed to be coming out of the fog he had been in before.

"'Course you'd say that," I said. "She's your stuff."

"It ain't that, Zelmont." He grabbed his side and I was just about to leap on him when he waved me off. "Even if Ysanya wanted to tell him about our plan she knows she'd be dead if she did. How else could she explain what we were up to unless she copped to me and her gettin' it on?"

"Then who?" I wanted to know. Talking about it made me feel like I might walk out of this storm drain and get to spend my cash. Talking about it kept me from imagining that Wilma had got the best of Danny and was gonna sneak back here in the middle of the night with me and Nap conked out. Then she could pop the both of us and be off livin' large in Switzerland or some place like that. Me and Nap cold as motherfuckahs in the ground.

"Could it have been Weems?" I moved to sit against the side of the pipe again so I could stretch my legs out and they wouldn't cramp so bad.

"How would he know anything?" Nap asked.

I guess Wilma hadn't told him everything. That was good.

"Forget it."

"I think it was just Stadanko being careful." Now Nap's voice sounded far away. "Remember, this run was going to have to last him, so he had to be thinking how vulnerable he was. All that money moving over all those miles...." He stopped, getting his strength. "...from the various stops the truck had to make to collect the dough." Nap quit talking like he was used up.

"We'll find out." I listened for anything. The rats were moving around and there was water dripping back there in the deeper darkness too. It was getting cold. How long did we have to wait?

"I'm going to use some of my money to start a scholarship."

I laughed. "Now I know you must going crazy, Negro."

He moved his head from side to side. "No, man, if I get out of this I know I have to atone."

"You been watching Reverend Fred Price again, huh?"

"I'm serious as cancer, Zee. I have to make up for what I've done. That's why God let me be shot up, so I could realize what I had to do." He stopped for so long I thought he'd passed out again. But then he went on.

"Don't you remember when we were kids and we were so excited to play? How it felt to be standing in line and be picked for dodge ball or baseball? How the other kids knew from seeing us before that we had something, that extra spark, the promise of talent that made them say to themselves, "Yeah, I have to make sure that guy is on my team"?

"And getting to be a star in high school," I said. I didn't want to think back but couldn't help it.

"The world was ours for the asking," Nap said. "But we still played because we dug it, man, because the game was something that set us apart from the crowd. We felt good going down the field with the other guys 'cause we knew we were part of a team, part of something special."

"Yeah, you're right, Nap."

"God wants me to do better, Zee. He wants me to help make the same thing possible for some poor kids. I have no choice."

Talk of being all holy always got under my skin. And it was worse with us sitting in the dark, shivering and hungry and wounded. That's how them Christians wanted you to be, all racked up, shit looking lost. So naturally you had to call on de Lawd to save your pathetic ass 'cause who else would come and wipe your nose in the middle of the night?

"Man, Burroughs gonna dig the slugs out of you, then shoot you up with some of his homemade happy formula. After that, you'll be thinkin' about all the pussy – oh, I'm sorry, in your case, Nap, all the poon tang and hairy booty – you'll be gettin' with your new money."

Nap kinda coughed, trying to laugh. Then there was a pause.

"I did it, Zee, I killed Davida."

"You trippin."

"She knew about me and Ysanya."

"How?" I flashed on that tape I'd seen of Davida back at Stadanko's cabin and figured he might be telling me straight.

"Pablo, of all people. He didn't mean it, of course."

"Oh, Pablo was knockin' boots with her too, Nap? I thought he only liked to be poled."

Nap coughed and laughed that time. "He does. But they were drinking together at the club one night. You know, chicks like talking to queens as if they have some special insight into the female condition. Anyway, the lad really can't hold his liquor, and he blurted out about me and Ysanya."

"Why'd you tell him for anyway?"

"Another bad move in hindsight, but pillow talk has done many a man in, I suppose. So he blabs this to Davida, and you know that girl, no matter how tipsy she was, if it was an angle she could use to advance her career she'd hold onto that information."

"You got that right, home." We didn't say anything for a minute, the only sound coming from the rats and the water. I looked to the left and could see one of the little vultures climbing on a stack of money. Guard rat.

"Davida sweated you for cash after that, didn't she?"

Nap tried to sit up but couldn't. "I offered to make her a partner, but she said it would take too long to get her dough. She knew this producer was playing her, Zee. All she wanted was enough scratch to finance her album. She didn't really want much. And she was never nasty about it, you know how she was."

"Yes I do."

"She'd call up asking me for a little more or maybe to make a phone call for her."

I wasn't sure, but it seemed I heard a car driving around.

It had been five hours since we'd holed up in here. Could there still be cops outside, going over the ground again and again?

What if they brought back dogs?

"So how come you offed her, Nap?" I suppose I should have been upset but I wasn't. I was pissed that Fahrar that motherfuckah was on me like white on rice, but I didn't expect Nap to call him up and confess.

"She wasn't getting where she wanted to go." Nap's breathing didn't sound too good. "She called me all wound up that Tuesday. I could tell she'd been doing some lines."

That was the day we'd had our fight, but I didn't say anything.

"She was threatening to tell Stadanko if I didn't come up with some real money."

A car door slammed and I could hear footsteps. "Hush up, Nap."

"I decided I'd meet her way out so no one would see us." Nap kept talking, his voice very soft. I listened for anything.

"I don't really know what happened, Zee. She wouldn't believe how deep I was into Stadanko and Chekka. She was too wound up, she'd been doing more coke. Then she offered me sex right there, in the parking structure right behind the building we were at. This was during working hours, man." He coughed some more. I heard another car stop and I got scared. "Of course I was game, the riskier the better, right?"

"Right." It had to be cops.

"We were going at it on the hood of her car. You know how she liked it, rough and rougher."

"So it was an accident." I moved closer to where Nap was laying.

"It would be good if I could think so." Nap starting crying. "But as were doing it, as I had her panties around her throat, getting her off, she laughed, saying she was going to fuck me all kind of ways." He hacked up who knows what from his lungs. "I just wanted to be done with her. We had this job coming up. She would have been a problem for both of us. Her harassing me could go on way too long."

I heard voices up top. I got close to Nap. "I understand, man. She got on my last nerves too. But right now you gotta be quiet until I make sure who's up there."

If he heard me it didn't make any difference. He let his side go, grabbed his head, and started wailing again. "Aw, man, God wants me to do better, Zee. He's taken me to the brink to teach me right from wrong." From somewhere strength came into him and he grabbed me, holding me close to his chest. "We've got to repent, Zee. We've got to use the money for more than just us."

He was hollering so loud I didn't know what to do. I heard the footsteps again, and it sounded like someone was coming down the hill. "Shut up, Nap, you've got to shut up," I whispered in his face, scared like crazy.

Nap got me in a bear hug, his big arms suddenly filled with an energy I was shocked to see he still had. The pain in my back almost made me pass out as Nap crushed me. "Nap, Nap, come to yourself, man."

"Jesus is calling on us, Zee. He knows what we've done."

"Nap," I cried out despite the footsteps. My hands went to him in the dark, his sweat and blood all over me. His breath was rotten and he had me very tight in his grip. I pushed back against him, trying to pry myself loose. Our bodies shifted and I got leverage over him.

"Nap," I said, gritting my teeth.

"Zelmont," his voice boomed in the pipe. The rats got excited and started scooting all over the place.

His arms were like steel around me and I had top get my hands under his jaw and push away. His body shook and he let out air like a bad tire. Then his grip went limp and I rolled clear.

"Zelmont."

I looked over where Nap was lying still. "Zelmont," the voice said again. It wasn't Nap. It was Wilma.

"In here." I could barely talk.

"We're coming."

Pretty soon a light came through the grate of the water pipe. I could hear Wilma's feet crunching on the earth as she came closer to the entrance.

"Zelmont? We've been driving around for a while. The cops removed the trucks, and in the dark we couldn't tell which drain pipe you two were in."

"Where's Burroughs?"

"He came with Danny. I thought it would be better to bring two cars just in case Nap had to be stretched out. Danny drove Burroughs' station wagon."

"That's good," I said.

I half crawled over to the entrance. Together we removed the grate. "I guess that old bag of bones ain't gonna come down the mountain."

She was shining her light past me, like she thought me and Nap had buried the bundles somewhere. "Is he okay?"

"He's dead."

"Shit." She was thinking what I was, that Danny was gonna go straight off.

"What happened?" She came into the pipe.

"He went nuts, kept talkin' about how he had to get right with Jesus. He told me he killed Davida."

She put the light on me, studying my face. "I assumed – "

"You and everybody else, Wilma. Me and Nap struggled some. He'd grabbed me, damn near busting my back. I don't know if me fighting with him caused him to die sooner. But we need Burroughs to come down here and say Nap died of the bullet wounds."

She stared at me then nodded her head. "I'll go up and tell them he's barely hanging on."

"If you can, on the QT tell Burroughs there's more money in it for him to do as we say."

"He was Nap's friend, too."

"Nap can't pay him, we can." At that moment I couldn't afford to feel anything about Nap.

It took some doing, but with Danny's help they got Burroughs down the hill. The old scarecrow was at the entrance of the pipe, the moon lighting him from behind. He looked like death himself come to call.

"You better hurry, he don't look good." I stood back as Danny rushed in.

"Nap, I got the doc here, Nap, is you awake?" Danny was all over him, slobbering and carrying on. Wilma had her flashlight on us.

He looked up at me like a little kid lost in Disneyland. I had on the face I wore when I didn't want a defender to know anything I might be up to.

The ancient pill roller got on his knees and bent over Nap, going over his body with his stethoscope. Burroughs' long, hinged fingers were like insect legs dancing over the big man's form. Under his breath I could hear him talking to himself. Danny stood to one side, a flashlight in his left hand. He kept his right free for the gat I knew he had on him under his sweat top.

"One of the high velocity shells shattered his clavicle, and another drove part of his ribs into his stomach, puncturing the lining. He bled into his stomach over time, eventually choking on his own blood and bile." Burroughs' voice was the same as it always was, flat with no emotion. What would Danny think?

The youngster put the light dead on Burroughs, then on me.

I didn't look away, I didn't want to seem guilty.

Wilma stood between me and Danny. "We have to move Napoleon because if the police find him they'll know we did the robbery. Dr. Burroughs will attend to your brother's body, and see that he's cremated properly."

"We ain't gonna bury him?" Danny said softly.

"Danny," I said, "we gotta think clearly now. We have to get rid of the body."

I helped Burroughs get up. He looked at me sneaky behind his glasses but didn't let on anything. If Danny went buck wild, he'd talk to save his skin. But otherwise he could be depended on to go along with the flow 'cause there was the promise of bigger ducats in it for him.

Danny was massaging his face with one of his hands, pacing back and forth at the entrance of the big pipe. I guess his shock was wearing off 'cause he was pointing and shaking his finger at us. "See, see what happened when I went along with you motherfuckahs? My brother is dead…dead, goddammit." He pulled out the piece but I didn't make a move, even though I felt I could have. This was one time when talk, not head ringing, was called for.

"What are you gonna do, Danny? Dust all of us and run off with the money by yourself?"

He stopped moving around, bringing the piece up on me. "What if I do, Zelmont? Nap ain't around to protect your ass now, is he? You the one that let him down, wasn't you? How I know you didn't fuck up and he died 'fore he was supposed to?"

If Burroughs was staring at me, I didn't let on. "Nap died from his gunshot wounds, Danny. I know you've been around enough to know how that can go, how at any minute the bullets sitting there in the wounds can cause all kinds of shit to happen. You must have had a homeboy go out like that before."

Danny wasn't about to let logic get in the way of his mad-on. But in some part of his eight-ballin' head he had to be wondering how a small-timer like him would move all that cash. He needed Wilma, at least. Now she had to buy my life.

"Whatever you decide, Danny," Wilma started, "you're going to need Zelmont to help you move the body back up to Dr. Burroughs' car. I assume you know you can't let one of your boys in on this."

"You let this dope fiend skeleton in on it." He jerked the pistol at Burroughs.

"He's used to this, Danny," Wilma said. "What happened to Napoleon was unfortunate, but it has happened. It's nobody's fault. And if you decide you don't need any of us, then get the killing over now, stop screwing around."

I wasn't sure that reverse psychology bullshit was the right angle with a hothead like Danny, but there was nothing I could do. She either convinced him or we – at least me and the doc - would be sucking on his gun in a few ticks.

Danny didn't speak. He stood there, staring at his brother.

Then, slowly, he cranked his head to look at the stacks of bills. He moved more into the pipe, giving me the stare-down. "Let's get him out of here," he finally said.

It took a lot of effort from the four of us to get Nap up the hill. Even Burroughs pitched in, more out of fear of Danny than greed for what he was gonna charge us afterward.

With a lot of stops and starts we got Danny up to the station wagon. Burroughs had brought along some kind of liquid he used for cleaning his tools. I used that stuff to swab out the pipe as best I could so there wasn't much trace of his blood or our fingerprints. You never knew, the cops might come back and find the hiding spot. No point in giving them a head start on finding out who died in there.

We got the bundles up and headed back to the Seven Souls Clinic in Burbank – me and Danny in Wilma's car, the doc and her in the station wagon with Nap's body. I was sweating something fierce what with all those cops and sheriffs running around. But damn if that old pharmaceutical junkie Burroughs didn't bring us luck. We made it back to his place without being stopped.

Burroughs had me get a gurney and we wheeled Nap in through a side entrance, a sheet draped over him. We left him in a room with nothing in it except a white metal trash can and a scale. He locked it up and we went into his office. The bundles were in there too.

Wilma cut a bundle open with a pair of snips he had on a shelf.

She counted out seventy grand in fifties and hundreds. "This do it?" She handed the money over to him. He sat behind his desk, rocking back and forth in his chair.

"Well," he said, picking up the cash. "There has to be some compensation for all my exertion." He licked his lips like a lizard flicking his tongue for a fly.

"Fuck you." Danny stepped up and tapped the gat quick against Burroughs' large forehead. "Exert this, motherfuckah."

I had to hand it to him, that ole zombie kept his cool. He took off his glasses and closed his eyes like he was waiting to be sent to that big pharmacy in the sky.

"Danny," Wilma said, putting a hand on the boy's arm.

"Give him another $30,000," I said. "Stop playing Snoop Dogg every time something don't go your way, Danny. This is business."

He mumbled at me and Wilma and quietly put the gun away.

Burroughs opened his eyes, and I swear for a second there he had a disappointed expression in his eyes. I counted out his bills and handed them over.

"I shall take care of everything on my end." He sat back, examining us like I'm sure he did when he was getting ready to cut a body open.

We split in Wilma's car, the bundles in the trunk. We were goddamn millionaires. We'd taken money from a dude that couldn't report it and who'd soon have even bigger worries to occupy his time. 'Course there was still his wild-ass cousin Rudy to deal with, but I wasn't worried about him right then. My cut was gonna be two, three million. I could get my thing going again, get myself set up sweet. Maybe I'd take over the Locker Room and franchise that bad rascal, then let the pussy and money roll in.

But something didn't feel right, and it wasn't just 'cause my best friend was lying on the slab.

hen I got back to my pad in Lennox, I grubbed on three cheeseburgers and two large orders of fries I'd bought at the Jack-in-the-Box on Imperial. I had some Scotch left in the cupboard, and would have zonked out on coke if I had any. I couldn't believe it but I was glad Wilma had hinted she was too tired and too wired for sex. The only thing I wanted was food and sleep.

As the sun came up, I went to bed and tried not to think about Nap. Or that Wilma was sitting on the cash, her with the only safe place to keep that paper.

For the next few days everything seemed to be happening in a world I was only a visitor to. I was too paranoid to stay at my shitty apartment but too broke to go anywhere else. Wilma had leaked information to the contact she had in the Justice Department before we did the robbery. The day after the job there was a piece in the L.A. Times sports section about the charges coming down on Ellison Stadanko. And there was a companion story inside about an investigation into Rudy Chekka, reputed mob boss.

That night I was sitting in the Proud Bird on Aviation watching the TV that hung over one corner of the bar. On the news was coverage of Stadanko at a press conference. He was with his lawyers and was denying everything. His old lady wasn't next to him.

A hand came down on my shoulder. "Shame, isn't it?"

"Assholes always get what's due them, Fahrar." I drank my drink, not bothering to look at the chump.

"How you been keeping, partner?" He sat down on the stool next to me.

"I've been just fine, pardner." Now there was a piece about an ice skating bear on the news. A chick at the other end of the bar cracked up at this. "I know you don't expect me to buy your funny-eyed self a drink."

"That might be construed as a bribe." He took off his hat and placed it on the bar.

"Ain't there someplace else your half-breed ass can get a drink at?"

"And miss your witticisms?" He leaned over the bar and ordered. "Give me a rum and coke with a lime in it, okay?"

The bartender, a big tittied woman with a weave that needed repair, nodded and made his drink. Fahrar sat there, watching TV and getting under my skin as she made his drink. She put it on the bar for him and he paid her. Cheap civil servant motherfuckah tipped her a quarter.

"Two men are sitting over in the jail ward of County Hospital." He slurped his drink.

Finally we were getting to it.

"As you must know, these Serbian gentlemen were pretty fucked up. One of them in particular has got a smashed pelvic bone, busted spleen, nuts hanging all low." He shook his head from side to side. "The poor bastard may never walk right again."

I finished my Maker's Mark but didn't want to order another one. No sense getting too loose and end up slipping with this nosey fuck. "Ain't that something. Man, you oughta write that up and sell it to *Cops and Donuts Monthly*."

Fahrar's yellow eye zeroed in on me over the top of his glass as he drank. "Naturally these tough boys aren't saying diddly. And their employer, Ellison Stadanko, claims no knowledge of what these ruffians could have been up to carrying firearms on the garbage truck. He's as perplexed as the rest of us why it is that five men, three of whom were in bio-hazard suits, were on one garbage truck."

"*The Times* had a piece today saying Stadanko may get jammed up by a grand jury." What the fuck, I ordered another Maker's.

"Since when you start reading the newspaper?"

I was gonna say, "Since your mama started bringing it to my crib in her teeth," but decided to chill. "I always been into self-improvement."

"Like nine million worth? 'Cause that was the take you strokes pulled down, Zelmont. Stadanko is boxed in and is going to be sweating under the federal lights soon. That's smart, so smart I know your ducking and dodging self couldn't have thought it all out on your lonesome. No, it would take someone who had a knowledge of how to drop the right clue in the right back channel in the legal labyrinth of D.C."

"Really?" The bartender had turned the TV to a channel featuring a marble shooting championship. Damn.

"Did you know that Wilma Wells clerked in the law firm that Brooks Weems has in D.C.?"

He got a reaction that time. The surprise was all over my face.

"Yeah," the snake fuck smiled. "Brooks is the older brother of the football commissioner. Isn't that quite the coincidence?"

"Life is full of them, my mother always said." Come on, Zelmont, don't let this chump rattle you. But damn if he hadn't blind-sided me. I sipped my drink and tried to look like I still had game.

"You seen Napoleon around lately?" He thumped his hat with his finger.

"Naw, you ask his brother?"

"He said he hadn't seen him for a few days. He said that maybe he might be back East on some kind of business, but he wasn't sure."

"There you go." The bartender had switched the channel again. Now there was a cop program playing with somebody I recognized. It was the Asian dude I'd done the syndicated shows with a while back. The sound wasn't on but it seemed like he was the star. Good for him. We were all getting over.

"There was a fair amount of blood on the roadway, Zelmont. Quite a few spent shell casings too. And flash grenades. But you knew that."

"I did, huh?"

Fahrar had more of his booze. "Some of that blood matches Napoleon Graham's blood type."

He must have gotten Nap's medical record from the league.

But so what? He didn't have a body. "I'm sure a lot of people match his blood type."

"How about his DNA?"

"You can cut it out, cop. I read in the paper the samples swabbed from the roadway were hard to break down. There's all that oil, gas, and what have you mixed in, plus it got absorbed. They quoted a biologist from UCLA who said all that debris or whatever messes up an exact match."

"Sounds like you studied that part of the article back and forth."

"Don't it?"

Fahrar got off the stool, holding the drink in one hand, his hat in the other. "When you see Napoleon, let him know I'd like to talk with him."

"Oh, sure."

He looked at the glass in his hand like he'd lost the taste. He put the drink down, not finishing it. "Every step you take." He snugged his hat on his head and drifted out of the joint.

I pushed both my hands against the edge of the bar, gripping it hard. I suddenly felt like I was gonna slip away into a hole and this was all I could do not to disappear forever. I got up and moved through the noise of the Proud Bird to the pay phone near the bathrooms. I figured it was better using that than my cell.

I dialed Wilma's number at work, her inside line. Her machine answered and I hung up. I dialed her at home, then on her cell phone and got no answer. Maybe Fahrar had told me about Wilma working for Weems' brother to see if we'd fink out each other. Maybe it was a lie and he was waiting outside to tail me like he'd shown he could do and catch me confronting Wilma.

I put the phone back and tried to catch my breath, get my bearings. We hadn't really talked about what we were going to do to explain Nap's absence. None of us had a solution anyway. I walked back to the bar and had my whisky without tasting it.

Wilma had said we should just go about our business as usual for the next few weeks. For Danny that meant running the Locker Room, for her the lawyer thing. And me? Hell, I was only the cat who saved the day, and here I was drinking away what little folding money I had at the moment. She said we'd square up our shares soon as her trap closed in on Stadanko. Well, shit was sprung on the motherfuckah now and we hadn't heard peep. Correct that, I hadn't heard nothin'.

By the time I had my fourth Maker's, I was imagining that Wilma and Danny had skipped out on me with all the haul. I gave a crooked smile to the sucker looking back at me in the bar's mirror.

"Say, handsome, ain't you Zelmont Raines?" She was older than me by at least ten years. But she had nice legs sticking out of the skirt that was too short for her plump legs. Plus, I liked the blonde dye job she'd given her hair, not to mention her overlapping front teeth.

"I'm he. What you having, dark and lovely?"

About an hour later we were grinding on the stairway leading up to my apartment. She had one leg wrapped around my hip and I had her dress hiked up, my hand rubbing between her legs.

I breathed some words, drunk and hot and wanting to get my money and get the hell out of town. Fuck Wilma and her scheming self.

"Let's get inside," she whispered in my ear, slobbering and nibbling on it with her tongue and teeth.

I mumbled something else and was untangling myself from her when I got that feeling. The one that told me a cat was about to jack me from behind while I had my eye on the ball. I stopped getting my nut on and tuned my radar outwards.

"What's wrong, baby? Your wife coming home?"

"Shhh." I put a hand on her lips. She bit my fingers, still thinking I was fooling around. Somebody was coming up the stairs, and they were on a creep. We had stopped in the middle of the second flight of stairs that ran up a kind of inside shaft of the apartment building.

Below me the stairs turned the corner and continued down to the first floor and the sidewalk. The stud had to be at the corner. Good thing the cheap sumabitch landlord hadn't bothered to replace the lights that were supposed to be in the stairwell.

"What, baby?" she said again.

I heard the step and threw the chick down where I figured he was standing.

"What the fuck you doing?" she screamed. As she went down, I went right behind her. She collided with the creeper, who'd started backpedaling too late. The two went over.

"Motherfuckah, I'm going to cut you," she said.

I jumped over her and onto the dude she was halfway on. We slid down part of the first set of stairs. He was big, muscular.

This boy was no mugger. Somebody I knew had sent him to do me in.

"Niggah, you don't know how to treat a lady, do you?"

Homegirl was still going on.

Me and the dude were tussling, trying to get to our feet. He beat me to it and caught me good in the side with the tip of his shoe. I fell and reflexively brought up my arm. A heavy piece of metal crashed down on it and I yelled out.

"Oh, Zelmont, you in trouble, ain't you?" She finally got the picture.

I rammed forward, but this chunky clunk knew what to do. He brought a knee up, catching me under the chin. I sagged down and got clubbed in the shoulder blades as I ducked my head out of the way. Otherwise he'd have taken it off at the root with his metal club.

"Don't worry, honey."

There was a swish of air and then it was the other cat's turn to holler.

"Skank," the dude said, holding his leg. We were at the bottom of the stairs, a little light coming in from the moon and street lamps. My opponent was dressed in a nylon workout suit I had seen before. But I didn't have to guess since he wasn't wearing a mask. It was Coach Cannon.

The blonde was holding a hook knife, which she'd used to slash him across the leg. Her top was torn. She must have ripped it tearing the knife loose from her bra. Well, a girl had to be careful, I guess. She was dancing around like a welterweight, jerking the knife in the air like she had the shakes. She didn't know what to do next.

Cannon did. He backhanded her with the pry bar he was holding. She flew back against a wall and went to the ground like wet laundry. But that had given me enough time to get moving, and I dropkicked the coach in the chest just like I'd seen Wild Man Tank do in one of those cage matches.

Cannon staggered back against the wall of the stairwell. I got up and slugged him.

"Goddammit," he wheezed.

I hit him two more times on the back of his neck with my hands held together like a club. The bear of a man sunk to his knees, still holding onto the hunk of metal. So I brought my elbow down straight on his dome. That disoriented him enough for me to make a grab for the pry bar.

"No." He was on one knee, holding onto the bar with both hands. I was pulling on it with both my hands. We were like Malone and Jordan back in the day tussling for the ball. But I had an advantage 'cause I was at a better angle, and I snatched the bar away. Quickly I chugged him under the chin with the end of the bar, stunning his ass.

I leapt on him, pressing the bar against his throat. "Who the fuck sent you, Cannon?"

"I had to do it, Zelmont."

"Give me an answer 'fore I cave your skull in." I pulled him up, the bar resting against the side of his face.

"Chekka, Chekka sent me after you." He started sobbing like a little girl. I can't stand a man crying. Man got to own up.

"Stop it." I slapped him with the bar, but not too hard.

"Why, what's he got on you?"

"My oldest boy, you've heard about his gambling habits. Chekka got him in debt by advancing way too much to him. Must be more than five hundred grand." He started crying again.

"You the head coach of the Barons, man. I know you can come up with some of that green."

Cannon shook his head, his beard wet with sweat and tears.

"He's got more on the boy, real bad stuff." He shook his head again. "I didn't want to do it, Zelmont. But Chekka said he'd have my son crippled if I didn't."

"Chekka told you to kill me?"

"No, you know I couldn't do that. He wanted me to scare you. He wants the money back. If his cousin was going down he needed it to get away. Seems with Ellison pissing in his soup about the Justice Department, most of the boys are out looking for other work or trying to break off part of the enterprise for themselves."

The hook knife chick groaned.

"So why did he send you to mess me up? Don't tell me he couldn't get one of his Serbian slobs to throw in for old times' sake."

"To delay you, my friend," Rudy Chekka said, his voice coming from behind me.

I got off Cannon and turned around. Chekka had on a slick black leather jacket, black shirt, and glossy tan tie. To top it off he had a black pistol in his hand.

"I use coach, I don't owe him money. I use any of my countrymen, then I got to pay out." He made a circle in the air with the gun. "I have learned in this country it is better to have a short memory when it comes to who your friends are."

"How'd you know it was us?"

"Unlike the cops, I don't need proof. Garvak, the one you kicked in the truck, described the size of one of the men, and it matched Napoleon Graham. And of course how the other gunman was so concerned for this wounded man's condition." He smiled, stepping closer. "And that championship run up the hill could only have been you, Zelmont. Now let's get that money, yeah?"

"Sure."

One of my neighbors was coming home. I recognized the putt-putt of the beat-to-hell car that always dropped her off at this time. She was Guatemalan or something, and she worked swing at some bindery. The car door closed and her footsteps were coming down the walkway.

"Oh," she said when she came into the crowded stairwell.

"Hi," I said, moving to the side.

Chekka looked at Cannon, who was picking up homegirl off the ground.

"Hey, baby, I told you to be cool on that Hennessy." He was bent over, trying to lift her cold-cocked ass up.

The little Latina started hurrying up the stairs, smiling nervously at us as she went. I was gonna toss her like I did with hook knife woman, but Chekka was wise. He patted the gun in the deep pocket of his leather coat. I let the chick go on up.

"Let's go." Chekka twitched his head toward the street.

Cannon let my girl drop with a thud. That was cold.

"Who's driving?" I asked.

"The coach. You and me will ride together in back."

"Great."

So off we went to fuckin' Oz. Now maybe Dorothy and Toto and the Tin Man might have had an idea of where to go, but I sure as shit didn't. I didn't know if Wilma was in town or had skipped off, making me the biggest dope of all time. I was more upset about that than the fact Chekka had a rod on me and was gonna gat me as soon as he figured out I had no clue as to where the dough might be.

"Where we going, Zelmont?" Cannon played with the rear view mirror, looking at my face in it. "You give up the money and everything's cool, right?" He started his ride, a Navigator with a dented bumper. He clicked the automatic floor shift into place and we took off.

"Of course." Maybe coach wanted to really believe Chekka so it would make his guilty conscience feel better. But both of us knew Chekka wasn't planning on letting me so much as scratch my balls for one second after I showed him to the swag. As if I could.

"We gotta jet down to Alhambra."

"Why?" Chekka jabbed me in the gut with the barrel of the gun.

"That's where we hid it, at this clinic that Doc Burroughs owns a piece of."

"Who is this?" Chekka growled.

"He's a needle freak players go to when they're starting to lose their edge. It makes sense, Rudy."

"Very well," he said, sounding like he bought the lie.

We rode along, the night passing by with me trippin' off the notion that it might be my last look. But I figured I still had one chance left, and I made my move as we hit the onramp to the 105 going east. I kicked out with my heel at the floor shift, hoping to send the car into reverse.

"Watch it," Chekka screamed.

As I kicked, I had fallen against Chekka, hoping to wrap up his gun hand. My move worked, and the Navigator shuddered into backward motion. Someone driving behind us had to swerve wickedly as the Navigator smashed into the concrete wall lining the onramp. I kept kicking as Cannon tried to get the car going forward.

Meanwhile me and Chekka were mixing it up. I had a hold of his arm and was shoving myself against him for all I was worth.

The gun went off and ripped a hole through the roof. Cannon had the SUV in the right gear again and got going.

"Nigger," Chekka hollered. He hit me on the side of my face with his free hand.

But I did what he wasn't expecting. I lurched forward, holding onto him as the car took off up the ramp again. We were moving onto the freeway and our bodies slipped into the opening between the two front seats. Cannon put a hand on the gear selector to keep it in place, but that meant he had to steer with one hand while me and Chekka went at it.

"Get him off me." Cannon batted at me with his arm while he concentrated on keeping the car straight.

The gun went off again. The bullet penetrated the front Windshield – a spider web spreading out from the center where it had punched through the glass.

Me and Chekka were all over the back seat, throwing blows and yelling at each other. Traffic kept whizzing by us. Maybe the people in those cars didn't see what was going on inside, or maybe they did and figured what with all the road rage in L.A., it was best not to get involved. I threw another kick, catching Cannon upside his temple. At the same time, Chekka got me good in the stomach and I went slack for a moment or two. He was bringing the gun around on me. Thinking he was gonna pop one of my knees, I twisted my body and threw all my weight against him, grabbing his arms with whatever strength and determination I had.

"Get him settled down," the coach yelled. He was looking back at us and swerved the car into another lane. A big-wheel truck blasted its horn at us.

Like it was when I was on the field, the action seemed to slow down. I was in the zone and could sense an opportunity present itself as Chekka brought the gun up. I could hear my heart thumping in my ears and the blood rushing like quicksilver through my torso. As his finger twitched on the trigger I rammed his forearm with the heel of my hand. Chekka's gun now pointed at the back of the driver's seat and the barrel jerked when the bullet left it. The shot went through the seat at an angle.

"Fuck, you idiot, you shot me." Cannon gritted his teeth but managed to keep both hands on the steering wheel. I did my best to grind my foot into the wound in his stomach, and also tie up Chekka's gun hand.

"Zelmont, for Christ's sake," Cannon shouted, beating at my foot and ankle with his hand. Chekka got on me and I rammed against the back of the passenger seat. Our weight made the seat back snap forward, and I shot up against the dash. Cannon was trying to control the car as he drove on the freeway, but I could tell out of the corner of my eye the wound was bothering him.

"Black nigger," Chekka screamed. He pumped off another shot, blowing out the car's radio.

"Watch out," Cannon hollered. The blood was leaking from his side and had stained his shirt and pants.

I grabbed Chekka and rolled us into Cannon.

"Goddammit." The steering wheel came loose from the coach's hands as we plowed into him. The SUV swerved toward the concrete divider as cars hit their breaks and tires screeched. A driver rear-ended us as the Navigator bounced off the divider. The SUV shot back into the number two lane as some chick in a red Mustang came barreling along. She made to zoom around us but clipped the coach's vehicle on the ride side, dead across the door.

By this time more cars were honking and screeching to a halt. The chick in the Mustang was pointing at us to pull over, like three dudes duking it out in a Lincoln Navigator was something ordinary.

I got hold of the steering wheel and whipped the front end into the Mustang. The cars came together in a 'V' and slid along the freeway. A Lexus rammed into the Mustang's bumper and the Navigator went up on the divider going too fast. The damn truck skated along on two wheels and then tipped onto its side. This was getting to be a habit. Our momentum kept us going and we came to rest only after we slapped into the rear of a pick-up truck.

The front windshield exploded as I got a grip on Chekka's jaw. I propelled the top of his head into the door handle and didn't wait to see if he was disoriented or not. I latched onto the coach and started to wiggle past him to get out of the driver's side window, which was now pointing up toward the night sky.

"Zelmont, you've got to help me." His seat belt was still clicked in place. He had his head back on the seat, holding himself with his arms crossed. It was as if he were afraid his spirit might leave him forever. I flashed on Nap, begging me too.

"You was about to bust my head open a few ticks ago there, coach."

"That was only to scare you, Zee." Cannon was sounding too friendly. Bastard was scared. "You know I'd never really hurt you." He started breathing hard, coughing blood and spit. "I've never been shot."

"Neither have I, coach, and I intend to keep it that way." I started to climb past him again. I could hear people outside.

Soon the law would be here.

"Zelmont," he said, pawing at me with his beefy hands.

"I'm here, coach." I leaned in close like I was gonna help him get loose. Instead I hit him a couple times, knocking his conniving self unconscious. I had to kick out what was left of the driver's side window 'cause it was up and was an electric number. Then I pulled myself loose. A crowd was around, including the irate broad with the Mustang we'd fucked up.

"You are in big trouble, mister." She shook a finger under my nose as I heard sirens getting close. A lot of eyes were on me in the dark. Several cars were stopped and traffic was backing up in the lanes on our side of the divider. That was good 'cause it meant the cops would have to go around the other way to get to this spot.

"These men kidnapped me." I leaned against the Navigator, looking all dazed and shook up and shit. That got some whispers going in the crowd. "Can somebody get me to an ambulance?" I started massaging my stomach. "Something doesn't feel right."

The Mustang chick, who was tall and had a sweet-looking pair of jugs on her, stared at me, not knowing what to do.

"Why don't you sit down until the police and emergency personnel arrive?" a woman in a flower print vest said, trying to be kind.

I could see the blue and reds blinking behind the sea of cars that had backed up.

"Yeah, that's a good idea." I stumbled over to the divider and leaned on it but remained standing.

Mustang Sally and a couple of young studs, no doubt hoping that being a Good Samaritan might earn a phone number from her or more, stood close to me, making sure I wasn't going to book. Then Cannon saved my ass. He came to and started bellowing.

"See, I told you they were up to no good." I pointed at the truck like a little kid telling on his sister.

"Help me," Cannon begged, his voice getting real weak.

The two studs had to prove their manhood. They looked at each other and marched over to the coach's SUV with some of the others who were standing around.

I pushed Mustang Sally to the ground and went over the divider into oncoming traffic. There was braking and cursing as I dashed across the lanes, hoping like hell I'd make it. An MTA bus almost flattened me. The driver, a woman with long braids that went flying everywhere as she rode the air brakes, stopped about four inches from my popped-out eyes. We looked at each other with our mouths wide open, my face all bright in her headlights. But her sudden stop made other cars slow since they didn't know what was going on. I took off again toward the bushes and trees on the side of the freeway, my fear of getting caught bigger than my fear of getting run over. My hip was acting up some, but I got across just as a Highway Patrol car pulled up.

I went down the hill through the bushes and such on the side of the freeway and came to a cyclone fence at the bottom. I went up and over and was now on a dead-end street of small houses. Every last one of them seemed to have a dog that didn't mind barking. There was too much drama going on, and I had to get away and figure out my next move. I knew I was getting played, but not exactly how. I wound up near Hawthorne Boulevard and caught a bus heading north. I tried my cell but the battery was out. The cops would be all over my pad and fan out from there, so I knew if I went south toward the crib I would get nabbed for sure. I got off at 165th Street and called Isabel from a pay phone.

"I need a ride, sweetness, can you do that for me?"

"I bet it has something to do with this business on the 11 o'clock news."

"That's right." What was the point in trying to scam her?

She didn't say anything for a few seconds. "All right, Zelmont, I'll come get you. I'll come for you wherever you are."

"You're all right, Isabel."

"'Bout time you realized that."

I waited outside an all-night supermarket for her, sweating because it was humid and I was on edge. I watched cars and trucks and buses go by on the street. Somewhere out there was my money, and Wilma was lording over it. Maybe she'd already split with the whole take. Fine. I'd keep after her until I couldn't search no more and then I'd still keep looking. I was gonna get what was due me.

i recouped at a fat farm in Hesperia up in San Bernardino County. It was co-owned on the sly by Burroughs and Monique Gold, a retired actress who did all these second version *Twilight Zones*, episodes of the original *Knight Rider* and what not. She always had on a ton of black mascara and still wore her dyed coal black hair way up in some kind of cone effect. I'd been to the place a few times in the off-season when I was the top dog 'cause they had a complete gym, sauna, massage, and whirlpool facilities. Back then it made for a good hideaway from reporters who were always getting in my face, and I sure didn't think Chekka, Weems, Trace, or anybody else would find me at this joint.

It was hotter than Galatus' breath up there. I worked out on the machines and did laps in the pool, which was shaped like a giant teardrop.

"Representing the tears I shed for Hollywood," Monique said. She had to be pushing 70, and as usual was holding a club glass in one hand and a thin cigar in the other. She stood at the edge of the pool in heels and a robe with leopard spots. The wraparound she had on was too short for a Barbie doll. But I had to admit, she had pretty good legs for an old girl.

"How many times a day you say that line, Monique?" I hauled myself out of the pool, sitting on the edge. A few of her clients were also doing their laps and splashed water like walruses.

"Many times, many times, darling." She put her glass on a table with an umbrella in the middle of it. She grabbed a towel from a chair next to it and bent down. Monique dried my back and shoulders.

"You've managed to keep your figure, sweet boy." She talked with the cigar hanging from her red, red lips. As usual she had on a fistful of mascara over her dark eyes and enough hairspray to knock out mosquitoes from twenty feet away.

"What else have I got, Monique?"

She looked me up and down, puffing on her cigar. "You've got that right, darling."

"Better be cool. Some of your high-end customers might not dig you flirting with Mandingo."

"They'd only be jealous. Maybe I'd have to share you." She kissed my shoulder.

I got up and was surprised to find the hip joint had moved wrong when I was sitting. I gritted my teeth in pain. The goddamn thing was getting to be unpredictable. Guess all the stress I'd been putting my hip through lately was starting to add up. Now it looked like I was gonna have to get that operation after all.

"You've been aggravating that condition." She touched my hip.

"How do you know?" Irritated, I started to walk off.

"Come with me," she said.

"I ain't got time for no games, Monique."

"No games."

I followed her into the main building, which was done up like a temple you'd see on an old rerun of *Ben-Hur*. We went into her office. It looked like a set from that cable show about ancient Rome.

"Here." She pointed at a shelf filled with weird-ass statues in the shape of half-animal, half-human creatures that had wings and horns and so on. Same kind of shit Nap had in his office.

"That's real nice, Monique."

She picked a good-sized statue off the shelf. It looked like a bear, but had long fangs and bat wings. "This is Nap."

"Your wig hat's on too tight, girl."

"Burroughs does illegal cremations and has the remaining ashes mixed with clay and resins, then baked into these statues. So even if the law should suspect, they'd never be able to find a trace of the missing person."

She held the creature out for me and I took it in both of my hands. I didn't know what to say.

"I thought you knew and that's why you came up here. But for the last three days you never said anything about it as you pushed yourself through your exercise routine. I figured it was only right I tell you. I suppose I'm just sentimental." She sat on her desk and crossed her legs, showing a lot of thigh.

I was staring at the statue's monster face, looking for some sign that it was Nap. All it did was make me mad at Wilma again. It was her fault Nap had been shot, her fault me and my ace had tussled. I put the thing back on the shelf, looking closely at the other figures.

"Not everyone represents somebody real," she said, "but there's enough on those shelves from over the years."

"Thanks, Monique."

"Sure, Zelmont."

I walked out and went into the sauna. Sitting there with the towel around my waist, I cried real quiet to myself. The other people in there noticed, but nobody asked me what I was going on about. Not that I could have told them if they had.

"e are pleased to announce that Wilma Wells is the new general manager of the Los Angeles Barons. As such she will also enjoy stock options which, when exercised, will make her a minority partner in the club."

If I hadn't been prepared to be blind-sided I might have gone straight playground while driving the car Monique lent me back to town. As it was, the announcement on the all-sports radio station, a live report from the Coliseum, made my head knot up inside. That smart bitch had jooked me good. I wondered what was Danny's part in all this. I couldn't see that roughneck hanging around in the front office, grabbing coffee and a bagel for the queen bee.

Weems was talking. "We are of course hoping that Coach Cannon pulls through. He's undergoing more surgery today and all our prayers go out to him. We are comforted by the knowledge that one of the men responsible for his unfortunate condition has been arrested...."

I tuned him out and kept driving. A little while later, the two clowns on the sports station took phone calls about how this was gonna change the game, how Wilma was making history as the first black woman to hold such a position in the NFL and so on, yakatty and blah. She had made history, all right. But if I had anything to say about it there was still another chapter to be written.

I got back to town around two and went straight to the Barons' offices in El Segundo. I parked in the lot fronting the main building, putting the car way back so I wouldn't be spotted. I knew which office she'd have. It would be the one that had belonged to Stadanko. Of course she'd be redecorating it soon.

I hadn't worked out much of a plan. My idea was to bogard my way inside, find Wilma, and beat her down until security pulled me off her. Then I'd go to jail and spend the next twenty years contemplating what I was gonna do when I got out. Eventually I'd get paroled, go find Wilma, and beat her down again until I was too tired to lift my arms. Simple but effective, as coach liked to say of the best plays.

I sat there running that scenario around my skull and decided that even though it was late in the game, maybe it was time to get on the good foot. I split and drove to the Proud Bird. I got a ginger ale and sat in a corner booth, the early evening creeping in with the customers. On the TV over the bar the four o'clock news was showing the report announcing Wilma's new gig. I went over to hear it.

"…I think this is the best move we could make under the circumstances." Julian Weems was showing his wolf teeth as he talked. Wilma was standing next to him, and Trace was in the background. One big happy fuckin' family.

Weems was talking. "Ellison Stadanko has graciously stepped aside to concentrate on his current legal battles. In that void the team owners, who I brought together in an emergency meeting, have unanimously selected a sterling individual with a keen mind and impeccable credentials. I can only add that it's about time we did the right thing and handed the reins of power to a young woman who represents the future."

The clip ended. Some dudes sitting at the bar started yapping about whether this was good or bad for the Barons. I went back to my corner.

Eventually I headed back to the apartment. It was as neat as I'd left it. Chekka hadn't had a chance to toss it, plus they knew I wasn't stupid enough to leave several million laying around like stank laundry. The couch looked good and I laid down, wondering how I was gonna get my share. After a while I got up and drove over to the Locker Room. The place was open and I walked inside.

"Danny around?" The bouncer had his back to me and was talking to a couple of honeys in straining tops.

"Who's that, sir?" The dude had turned around, and I got a real good look at the flaming cross tattooed on his cheek.

"The brother that owns this place."

"I wouldn't know about that, sir."

"Then how is it you're doing duty here?"

"That would be on Mr. Trace's say-so, sir."

"Oh." I went further inside, expecting things to look and sound different, but they didn't. There was bumpin' music on the speakers, booze at the bar, and fine mamas flowing about the joint. Then I spotted a big man with his back to me at the top of the stairs, standing where he always did by the rail.

"Nap," I said to myself, gulping hard.

The man saw me and waved so I walked up there, everybody around me moving in some other dimension. Had everything been a dream? Was I laying on the field in Barcelona, a concussion ringing the bells in my head? Naw, the truth was scarier.

"How's it going, Zelmont?" Trace was G'd up in a crisp new Hugo Boss suit and polka dot tie. He touched the flaming cross on his cheek.

"Where's Danny Deuce?"

"I understand he had to leave the hereabouts in a hurry."

Trace looked at a chick walking past us in a very un-Christian way. "It seems the younger Mr. Graham is wanted by the authorities for a possible connection in a murder. A rumor has been going around that he had his brother killed to take over the club. Something to do with Stadanko and his illicit affairs."

I knew, and maybe he knew, the cops could have only got that 411 from Wilma. But what did it matter? She'd had this worked out from the word go.

"So Weems has taken over this place?"

"Miss Wilma has. I'm considering a new direction."

"I guess you would be. But don't you want to get back at her for what she did to your boy at the cabin?"

Trace jerked his head like he was shaking off a fly. "Let's just say I got an understanding of the order of things since that time."

"Ain't that something?"

"Yes, I believe so." The bouncer came up the stairs and whispered something to Trace. I might as well have been invisible. He wasn't mad about Wilma capping his buddy, wasn't upset at having to dig the grave for the dude, and he could care less about me. He was in tight. I guess the Lord had told him night clubbing was his calling. Or maybe Wilma would turn the place into one big 24-hour gospel-and-grits diner. I left, not knowing what to do.

If I hung around town, Fahrar or some Joe Friday wannabe was gonna clap cuffs on me for sure. But the thing was I had to get to Wilma. She must have used the money we ripped off to buy herself into the GM/part owner position. Shit.

I drove by her pad, but like I expected there was a for sale sign stuck in the lawn. I peeked in a window between a gap in the shade. The house was stone dark and it looked like she'd never be back. I got in my ride and drove around some more, lost in a city I knew by heart.

Time passed and I took to the hills that led to my pad. The home I used to have. That house too was quiet and shut down. No one lived there either. With Candy and Dandy gone, the place looked like any other square's crib. Fuck it. I broke in by going over the rear wall and through the side door that never did sit right in the frame. I messed up the knob and the lock, but that was someone else's worry. Naturally the real estate people wouldn't be keeping up the subscription to the alarm service.

Most of my stuff was either in storage or, like my bumpin' music system, had been sold off. There was some mail on the kitchen counter. One was a letter from Terri. Having nothing else to do, I opened it. She'd sent a note saying maybe I should come down there and see her and the baby. That my sending her that dough must have meant I was ready to be a father. She'd tossed in a picture of her and the baby, and I held it up to a window to get a better look in the moonlight. Terri was still fine, just about busting out of the stretch top she had on. Then there was that kid standing in front of her. He was taller than a regular six-year-old, with wide shoulders and a smile of teeth. Good-lookin' kid. He was my son. My son.

I stumbled through the house, holding the photo in one hand, then crumpled it 'cause I was angry at myself and angry at Wilma. There was no couch in the front room anymore. I made a pillow of my shoes and curled up on the floor. People think it doesn't get cold at night in Los Angeles. It gets plenty cold.

In the morning I snuck out and went down to Hollywood Boulevard to get some food at a little cafe where the owner knew me. Then I went back to the Locker Room. I parked on Georgia to have a full view of the place. Around a quarter past eleven, Wilma pulled into the lot in her Phaeton.

"Where's my cut, Wilma?" She'd been getting something out of the trunk when I came up behind her.

"I'm going to take care of you, Zelmont." She straightened up slowly and turned around. Wilma was clicking in a long skirt and a loose silk top. She looked like new money and smelled of flowers.

"Uh-huh, like you took care of Danny."

"He was tripping, Zelmont. He was threatening me in public, blabbering on about what we'd done." She closed her trunk quietly, holding the leather case she'd gotten out of there. She was ready for business. "He was a liability. He had to be dealt with."

"This was your plan all along, wasn't it?"

"Yes." She didn't say it like a challenge, just a fact.

"And you never meant to make good to any of us."

"That's not true. The money is safe. Chekka is being grilled and Fahrar has his suspicions about the hijacking, but so what?"

"Where do I fit in?"

"However you want."

I knew she was bullshittin', but it sounded good to hear her say it. "I want what's mine."

She got close. "That can mean a lot of things." She kissed me.

"The money," I said pulling back from her. Maybe I'd get a plane ticket and go see Terri and the boy. Do something right like Nap wanted.

"Very well."

We met that night at the Coliseum. I'd been looking at the headless statue with the torch in front of the peristyles when she drove up. She got out of her car, hefting a gym bag.

"What will you do?"

She handed me the bag. It felt heavy. I opened it. The dough was in there. "Make a few things right." I zipped the bag closed and walked up the steps to the peristyles. I looked out over the field. In some corner of my head I could hear the crowd. Wilma came up behind me.

"You and Weems were partners in this, weren't you?" The field was a beautiful, sparkling green in the low lights they kept on along the edge of the dome. You could run forever on a field like that. I walked down the steps toward the dirt track that circled the grass. I didn't care what her answer was.

"That's not how it started out, Zelmont." She kept up with me, a few steps behind. Must be the first time she had ever followed a man. "But Julian had his investigation of Stadanko going too."

"That's why he sent Trace and Randy up to the cabin, to look for what we were looking for." I stopped halfway down, taking in the view. The crowd's energy was starting to build. Just win, baby. "But when you capped Randy that was a message to him you weren't gonna ride the pine." I glanced back at Wilma. Her skirt and blouse were fluttering in the wind...man, what a sight.

"Yes. Julian and I met after the cabin incident. I convinced him to lay in the cut as you'd say, and let me take the risk of getting rid of Stadanko and Chekka rather than him."

I walked down to the field. She was still behind me. It was on the field I would be free. "You don't give a shit about the money, do you, Wilma?"

"Nine million is barely enough to keep the club in jock straps and shoulder pads, you know that."

"But you needed the robbery and the files as a way to expose Stadanko." We were walking across the outer track. To my right was the tunnel the Barons came out of at home games. The ghost people in the stands were cheering again. Zelmont Raines was back in the formation.

"That's true."

"You can't trust Weems." It felt as if I were standing outside of my body, watching the two of us. "He'll turn on you faster than a pit bull poked in the eye since you've done his dirty work."

I heard her pull the gun from her handbag. It was probably the piece she'd killed Randy with at the cabin. Later she'd no doubt link it to Danny. "Let me worry about that, darling."

"Look like you don't need your old partners, huh?"

"You won't run away run like Danny or be scared shitless like Ysanya. And I know you can't be confused like poor Pablo."

"Ysanya must be terrified. Nap ain't around and her old man is going down."

"She got a call in the middle of the night and took off with whatever she could carry."

"The only thing I'm running for is the glory, Wilma. The Locker Room should be mine along with a piece of the Barons' action. I deserve that much for all the hell you put me through."

She raised the gun. "You're right."

The crowd was chanting my name, the sound filling up the stadium. I turned away from her and took off down the field. I weaved and dodged, both my hips churning like well-oiled rocker arms. I threw the bag in the air and leaped up, spinning like I'd done in the Super Bowl. In mid-air I caught the bag with one hand, my other arm cocked at the elbow so I could twist and set my body right.

Wilma's bullet caught me dead center in the chest and the impact screwed up my landing. I was coughing blood even as I hit the deck. I could hear her high heels on the stone steps echoing up to the peristyles and out of the Coliseum.

I still had a hold of the bag, and through a haze I could see the goal posts. I staggered, then got my second wind. I felt great. Head up, shoulders forward, I was a human freight train.

In the stands my mother was clapping. Terri had brought our child and Cody was laughing with joy at his father. It was beautiful. This was the way football was supposed to be, clean and pure like when I was eleven and played Pop Warner just for the love of the game. Before the scouts, the slaps on the back, the classes you were allowed to skate through, the coach in high school making his dreams yours, the alumni big wheels, the agents, the hangers-on. This was what the sport was all about, you and the ball and the goal line.

The crowd was on their feet, urging me on. They were chanting my name over and over.

It was so beautiful.

I fell to the field, breathing in the fresh watered grass. I was gonna hold onto that bag forever.

The End

a note about the type

Minion was designed by Robert Slimbach in 1990 for Adobe Systems. The name comes from the traditional naming system for type sizes, in which "minion" is between nonpareil and brevier. It is inspired by late Renaissance-era type.

FRIENDS OF PM

These are indisputably momentous times – the financial system is melting down globally and the Empire is stumbling. Now more than ever there is a vital need for radical ideas.

In the year since its founding – and on a mere shoestring – PM Press has risen to the formidable challenge of publishing and distributing knowledge and entertainment for the struggles ahead. We have published an impressive and stimulating array of literature, art, music, politics, and culture. Using every available medium, we've succeeded in connecting those hungry for ideas and information to those putting them into practice.

Friends of PM allows you to directly help impact, amplify, and revitalize the discourse and actions of radical writers, filmmakers, and artists. It provides us with a stable foundation from which we can build upon our early successes and provides a much-needed subsidy for the materials that can't necessarily pay their own way.

It's a bargain for you too. For a minimum of $25 a month, you'll get all the audio and video (over a dozen CDs and DVDs in our first year) or all of the print releases (also over a dozen in our first year). For $40 you'll get everything that is published in hard copy. *Friends* also have the ability to purchase any/all items from our webstore at a 50% discount. And what could be better than the thrill of receiving a monthly package of cutting edge political theory, art, literature, ideas and practice delivered to your door?

Your card will be billed once a month, until you tell us to stop. Or until our efforts succeed in bringing the revolution around. Or the financial meltdown of Capital makes plastic redundant. Whichever comes first.

For more information on the FRIENDS OF PM,
and about sponsoring particular projects,
please go to www.pmpress.org,
or contact us at info@pmpress.org.

PM PRESS was founded in 2007 as an independent publisher with offices in the US and UK, and a veteran staff boasting a wealth of experience in print and online publishing. We produce and distribute short as well as large run projects, timely texts, and out of print classics.

We seek to create radical and stimulating fiction and non-fiction books, pamphlets, t-shirts, visual and audio materials to entertain, educate and inspire you. We aim to distribute these through every available channel with every available technology – whether that means you are seeing anarchist classics at our bookfair stalls; reading our latest vegan cookbook at the café over (your third) microbrew; downloading geeky fiction e-books; or digging new music and timely videos from our website.

PM Press is always on the lookout for talented and skilled volunteers, artists, activists and writers to work with. If you have a great idea for a project or can contribute in some way, please get in touch.

PM PRESS . PO BOX 23912 . OAKLAND CA 94623
WWW.PMPRESS.ORG